THE HEX IS IN

The Fast Life and Fantastic Times of Harry the Book

MIKE RESNICK

PUBLISHED BY:

UFO Publishing

1685 E 15th St.

Brooklyn, NY 11229

www.ufopub.com

Cover art: Tulio Brito

Graphics design: Jay O'Connell

Edited by: Alex Shvartsman

Copy editor: Tarryn Thomas

✽ Created with Vellum

CONTENTS

To Carol, as always,

And to the memory of Damon Runyon. I think he might have liked some of these stories.

PREFACE

A Bit of History

A few years ago, Mike and I saw a revival of *Guys and Dolls*—a play based on one of Damon Runyon's short stories. Over the next few months we both read a lot of Runyon stories; Mike loved them and so did I. When I couldn't find any new stories I hadn't read, I complained to Mike and thus, Harry the Book was born.

As you'll notice, Harry and his crew inhabit the same Manhattan as the *Stalking* books and very occasionally run into some of the characters from them. I think that adds a richness to the stories and it means that when you've finished reading these stories, pick up one of the *Stalking* books; they're longer but just as much fun.

I'm writing this on Valentine's Day. Mike wrote most of the "Harry" stories because I loved them and I nagged for more. I consider them Mike's valentine to me.

– Carol Resnick

Introduction
by Lezli Robyn

When I started re-reading *The Hex Is In*, the first thing I noticed was the unabashed joy that seemed to be woven in the writing of Harry the Book's story. To be the winner of five Hugos (from a record thirty-seven nominations!), the author of over eighty novels, three hundred stories, three screenplays, and the editor of over forty anthologies and fifty issues of science fiction magazines, Mike Resnick clearly had to be a natural-born storyteller and to enjoy his vocation. To truly know Mike was to know that writing was as integral to him as breathing. The aforementioned accolades were no small achievement, and a testament to Resnick's multi-faceted talent as an author and editor, but he had become so well-known for his serious works—his Kirinyaga stories and the like—that people often did not realize that what he loved to do the most was write humor.

And, damn, was he good at it.

If you ask many an author, they will tell you writing humor is *hard*. For most it is harder than writing an award-worthy story full of angst and heart and bittersweet resolutions, because the timing has to be just right. Yet, for Mike, writing humor pieces was second nature—he had the largest funny bone and the brightest twinkle in his eye I have ever known.

This was no doubt because Mike was the consummate entertainer. Many a night, Mike would be holding court at a convention bar, telling stories about the field and its authors with an almost space-operatic bravado and larger-than-life quality. He might have been the winner of many awards, but he always made his peers, writer children, readers and fans feel like they were the real winners just to be in his orbit.

Mike was just plain fun.

With his sharp mind and shrewd intellect, Mike was quick with humorous one-liners that lifted people up, even when they had been down. As his frequent collaborator, I was often privileged to read his work early. I've been incalculably sad at his passing away from cancer, and missing our daily communications even more, so re-reading this manuscript helped remind me of the emails I would receive from Mike in the middle of the night with the enthusiastic sharing of each new story the minute he had typed *The End* at the bottom of it. He wanted me to read them while he was still in the euphoria of having written them. There was something endearing about that almost child-like joy he experienced, his need for me to understand why these stories were important to him.

This book was no different. In fact, *The Hex Is In* was especially meaningful to Mike because it contained his wife's favorite ensemble of misfits. Carol was everything to him, and knowing how much she loved Harry the Book's escapades meant that Mike loved creating them for her—he put his whole heart into the effort, gifting these words to her, these larger-than-life characters.

And these characters definitely lived large. Along with Harry the Book, the bookie, you had Big-Hearted Milton, the mage with an almost shapeless blob of a nose and a red velvet cloak with the zodiac emblazoned on it; Benny Fifth Street and Gently Gently Dawkins, Harry's flunkies, often more of a hazard than an aid; Dead End Dugan, an impossibly tall zombie with bullet holes in his chest and head who spent the bulk of his time standing off in a corner thinking dead thoughts; and since so many scenes took place within the local tavern, no story was complete without the obligatory bartender, Joey Chicago.

Despite the almost-exaggerated descriptions of the rest of the characters, Joey Chicago was never described, so I was tickled pink when the publisher decided to use Mike's likeness as the physical appearance for the bartender on the back cover of this collection. For when you think about it, what is one thing that everyone knows about bartenders? They hold all the stories, everything they have ever heard within the bar. They are the storytellers in the making, the witness to all the drama unfolding, the re-tellers of all the bawdy tales. (The bawdier the better!) Even if Mike had not realized it, Joey Chicago was very meta for him, emulating the role he often held at conventions, in the bars at night. I would like to think that had been deliberate—Mike having also come from Chicago, just like the character—but even if it had not have been, I know he would be delighted with this take, given this is one of his last and lasting gifts to his wife.

While this book could easily have been called *The Fix Is In*, it is the hexes—all the things that could go wrong—that make Harry's story so lovable and funny. While the exaggerated personalities make the characters entertaining, it is their flaws that make them endearing, that help Mike's words get in under your skin to tickle your fancy and make you keep coming back for more.

So go forth and enjoy this tome. Be entertained and enjoy your memories of the man behind the words. They say that laughter is the best medicine. I also think that it is one of Mike's greatest legacies to his readers.

DANGER
KICK ME!
Tulio Brito

OCCUPATIONAL HAZARD

I have just given seventy-five-to-one against Lowborn Prince, who has not finished in the money since G. Washington chopped down the cherry tree, and I am wondering what kind of idiot puts five bills on this refugee from the glue factory when Benny Fifth Street walks up to me and whispers as follows:

"I saw you take that bet, Boss. Lay it off."

"What are you talking about?" I say. "Booking five hundred dollars on Lowborn Prince is as close as a bookie can come to stealing."

"Lay it off," he repeats.

"Why?" I ask.

He looks around to make sure no one is listening. "I just got word: the hex is in."

"Not to worry," I assure him. "I brought Big-Hearted Milton, my personal mage, along, just to be on the safe side."

"You don't understand," says Benny Fifth Street. "Don't you know who made that bet?"

"Some little wimp I never saw before."

"He's a runner for Sam the Goniff!" he says. "And you know the Goniff. He's never bet on a fair race in his life."

The horses are approaching the starting gate. It's too late to lay the bet off, so I just make the Sign of the Pentagram and cross my fingers and hope Benny is wrong.

The bell rings, the gate opens, and Lowborn Prince fires out of there like he's Seattle Slew, or maybe Man o' War. Before they've gone a quarter of a mile he's 20 lengths in front, and I can see that Flyboy Billy Tuesday has still got him under wraps. He keeps that lead to the head of the stretch. Then Billy taps him twice with the whip and he takes off, coming home forty-five lengths in front. By the time Billy has slowed him down and brought him back to the Winner's Circle the race is official and the prices have been posted, and Lowborn Prince pays $153.40 for a two-dollar bet. But I didn't book a two-dollar bet. I pull out my pocket abacus and dope out what I owe the Goniff, and it comes to $38,870, and I know that I have to pay it or the Goniff will send some of his muscle, like Two Ton Boris or, worse still, Seldom Seen Seymour, to extract it one pint of blood at a time.

I hunt up Big-Hearted Milton, who is sitting at his usual seat in the clubhouse bar. As he sees me coming he pulls five hundred-dollar bills out of his pocket and thrusts them at me.

"Here's your money," he says. "Fair is fair. I didn't deliver."

"That's fine, Milton. Now give me another thirty-seven grand and we'll call it square."

"That has never been part of our understanding," he says with dignity.

"Neither was letting a hex get by you."

"I *tried* to find you and give it back when I heard what was coming down," says Milton. "It's not my fault you were ducking out of sight because the cops were making the rounds."

"You *knew* Lowborn Prince was going to win?" I demand.

"I knew the hex was in. I didn't know who was going to

win, because I didn't know who the Goniff was putting his money on. There were three other longshots in the race. It could have been any of them."

"What went wrong?" I ask. "You've broken lots of hexes for me."

"Yeah, but they were from normal, run-of-the-mill mages. Not this time."

"Who the hell does the Goniff have hexing for him?" I ask.

"You ever hear of Snake Eyes Malone?" says Milton.

"Malone?" I repeat, frowning. "When did he get out?"

"Not *out*," Milton corrects me. "*Up*. They buried him in Yonkers, and that was supposed to be the end of it."

"So?"

"So he's a zombie now, and probably a vampire as well, and maybe a Haitian goblin as well, and my magic isn't strong enough to counteract his."

"Look, Milton," I say, "this is serious. If I take one more beating like this, I'm out of business, and probably out of fingers and other even more vital parts as well. What am I going to do?"

"You need a real expert to go up against him."

"A voodoo priest, maybe?" I ask.

"Yeah, that might do it," says Milton.

I gather my flunkies, Benny Fifth Street and Gently Gently Dawkins, and tell them we're leaving the track early, that we've got to find a voodoo priest before I can go back to work. Benny immediately suggests we buy plane tickets to Voodooland, but I explain that there isn't any such place, and Gently Gently says that he's got a friend up in Harlem who belongs to some weird cult and for all he knows it's a voodoo cult, and I tell him to offer his friend anything, but make sure he brings his voodoo priest to my place, and I'll be waiting there until I hear from him.

So I go home, and I send Benny out to bring back some

healthy food, like blintzes and chopped liver and maybe a couple of knishes, and then there is nothing to do but sit around and watch the sports results on my new twenty-inch crystal ball. The big news of the day is Lowborn Prince, and it is so painful to watch that I almost can't eat my blintzes, even though I have loaded them up with sour cream and cinnamon sugar, but at the last minute I decide I have to practice a little self-denial so I only pour one container of strawberries on them, and I spread the chopped liver over little poker-chip-sized pieces of low-cal rye bread.

Finally, at about eleven o'clock, there's a knock on the door, and it's Gently Gently Dawkins. He walks in, all three hundred and fifty pounds of him, and tosses his hat onto a table.

"So where is he?" I demand.

"He's on his way up the stairs," says Gently Gently. "He's an old guy. He don't climb as fast as I do."

"And you left him alone?" I yell.

"Believe me, no one's going to bother him," says Gently Gently, and just as the words leave his mouth in hobbles this stooped-over, bald, wrinkled, old black guy, and I would say he was dressed in rags but Ezekial the Rag Merchant would take offense.

"*This?*" I say. "*This* is what you spent all day looking for?"

"I'm pleased to meet you, too," says the old guy.

I turn to him. "You're really a voodoo priest?"

He shakes his head. "Do I *look* like an amateur?"

"Don't ask me what you look like and maybe we won't come to blows," I say. "If you aren't a voodoo priest, just what the hell are you and why are you here?"

"I'm here because this nice man"—he gestures toward Gently Gently Dawkins—"put the word out that he was looking for someone who could neutralize a Haitian zombie vampire's hex." He smiles and taps his chest with an emaciated thumb. "You're looking at him."

"Okay, you're not a voodoo priest," I say. "What *are* you?"

"The answer to your prayers," he replies. "Also, I happen to be the only *mundumugu* in New York."

"What's a *mundumugu*?"

"You might call me a witch doctor."

"I might also call you a crazy old man who's wasting my time," I say.

He makes a tiny gesture in the air with his left hand, and suddenly I can't move a muscle.

"Oh, ye of little faith," he says with a sigh. "I ought to leave right now, but Snake Eyes Malone is giving a bad name to both hexes and corpses. My name is Mtepwa." He extends his hand, and somehow I extend mine, even though I am not trying to. "And you are Harry the Book. I am almost pleased to meet you."

He snaps his fingers, and suddenly I can move again.

"I hope you didn't take offense, Mr. Mtepwa, sir," I say. "It's been a bad day."

"I understand," says Mtepwa. "But tomorrow will be better."

"It will?"

"It will, or my name isn't Cool Jumbo Cool."

"But your name *isn't* Cool Jumbo Cool," I point out.

"Details, details," he says with a shrug.

"Uh, I hate to seem forward," I say, "but what is this going to cost me?"

"I haven't decided yet," he says. "But whatever it is, I promise you'll be pleased with the price."

THE FOURTH RACE at Belmont is coming up, and I'm getting really nervous. Bilgewater, who couldn't beat my mother around the track, even if she was carrying 130 pounds on her back and running with blinkers, is 120-to-one, and this time the

Goniff doesn't even use a runner, he comes up and makes the bet himself: $1,800 on Bilgewater.

"That's a big bet," I note. "I'll probably have to lay some of it off."

"You can if you can," he says, and I realize that the word is out that Snake Eyes Malone has hexed the race and there is no way that any other bookie will take part of the bet. "I hear you've got a new boy working for you," continues the Goniff.

"Boy isn't exactly the word I'd use," I reply unhappily.

"I just want to do you a favor, Harry," he says. "Don't waste your money on another mage. I guarantee you that nothing in the field can beat Bilgewater. There's simply no way."

He utters a nasty laugh and walks off to his private box, and Mtepwa approaches me.

"That was Sam the Goniff?" he asks.

"That was him."

He looks after the Goniff, and nods his head. "I knew some-one who looked just like him—a long time ago."

"Maybe it was just the Goniff when he was younger," I say.

"I doubt it," answers Mtepwa. "This was before Colum-bus discovered America."

I wonder just how gullible he thinks I am, but we have more important things to discuss, and I tell him that the Goniff has all but admitted that Snake Eyes Malone has hexed the race and that nothing in the field can beat Bilgewater.

"Well," he says with a shrug, "if they can't, they can't."

"*What?*" I scream, and then lower my voice when every-one starts staring. "I thought you were here to put Malone in his place!"

"You have undertakers to do that," answers Mtepwa. "I'm here to make sure that his hex doesn't work."

"But if no one in the field can beat Bilgewater..." I begin, but then there's a cheer from the crowd and I realize that the race has started and I turn to watch it, and I immediately wish

I hadn't turned, because Bilgewater is already leading by ten lengths and as far as I can tell he hasn't drawn a deep breath.

I look at the rest of the field. Most of them are lathered with sweat, half of them are lame, and the rest spend more time watching the birds in the infield than the horses ahead of them.

"I should never have listened to Milton!" I mutter. "Voodoo priest my ass! I need a .550 Nitro Express and a telescopic sight."

"Be quiet," says Mtepwa. "I must concentrate."

I don't know why, but I do what he says. Bilgewater enters the far turn fifteen lengths in front, and Flyboy Billy Tuesday hasn't touched him with the whip yet, and then Mtepwa mumbles a little something that sounds like it's right out of *King Solomon's Mines*, and suddenly there is a big black-maned lion on the track, and he launches himself at Bilgewater, and the horse goes down and Billy Tuesday goes flying through the air and winds up in an infield pond, and the whole field circles around the lion, who is busy munching on the tastier parts of Bilgewater, and then the race is over and Benny Fifth Street and Gently Gently Dawkins are thumping Mtepwa on the back so hard I'm afraid they're going to damage him, and I shove them away.

The stewards post an Inquiry sign, and a moment later they announce that the lion has been disqualified and placed last, and the result is now official. And two minutes after that, the Goniff comes storming up to me, blood in his eye.

"I don't know how you did it," he says, and he's so hot I am surprised steam isn't shooting out of his nose and ears, "but it had better never happen again!"

"Don't bet on bad horses and it won't," I say cockily, because as far as I know this is the first bet the Goniff has lost since he was five years old (and no one ever saw the winner again).

"You listen to me, Harry the Book!" he says, shoving twenty large into my hand. "The Macho Kid is fighting Terrible

Tommy Tulsa at the Garden tomorrow night. I'm putting this on him to win by a knockout. If you pull anything funny, if you mess with my boy Snake Eyes Malone's work again, you won't be alive to gloat about it. Do I make myself clear?"

He turns on his heel and stalks off before I can answer, which is just as well because I have no idea what to say.

"Who is the Macho Kid?" asks Mtepwa.

"It is possible that he is the worst fighter who ever lived," I say. "At the very least, he is the worst fighter still licensed to get his brains beat out. He has fought forty-seven times, and has been knocked out forty-six times. His greatest triumph was when he lost a unanimous decision to Glass Jaw McDougal eleven years ago."

"I see," says Mtepwa.

"So what are we going to do?" I say. "The Goniff never backs down on a threat. If the Kid doesn't win, I won't be alive the next morning."

"No problem," says Mtepwa.

"No problem for *you*, Mtepwa," I say. "But what about *me*?"

"I've got twenty-eight hours to figure it out," he says. "And I wish you'd start calling me Cool Jumbo Cool. Mtepwa just doesn't seem right in this venue."

"Just get the Goniff and Malone off my case once and for all, and I'll call you anything you want," I promise.

"Every occupation has its hazards," he says. "You shouldn't let this upset you."

"I don't mind being upset," I tell him. "It's being dismembered that bothers me."

I AM JUST as upset when we show up at the Garden the next night. Mtepwa has gone into some kind of African swami trance, and only comes out of it an hour before the fight. I ask him what he was doing, and he says he was napping, that he's a 683-year-old man and he's had a lot of excitement and he needs his sleep.

"Did you solve our problem?" I ask.

"Well, actually, it's *your* problem," he explains. "Nobody's going to bother *me* no matter how the fight comes out."

"All right, did you solve *my* problem?" I say.

"I'm working on it."

"Well, work faster!" I snap. "If the Kid wins, I'm broke, and if he loses, I'm dead!"

"Fascinating problem," he says. "Rather like Fermat's Unfinished Theorem. Of course, if he'd simply paid me the five cattle and the virgin, I'd have shown him how to solve it."

"Will you please concentrate on Harry the Book's Unfinished Theorem?" I say pleadingly.

Before he can answer, I sense a presence hovering over me, and I turn and there is Sam the Goniff, smoking one of his five-dollar cigars, and with him is a guy who smells kind of funny and whose eyes seem to be staring sightlessly off into the distance and who has a lot of dirt under his fingernails, and I know that this has got to be Snake Eyes Malone.

"Hi, Harry," says the Goniff. "I'm glad to see you're a fight fan. I'd hate to think that I'd have to go looking for you after the Kid knocks out Terrible Tommy."

"I'll be right here," I say pugnaciously, but that is only because I know that hiding from the Goniff is like hiding from the IRS, only harder.

"I'll count on it," he says, and heads off to his ringside seat with Malone, and I notice that Seldom Seen Seymour is already there waiting for him, just in case he needs a little help collecting after the fight.

"Have you come up with anything yet?" I ask Mtepwa.

"Yes," he says.

"What is it?" I ask eagerly.

"I've come up with a sinus problem, I think," he answers. "Too much cigar smoke in here."

"What about the Macho Kid?" I demand. "If he loses I die!"

"Then he can't lose, can he?" says Mtepwa.

"But if he wins, I'm not only broke, but I haven't got enough cash to cover the Goniff's bet, and Seldom Seen Seymour will take me apart piece by piece."

"Then he can't win, can he?" says Mtepwa.

"I've got it!" I say, jumping to the happy conclusion. "You're going to shoot him before the fight starts!"

Mtepwa just gives me a pitying look, and turns to concentrate on the ring, where they are carrying out what's left of the Missouri Masher, and then the Macho Kid and Terrible Tommy Tulsa enter the ring, and the ref is giving them their instructions, such as no biting or kicking or low blows, and because this is New York he also tells them no kissing, and then they go to their corners, and the bell rings and they come out and Tommy swings a haymaker that will knock the Kid's head into the fourth row, but somehow his timing is off and he misses, and the Kid delivers a pair of punches that couldn't smash an empty wine glass but suddenly Tommy's nose is bleeding, and he blinks his eyes like he can't believe that the fight is thirty seconds old and the Kid is still standing.

But the Kid is still on his feet at the end of the round, and it later turns out that one of the three judges actually gives him the round, and another calls it even, and that is the way the fight goes for three rounds, but I am not watching the fight, I am watching Sam the Goniff, and between the third and fourth round he somehow gets the Kid's attention and holds his fist out with his thumb down and I know he has just signaled the Kid to end it in the fourth round.

I am not the only one who has seen it. Mtepwa is staring right at the Goniff, and he just smiles, and I know he's got something up his sleeve besides his arm, but I don't know what.

The bell rings and the fighters come out for the fourth round. Terrible Tommy connects first, a blow to the solar plexus that should double the Kid over in pain, but instead Tommy screams and pulls his hand back like he's just broken it punching a concrete wall, and then they circle around until the Kid's back is to me, and suddenly Mtepwa starts mumbling again, and the Kid throws his money punch, and I look, figuring this is the end and Terrible Tommy is going down for the count, but it's *not* Terrible Tommy, it's the Goniff, and he takes the punch on the point of his chin and goes reeling around the ring, and the Kid starts pummeling him, and it occurs to me that the Kid looks a lot more like Rocky Marciano and a lot less like the Macho Kid.

Every time he delivers what looks like a knockout blow, Mtepwa starts mumbling again, and no matter how much punishment the Goniff takes he stays on his feet. Finally the Kid winds up and knocks him through the ropes and he falls to the floor right in front of me.

"Is there something you'd like to say to me before you climb back into the ring?" I ask pleasantly.

"I ain't climbing back in there!" he mutters through bleeding lips.

"Yes you are," says Mtepwa, and against his will the Goniff gets to his feet and turns to face the ring.

"All right, all right!" he says. "I cancel the bet!"

"You don't even have to cancel," says Mtepwa before I can stop him. "Just promise you'll never bet with Harry again, or use Snake Eyes Malone to hex a sporting event."

"I promise," says the Goniff.

The instant the words are out of his mouth he collapses, the referee declares the Macho Kid the winner, and the Goniff is carted off to the hospital.

"Thanks for nothing!" I say to Mtepwa. "We didn't cancel, so I still have to pay off! The bet was that the Kid would knock Terrible Tommy out, and he did!"

"The evening's not over yet," he replies, and indeed it isn't, because the Kid fails a urine test (which doesn't surprise anyone, given that he made it all the way to the fourth round), and the fight is declared a draw—not a non-contest where I would have to return the Goniff's money, but a draw, where everyone who bet on either fighter loses and only those who bet there'd be a draw win.

AND THAT'S THE STORY.

Well, not quite all of it. Mtepwa changes his name legally to Cool Jumbo Cool and sets up shop in Port-au-Prince down in Haiti—but not before I pay him his fee, which was supposed to pay for the overdue rent on my office, so I am now conducting my business out of Joey Chicago's Three-Star Tavern. Big-Hearted Milton practices the black arts on a couple of poker games—he calls them the black-and-red arts, since they involve all four suits—and gets back in my good graces again, even if I did lose a couple of friends who couldn't believe that I could draw three consecutive straight flushes.

I even hire a third flunky, Dead End Dugan, because when a bettor is reluctant to pay what he owes, it's nice to have a six-foot-ten-inch zombie on the payroll to remind him of his obligations.

As for the Goniff, the last I hear of him he has moved out to California and gone into politics, which just proves the old adage: once a crook, always a crook.

VISITORS' NIGHT AT JOEY CHICAGO'S

So I'm sitting there in Joey Chicago's Three-Star Tavern, nursing an Old Peculiar, and doping out the odds if Belmont comes up muddy after the rain we're expecting, when an annoying high-pitched voice says: "Gimme a bourbon martini and make it snappy!"

"Ain't no such animal," says Joey. There's a pause, and then he says, "Ain't no such animal as you, neither."

"Watch your mouth, Mac," says the voice, "or I just might put my fist in it."

I look up, and what should I see but an ugly little demon, maybe fifteen inches high, standing on the bar, paws on hips, glaring at Joey.

"Harry," says Joey to me, "where the hell has Big-Hearted Milton gone to?"

"He's in the john," I say. "He's hexing a rasslin' match. He says he thinks better in there."

"Well, you tell him if he wants me to keep paying him for protection, he'd better get his ass out here."

"What about my drink, Mac?" snaps the demon.

"Keep your shirt on," says Joey. "I'm working on it."

"I ain't got no shirt," says the demon.

"Harry," says Joey, "are you gonna get Milton or are you going to spend all night listening to me argue with this disgusting little critter?"

"Keep a civil tongue in your head!" says the disgusting little critter. "I get mighty ugly when I'm riled."

"You ain't so good-looking even when you're not riled," says Joey as I walk into the men's room. Milton is sitting there on the floor, fully dressed, mumbling some spell at a pentagram he's drawn on the floor.

"Come out to the bar," I say. "Your urgent assistance is required."

"In a minute," says Big-Hearted Milton. He mutters one last spell and then stands up. "Okay. Now Rikki Tikki Tavi is going to beat Monstro Ligriv in straight falls tomorrow night at the Garden. I figure we should clean up, because everyone knows it's Monstro's turn to win."

"We'll worry about that later," I say.

"Harry the Book isn't interested in a sporting event?" he says, arching an eyebrow. "You gonna start taking bets on the stock market, perhaps maybe?"

"Just pay attention, Milton," I said. "There's some kind of strange creature in the bar, demanding a bourbon martini, and Joey Chicago wants you to make it go away."

Milton's face goes white as a sheet, and he has trouble catching his breath. "A bourbon martini?" he repeats. "Is this a redhead named Thelma?"

"No, it's an ugly demon from some mystic world."

Milton relaxes visibly. "Okay, no problem," he says. Then: "You're *sure* it's not a Thelma?"

"I'm sure," I say. "Now come on. I'm the guy who convinced Joey to hire you for protection, so if you don't vanish this demon, or at least turn it into something friendly with a bankroll to bet, it'll reflect badly on me."

"Why do you care?" asks Milton.

"I'm using the third booth in the bar as my temporary office."

"They evicted you *again*?" he says, though since this is the fifth time in three years I don't know why he looks so surprised.

"A temporary setback," I say with dignity. I make a face. "The Boston Geldings haven't beaten the point spread in two years. How the hell could I know they were going to get hot against the Syracuse Ridglings?"

"You could have asked," says Milton, looking very self-important.

"You could emerge from the damned bathroom more than once a day," I shoot back.

Then we are in the tavern, and Milton takes a look at the little demon, which is sitting cross-legged on the bar, munching on a pretzel.

"About time," says Joey Chicago. "Make him vanish, Milton. When I wouldn't serve him, he went around spitting in all my customers' drinks."

"I don't see any customers," replies Milton, looking around.

"Would *you* stay if someone kept spitting in *your* drink?" demands Joey. "Just make the little bastard vanish."

"Piece of cake," says Milton. "Where does he come from?"

"How the hell do I know?" says Joey.

"I can't send him back if I don't know where to send him," says Milton. He turns to the demon. "Excuse me, kind sir, but what realm do you reside in?"

"I'll never tell!" snaps the demon.

"Well, so much for sending him back," says Milton with a shrug.

"You mean I'm stuck with him?" demands Joey. "I want my protection money back. First thing in the morning I'm hiring Morris the Mage."

"No, you're not stuck with him," says Big-Hearted Milton,

who has never offered a refund since T. Rex was a pup. "I just said I couldn't send him back."

"You're going to take him home with you?"

"So he can spit on *my* chopped liver and in *my* matzo ball soup?" says Milton. "Don't be silly."

"Then what are you going to do?"

"I can't send him home," says Milton, "but I can encourage him to go home on his own power."

"How?" asks Joey curiously.

"Like this," says Milton, snapping his fingers.

Nothing happens.

"What's Morris the Mage's phone number?" says Joey disgustedly.

"Oh, ye of little faith," mutters Milton. He mumbles something that wouldn't make any sense even if he was saying it clearly. Then he snaps his fingers again, and suddenly there is a very bright blue *something*, about the size of a bulldog, but with scaly skin, three-inch claws on its front feet, two rows of razor-sharp teeth, bloodshot little eyes, and halitosis. It is standing on the floor, and suddenly it sees the demon on the bar. It flaps wings I didn't even know it had, flies up to the bar about ten feet from the creature, gives a high-pitched hum that sounds more ominous than a growl, and begins approaching it.

"Omygod omygod omygod!" shrieks the demon.

The blue thing launches itself through the air, and the demon vanishes about a fifth of a second before it reaches him. (Okay, so maybe it was a quarter of a second, or a half, but bookies who hang out at the track measure everything in fifths of a second, so don't hassle me, okay?)

"Well, that's that," says Milton. "One problem presented, one problem solved. I'm going back to the men's room."

"Uh ... Milton," says Joey, pointing to the blue thing, and we see that it has just downed a bottle of vodka and is going after Joey's bottle of '73 Dom Perignon, which is the only bottle he has ever owned and is just for show. Joey tries to shoo it away, and it just snarls at him.

"Milton," says Joey nervously, "thank it and send it on its way."

"It's not that easy," says Milton, frowning.

"Why the hell not?" demands Joey.

"Bringing them here is easy; sending them away isn't."

"What are you talking about?" says Joey. "A spell's a spell."

"Some are more complex than others," says Milton.

"I *knew* I should have hired a union wizard!"

"Do you know what they cost?" says Milton.

"Less than this *momser* is going to drink before I get rid of him, I'll bet," snaps Joey.

"I'll get rid of him," says Milton. "I just can't send him back to where he came from."

"I don't care where you send him," says Joey. "Hell, send him to visit my ex-wife and the bastard that *yenta* ran off with!"

Milton rolls up his sleeves. "Stand back, everyone!" he says.

"What do you mean, 'everyone'?" says Joey. "Except for Harry the Book, who's running his business out of the third booth here, everyone's long gone."

"Silence, mortal!" says Milton.

"You're as mortal as I am," says Joey, "and if you don't vanish this beast pretty damned fast, I'm gonna give you one hell of a kick in your most mortal part!"

"All right, all right," says Milton. He turns to me. "Harry, how much would you say it weighs?"

"Maybe forty-five pounds," I tell him.

"Mammal, reptile, or dragon?" he asks.

"Yes," I say.

He frowns. "Okay," he says. "Here goes!"

He mumbles something that almost rhymes, but it is in no language I have ever heard and makes even less sense than French, and then his eyes roll back in his head and his arms stick out straight ahead of him and he goes into a kind of swami trance, and suddenly we hear an ominous and portentous *gulp!*, and we look at the bar, and there is this thing that looks kind of like a leather gorilla, except that it's got an extra pair of arms and a third eye right in the middle of its forehead, and it is chewing and making crunching noises, and a few blue scales kind of dribble out of its mouth.

"Man, that was *good!*" he growls. "I haven't eaten in 253 years, give or take an afternoon." He looks at Joey's stock. "What have you got on tap?"

"Old Peculiar and Old Washensox," says Joey in kind of trembling tones.

"I'll have a keg of each!" says the leather gorilla. "By Merlin, it feels good to be free again!"

"Uh … Milton …" says Joey.

"You said get rid of it, I got rid of it," says Milton defensively.

"Milton," I say, "I know you're not a betting man, but I'll offer you seventeen trillion-to-one that I know what Joey's going to ask for next."

The gorilla gets tired of waiting, so he climbs down behind the bar, lifts a five-gallon keg, and chug-a-lugs it. "I could get to like this place," he says.

"Make me an offer," mutters Joey.

The leather gorilla belches. It is so loud that six glasses shatter. Then he turns to Milton. "I intuit that you're the one who brought me here."

Milton tries to answer, but he's shaking so badly nothing comes out, and he just nods weakly.

"You conjured me to kill the Spedunker, right?"

"The blue thing with the wings and scales," says Joey.

"Yeah, a Spedunker." Suddenly the gorilla grins. "Now I'll bet you're trying to figure out how to get rid of me."

"I would never do such a thing," says Milton. "Honor bright and pinky to the sky, the thought never crossed my mind."

"Your nose just grew seven inches," notes the gorilla.

Milton's hand goes to his nose. It is the same almost-shapeless blob as usual.

The gorilla throws back his head and laughs. Three mice who have been attracted to all the strange new smells faint dead away. "I was just pulling your leg," he says. "Or maybe I should say I was pulling your nose!" He laughs at his own joke, and two of the overhead light bulbs burst.

"Now that you've had a snack and a little something to wash it down with," says Milton hopefully, "maybe you'd like to go home and take a nap?"

"Go back to that tiny cave where I was imprisoned for millennia?" demands the gorilla angrily. *"Never!"*

"Harry," says Joey, "go find the phone book and look up Morris the Mage's number."

"Relax," says the gorilla. "I find you even more distasteful than you find me. I'm off to explore this strange new world. Where's the nearest whorehouse?"

"For gorillas?" I say. "I don't think there are any."

"Yes there are!" says Milton quickly. "There are three of them in Brooklyn."

The gorilla turns to Joey. "Loan me a fiver," he says. "I came out without my wallet." He frowns. "In fact, I came out without my pants."

Joey opens the cash register and gives him a ten-spot. "You'll want to visit a Brooklyn bar when you're done," he says hopefully.

"Thanks, fella," says the gorilla, grabbing the sawbuck. "You're okay."

He lumbers to the door, starts to walk out, and bounces back to the middle of the tavern.

"What's going on?" he demands, looking right at Milton.

"I should have thought of it," says Milton, frowning. "The spell brings you here, but it doesn't let you leave. You're just here to eat the Spedunker."

"I *ate* the Spedunker," snarls the gorilla. "Now I've got urgent business in Brooklyn."

Milton starts backing away from him. "I don't know a spell to let you out," he says. "All I know is how to bring you here."

"Well, you'd better think of something fast," says the gorilla, slowly approaching him. "Because I'm getting hungry again."

"Gorillas are vegetarians," says Milton.

"So they'll penalize me fifteen yards," says the gorilla.

Milton screams a spell at the top of his voice, and before the gorilla knows it there is a seven-ton gryphon in the bar.

"Oh, shit!" says the gorilla, and vanishes just before the gryphon can reach him.

Well, you can figure what comes next. Milton summons a dragon to scare the gryphon away, and then he calls up a venomous hydra-headed chimera to frighten the dragon, and then he magics up a kraken to eat the chimera, and after two hours have passed I feel like I have watched the same movie fourteen times in a row.

"What now?" says Joey in disgusted tones as we watch the latest arrival, a creature that looks like a refugee from a movie with actors named Boris or Bela or Basil or something else beginning with a "B". The creature is considering which of Joey's bar stock to sample, and Milton decides to give it one last try, and he mutters and mumbles and goes into his swami again, and suddenly a trunk reaches out and holds the creature high above the floor, and it curses and cries and says that it has a wife and three kids and a mortgage and it hasn't sent in its insurance check yet, and the elephant loosens its hold for a second and the creature disappears in a cloud of gray smoke, which is very fitting because it was obsolete long before Technicolor movies hit the scene.

I am wondering what Milton is going to conjure to get rid of the elephant, who is so big that he is stuck half in and half out of the tavern, when one of the mice that fainted wakes up and squeaks a couple of times, and the elephant takes one look and trumpets in terror and backs out into the street, taking half of the front wall with him, and the last time I see of him he is making a beeline for Third Avenue, which is not going to help him much because that is Casey Callahan's beat and he doesn't allow anything to speed down his street, not even elephants.

"Well, that's that," says Milton.

"No," says Joey. "Pay me for all my bar stock and fix my walls and buy me a new bottle of '73 Dom and *then* that'll be that."

"Don't be so ungrateful," says Milton with dignity. "You asked me to solve a problem. I solved it."

"It's like solving a fist fight by turning it into World War VII!" snaps Joey. "Now, are you going to make restitution for damages or not?"

"I'm tapped out at the moment," says Milton, "but ..."

"No buts!" snaps Joey. "Get out of my establishment."

"I thought we were friends!" says Milton in hurt tones.

"You got it absolutely right," says Joey. "We *were* friends!"

"Okay," says Milton. "If that's the way you're going to be, give me one for the road and I'm out of here."

"Where's your money?" demands Joey.

"Put it on my tab," says Milton.

"We're mortal enemies," says Joey. "You ain't got no tab!"

"Hey, Mac," says a voice. "Is this guy bothering you?"

We turn to see the little demon who started the whole thing.

"You betcha," says Joey. "Make him go away."

The demon chants something in French or some other alien tongue, makes a mystic sign in the air, and *whoosh!*, Milton is gone (though he later turns up in a house of excellent repute in Brooklyn.)

"I'll have a tall one," says the demon.

"You got it," says Joey, drawing one from what remains of the tap. "By the way, I'm really sorry we hassled you before. You looking for work?"

The demon shrugs. "Doing what?"

"Protection," says Joey. "Keeping the riffraff out of my establishment."

"Sure, why not?" He extends a wiry little three-fingered hand. "By the way, my name's Louie."

"Louie," says Joey Chicago, "I think this is the beginning of a beautiful friendship."

THE HEX IS IN

So I am sitting there in the stands, and the Pittsburgh Pompadoodles are beating the Manhattan Misfits by a score of sixty-three to ten, which is not unexpected since the Misfits have not won a game since John Alden had a fling with Pocahontas, and I am silently cursing my luck, because the point spread is forty-six, and if the Misfits could have managed just one more touchdown I would not have to pay off any bets to *either* side.

But it is the fourth quarter and there are only twenty-two seconds left on the clock, and the Misfits are eighty-seven yards away from pay dirt, and the Pompadoodles have been beating them like a drum all day. And then, suddenly, Godzilla Monsoon finds a hole off left tackle, and he races through it, and two of the Pompadoodles defensive backs run into each other, and damned if he hasn't passed the midfield mark and is racing toward the end zone. Everyone is chasing him, but Godzilla's got a head of steam up, and no one gets close to him. Now he's at the forty-yard line, now he's at the thirty, now the twenty—and then, just as I'm counting my profits, a piano falls out of the sky on top of him, and the ref whistles the play dead on the eight-yard line.

Benny Fifth Street turns to me, a puzzled expression on his face. "You ever seen it rain pianos before?" he asks.

"Not that I can remember," I admit.

"I wonder if it was a Steinway," says Gently Gently Dawkins, who is sitting on the other side of me.

"What difference does it make?" I ask.

"Them Steinways are always a little flat in the upper scales," he says.

"You want to see flat, take a look at Godzilla Monsoon," offers Benny Fifth Street.

"You guys are getting off the point," I say.

"Was there one?" asks Gently Gently Dawkins.

"The subject was rain," answers Benny. "I suppose if it can rain cats and dogs, it can rain pianos every once in a while."

"The subject," I say, "is who wanted the Pompadoodles to beat the spread?"

"That should be easy enough," says Benny. "Who put some serious money on the Pompadoodles?"

"Everybody," says Gently Gently, chuckling in amusement. "The last time the Misfits won they were the New Amsterdam Misfits—and then they only won because the other team was attacked by Indians on the way to the game and never showed up."

I give what has occurred a little serious thought, and then I say, "You know, pianos hardly ever fall out of the sky on their own."

"Maybe it fell out of an airplane," says Gently Gently.

"Or maybe a roc was carrying it off to its nest," adds Benny.

"Rocks don't fly," protests Gently Gently. "They just lay there quietly, and sometimes they grow moss, which I figure is like a five o'clock shadow for inanimate objects."

"You guys are missing the point," I say. "Clearly the hex is in, and I paid my hex protection to Big-Hearted Milton. If the piano was going to fall on anyone, it should have fallen on the referee, who's been blowing calls all afternoon."

"Or the tuba player in the band," adds Benny. "He's always off-key."

"So why didn't Milton stop it, or at least misdirect it?" I continue.

"Speaking of Milton, here," says Gently Gently, handing me five one-hundred-dollar bills.

"If *I* speak of Milton, will you lay another five C-notes on *me*?" asks Benny curiously.

"This is a bet," answers Gently Gently. "I forgot to give it to you."

"From Big-Hearted Milton?" I say, frowning.

"Right. He gave it to me at halftime."

"But Milton never bets," I say. "It's against the rules of the Mages Guild."

"I heard they tossed him out for non-payment," says Benny.

"Which team did he bet on, as if I didn't know?" I ask.

"The Pompadoodles, of course," answers Gently Gently.

"Well, that explains why he didn't stop the piano," puts in Benny.

I get to my feet. "I'll see you guys later."

"Where are you going, Harry?" asks Benny.

"I got to pay off all the guys who bet on Pittsburgh, and then I have to have a talk with Milton."

"Where will you find him?"

"Same place as always," I reply.

So I do like I say, and pay Longshot Louie and Velma the Vamp and Hagridden Henry and all the others, and then I head over to Joey Chicago's bar, where my office is the third booth on the left, and I toss my hat there, and then go to the men's room, where I find Big-Hearted Milton sitting on the tile floor as usual, surrounded by five candles and half-singing, half-muttering some chant.

"Milton," I say, "we've got to talk."

"Why, Harry the Book—what a surprise," he says. "Wait'll I finish this spell." He goes back to chanting in a tongue so alien that it might very well be French. Finally he looks up. "Okay, I'm done. Did you bring my money?"

"That's what we have to talk about," I say.

"All right," he says, getting to his feet and snuffing out the candles with his shoe. "But I want you to know that I'm protected against spells, curses, betrayals, demonic visitations, and small nuclear devices."

"Are you protected against a punch in the nose?" I ask.

He frowns and looks worried. "No."

"Then let's talk."

"About my money?"

"About Godzilla Monsoon getting flattened by a piano."

"He'll be all right," says Milton. "It fell on his head. It's not as if it hit him in the knee or anything he ever uses."

"Why did it hit him at all?" I ask. "And just when he was about to wipe out the spread?"

"It wasn't my fault," whimpers Milton.

"Come on, Milton," I say. "The only time in five years you make a bet, and nine million pounds of music falls down on the guy who's about to make you lose?"

"I didn't do it."

"Maybe you didn't drop it," I say. "But I pay for hex protection, and you didn't stop it."

"It's too complicated to explain," says Milton. "Just give me my winnings and we'll agree never to discuss it again."

"Come on, Milton," I say. "You can tell me what's going on. We've known each other for fifteen years now."

"We've been friends for fifteen years?" he says, surprised. "How time flies."

"I didn't say we were friends. I said we've known each other. Now, what the hell is going on?"

He cups his hand to his ear. "They're calling you from the bar, Harry."

"The bar's empty, except for Joey Chicago, who was guzzling some Old Peculiar from the tap when I walked through."

He looks at his wrist. "Oh, my goodness, look at the time!" he exclaims. "I'm late for an appointment. I really must run."

"Milton, you're not wearing a watch," I point out.

"I pawned it," he says. "But I remember where the hands should be."

"Milton," I say, "I just want you to know that this hurts me more than it hurts you."

And with that, I haul off and punch him in the nose.

He hits the ground with a *thud*, pulls out a handkerchief to try to push the blood back into his nostrils, and climbs slowly to his feet.

"You were wrong, Harry," he says reproachfully. "It hurts me *much* more than it hurt you."

"An honest mistake," I say. "And now, unless you tell me what's going on, I am going to make honest mistakes all over your face."

"All right, all right," he says. "But let's leave my office and go to yours. I feel the need of a drink."

We emerge from the men's room and walk over to my booth, where Milton orders us each an Old Washensox.

"My treat," he says. "Joey, put 'em on my tab."

"I been meaning to talk to you about your tab," says Joey.

"Holler when it hits fifty," says Milton.

"I been hollering since it hit twenty, for all the good it's done me," answers Joey.

Joey brings us our beers, mutters the usual about firing Milton and hiring Morris the Mage to protect the place, and goes back to the bar.

"All right," says Milton, "here's the situation. I find myself a little short for money this year"—which is not a surprise; Milton has been short for money since Teddy Roosevelt charged up San Juan Hill—"and suddenly someone throws a beautiful gift in my lap."

"What was her name?" asks Joey, who was listening from behind the bar.

"Opportunity," says Milton.

"Not much of a name," says Joey, making a face. "I prefer Bubbles, or maybe Fifi."

"So tell me about this opportunity," I say, as Joey leans forward to get her measurements.

"Gerhardt the Goblin—you know, that little green critter who's always screaming 'Down in front!' at Tasteful Teddy's Five-Star Burlesque Emporium—anyway, Gerhardt approaches me one day last week and tells me that he's got a client who wants to put five hundred down on the Pompadoodles, but doesn't want to do it himself, and that if I knew anyone who would act as a middle-man, he'd get twenty percent of the winnings."

"And you don't know who you're working for?"

"I'm working for *me*," says Milton with dignity. "I don't know whose money I'm betting, but that's a whole different matter."

"Where can I find Gerhardt?" I ask.

"Beside Tasteful Teddy's?" says Milton. "He loves betting on the lady mud wrestlers over at Club Elegante." He lowered his voice confidentially. "They're the only wrestling matches in the whole city that aren't fixed."

"You know," I say, "I've been there a couple of times—just for the coffee, mind you; I paid no attention to the wrestlers at all—but I don't remember any of the matches having a winner."

"They don't."

"Then what's to bet on?"

"Which one gets naked first. How long before they're so

covered with mud you can't tell 'em apart. How many men say they just go there for the coffee. That kind of thing."

"Is there anything else you can tell me?" I ask.

"Not a thing."

"Okay, Milton," I say, getting up. "I'll see you soon."

"You're leaving?"

"Yes," I say.

"Where's my money?" he asks.

"Right here," I say, patting my vest pocket. "And it's *my* money."

"Aw, come on, Harry," he pleads. "Show a little charity."

"You insist?" I say.

"I do."

"Okay," I say. "Tomorrow I'll hunt up some charitable organization that repairs pianos."

Then, before he can say another word, I am out the door.

I stop by Club Elegante looking for Gerhardt the Goblin, grab a ringside table, and when he hasn't shown up by the seventh match, I decide to leave, especially because the next match features Botox Betty, who once broke her hand slapping my face over a friendly misunderstanding and a couple of intimate pinches, and Lizzie the Lizard, who shed her skin faster than French Fatima shed her clothes over at Tasteful Teddy's.

By the time I get to my apartment, Benny Fifth Street is already there, watching replays of the piano flattening Godzilla Monsoon just as he crosses the ten-yard line, followed by a hospital interview with Godzilla who doesn't sound any more punch-drunk than usual, and finally a statement from the winning coach to all the young Pompadoodle fans out there that they should never neglect their music lessons because today clearly proves that music *is* important to their daily lives, and without music they might only have won by forty-six points and disappointed all the big Pittsburgh plungers who bet on them to beat the spread.

Gently Gently Dawkins shows up just as we turn off the television—he was busy eating his fourth meal of the day, which puts him maybe two hours behind his normal schedule—and I tell them what Milton told me.

"Clearly it's got to be some Pittsburgh fan," says Gently Gently.

"Why?" I reply. "You don't have to be a Pittsburgh fan to fix a game."

"You don't?" he says, frowning, and I can see he's still a few thousand calories short of functioning on all cylinders.

"No," I say. "Maybe this isn't confined to Milton, or even to Manhattan. I mean, it's got to cost a lot of loot to get a wizard good enough to pull that stunt with the piano. Maybe we should see if anything like that has happened anywhere else."

"How should we go about it?" asks Benny.

"Start by calling Vegas. See if anything like today has happened when it looked like an underdog might win, or even just beat the spread."

"I'll do it," says Gently Gently.

"Are you sure?" asks Benny. "I don't mind making the call."

"No problem," says Gently Gently.

"Okay," I say. "The phone's in the next room."

"I know," he says, getting up. "So are the cookies."

"He eats three more cookies and a biscuit and you won't need Milton to hex the bad guys," says Benny, as Gently Gently leaves the room. "Just have him breathe on 'em, or maybe step on their toes."

Gently Gently is back out in less than a minute.

"That was fast," I say.

"It was all negative," he replies. "No one's dropped a piano anywhere." He pauses. "Some Acme Movers dropped a pipe organ carrying it into a church out there, if that helps."

"Not a whole lot," says Benny.

"Anyway, our contact's sorry, but no pianos. The only weird thing they've had out there is the tidal wave."

"A tidal wave?" I repeat. "In *Las Vegas*?"

"Yeah," he says. "Funny, isn't it?"

"Tell me about it," I say.

"No one was hurt," says Gently Gently. "It comes from out of nowhere and practically drowns Nasty Nick Norris just when he's about to pull a three hundred-to-one upset in their tennis tournament, and then as quick as it comes, it goes away. I think they would have been convinced it was a mass hallucination, except that they found half a dozen codfish and a sea urchin stuck in the net."

I pull out my abacus and dope out the odds that the tidal wave and the piano aren't related. Since the abacus can't compute any higher than a google-to-one, it melts.

"What have a Vegas tennis match and a New York football game got in common?" I muse.

Gently Gently raises his hand. "They're both sports?"

I ignore him and say, "We need to find the connection. Someone's paying a hell of an expensive wizard to rig these events, which means someone's making a bundle on them—someone who doesn't want his name to be known."

"That does not make a lot of sense," opines Benny. "So someone is paying a wizard. That doesn't mean he has to hide his own name. Anyone can lay a bet. Are you sure Milton wasn't holding something back?"

"Pretty sure," I say. "But even if he is, he knows that I am also holding something back from him"—I pat my wallet—"and we can trade whenever he wants."

"You mind if I turn on the TV?" asks Gently Gently.

"Trying to find out who's robbing us doesn't interest you enough?" asks Benny.

"It ain't that," explains Gently Gently. "But I got a sawbuck down on Loathesome Lortonoi in the seventh at Del Mar, and it's almost post time."

"You bet with some other totally illegal bookie?" demands Benny.

"It ain't ethical to bet with the illegal bookie I work for," responds Gently Gently. He searches for the right words. "It's a conscript of interns."

"Let him watch," I say. "It's easier than arguing with him."

The picture comes on, and the horses are already parading to the post.

"There's Loathesome Lortonoi!" says Gently Gently, pointing to a huge black horse who looks like he and his rider should be chasing Ichabod Crane around Spooky Hollow. "They shipped him out there just for this race. It's a perfect spot for him."

There are six horses approaching the starting gate. Four of them look like close relatives of Loathesome Lortonoi. The sixth horse looks like he should be pulling a death cart in medieval Graustark, or maybe be spread throughout a few hundred cans of dog food. Even the flies avoid him. His jockey looks like he wishes he could wear a brown paper bag over his head. The tote board says he's 750-to-one.

"Is that Pondscum?" asks Benny.

"No, it's just a little smudge on the screen," says Gently Gently.

"I mean the horse."

Gently Gently pulls a *Racing Form* out of his pocket and looks at it. "Yes, it is. Have you seen him before?"

"He was losing races back when I was in grammar school," says Benny. "He was the slowest, ugliest horse in the world even then."

The horses enter the gate, and a few seconds later the doors spring open and Loathesome Lortonoi comes out of there like a bat out of hell, and before they hit the far turn he's fifteen lengths in front. The next four horses are spread out over another thirty lengths. Pondscum isn't even in the picture.

They hit the homestretch, and now Loathesome Lortonoi is twenty lengths in front—and suddenly the crowd starts screaming, and the announcer gets so excited he starts whistling and cheering and forgets to say what's happening, but he doesn't have to because in another two seconds Pondscum enters the picture. He is going maybe ninety miles an hour, and it seems like his feet are hardly touching the around—and then I realize that his feet *are* hardly touching the ground, because somehow while rounding the far turn he has sprouted wings and is literally flying down the homestretch. He catches Loathesome Lortonoi with a sixteenth of a mile to go and wins by thirty lengths.

Gently Gently turns to me. "Is that fair?" he asks in hurt, puzzled tones.

"We'll know in a minute," I say. And sure enough, a minute later the result is official and Pondscum returns $1,578.20 for a two dollar bet.

I turn to Benny. "Who do we know out there?"

Benny consults his little book. "The biggest bookie working Del Mar is No-Neck McGee."

"Give me his number," I say, and a moment later I dial it and No-Neck McGee picks it up on the third ring.

"Hi, No-Neck," I say. "This is Harry the Book."

"Harry," he says. "Long time no see."

"No, I can see again," I tell him. "Wanda the Witch's spell only lasted a couple of weeks."

"So what can I do for you on this most terrible of days? Did you see what just happened in the seventh?"

"That's what I want to ask you about."

"I'm making a formal complaint to the Jockey Club."

"It'll never hold up," I say. "There's nothing in the rules that says a horse can't have wings."

"Just as there's nothing in the rules that says he can't have blinkers, or shoes for that matter. I'm basing my case not on the fact that he had wings, but that he didn't declare them prior to the race, the way you have to declare all other equipment. Is that what you're calling about? Did someone pull the same trick up at Belmont?"

"No," I say. "I just want to know if you had any big plungers on Pondscum?"

"I took just one bet on him," answers No-Neck. "Problem is, it was for six hundred dollars. That's why I've filed the complaint. Paying it off will break me."

"Who placed the bet?" I ask.

"An ex-jockey who hangs around the track all the time," says No-Neck. "Remember Charlie Romanoff?"

"Chinless Charlie?" I say. "Didn't he get ruled off the track for life?"

"Life or three hundred years, whichever comes first," answers No-Neck. "Anyway, he lays the bet, but he's never seen six hundred dollars at one time in his life, so I know he is someone else's stalking horse. Or is it stalking bettor?"

"Thanks, No-Neck," I say. "That's what I needed to know."

"Glad you called today," says No-Neck. "I have a feeling my phone will be disconnected by next week."

We hang up, and I turn back to Benny and Gently Gently. "I think I'm starting to see the light," I say.

"I don't know how you can," says Gently Gently. "It's almost nine o'clock at night."

"Give your *Form* to Benny and go into the next room for another cookie," I say, and he does so faster than Pondscum or even Godzilla Monsoon ever moved.

"I can tell by your face you got an idea," says Benny. "Or maybe it's just a stye in your eye. But it's *something*."

"It's an idea," I say. "It comes back to your question: why would someone hide the fact that he was laying bets? After all, betting is legal at the track and in Vegas, and it's almost legal with bookies."

"I already asked that," says Benny.

"The logical answer is that the hex was in, and he didn't want people to know that he was the one who made the bet."

"Yes, that makes sense," says Benny. "But we already know the race and the game and the match were hexed."

"But we know something else," I say. "We know that the kind of wizard who can cause a tidal wave or do the other things does not come cheap. So the next thing to do is find out who can afford three such wizards on the same day."

"There's hundreds of guys with that kind of loot just in Manhattan," says Benny. "It's like finding a blonde in a haystack."

"Don't you mean a needle?" I ask.

"I found a needle in a haystack once," he answers. "I've never found a blonde."

I couldn't argue with that, so I went back to the subject at hand. "We can work it from either end," I say. "We can narrow it down by finding someone who could afford all three wizards, or we can narrow it down by finding out just which wizards have the power to pull these stunts off."

"Too many either way," says Benny, as Gently Gently comes back into the room. "There's a third way."

"Oh?" I say. "What it is?"

"Pound the hell out of Big-Hearted Milton until he tells you who gave him the money."

"It could have passed through four or five hands before it got to Milton," I say.

"That narrows it down," says Gently Gently. "Who do we know who has four or five hands?"

I send him out to a chili parlor.

"You know," I say when he is gone, "I think the money is the key to it all."

"Of course it is," agrees Benny. "No money, no hexes."

"No," I say. "I mean, I think you hit on something before. There are hundreds of possible plungers, and dozens of possible wizards, but there's only one payoff, and that's the one I have to make to Milton."

"You're going to pay him?"

"Tomorrow," I say. "Tonight there's something I have to do. Get me Morris the Mage's phone number."

I talk to Morris, and we agree on a price, and he casts his spell and gives me the magic word, and the next morning I hunt up Milton in the men's room at Joey Chicago's, where he is sitting fully-clothed on one of the toilets, his nose covered in bandages, reading an ancient book of magic.

"Good morning, Milton," I say pleasantly.

"I ab nod talkig to you," he says through the bandages.

"That's too bad," I say. "Because I have sought you out to pay my debt of honor."

I pull out the money and hand it to him.

He smiles, gets up, puts the money in a pocket, and walks to the door.

"Thag you, Harry," he says. "I god to deliver this. I'll see you lader."

He walks out of the men's room, through the tavern, and out the front door, and I go back to the apartment, where Benny and Gently Gently have spent the night. (Well, Benny spent the whole night; Gently Gently made four more trips out for nine-thousand-calorie snacks.)

"Is it accomplished?" asks Benny.

"Let's give it an hour," I say.

Benny spends the time staring at his watch and counting down minute by minute. Finally it is time.

"He's got to have delivered it by now," I say, "and whoever he's delivered it to hasn't had time to get to a bank. So let's make sure he thinks twice before trying to rob Harry the Book again." I pause for dramatic effect, and then say: "Abra cadabra."

"That's it?" asks Benny. "Nothing's happened."

"It's not going to happen here," I say. "Turn on the news in another hour and we'll see if it worked."

Benny counts down from sixty to zero once more, and then turns on the television. The news is on all the channels: the estate of mafia don Boom-Boom Machiavelli has spontaneously caught fire and burned to the ground.

"And that's that!" says Benny, rubbing his hands together gleefully.

"Not quite," I say.

"Oh?"

"Milton never used a bank or a safe in his life, which means his share caught fire in his pocket. Find out what hospital he's in and send him some flowers."

"Any note with it?" asks Benny.

"Yeah," I say. "Tell him that if God had meant pianos to fly, He'd have given them wings."

Gently Gently looks surprised. "You mean He didn't?"

CHRISTMAS EVE AT HARVEY WALLBANGER'S

So we are sitting around Joey Chicago's Three-Star Tavern, with the wind howling outside the front door and sounding just like Velvet Voice Vinnie singing off-key. I am nursing an Old Washensox, minding my own business, which of course is dependent on whether Aqueduct comes up muddy on Christmas Day. Gently Gently Dawkins has been studying the crossword puzzle in the newspaper for the past twenty minutes, trying to come up with a four-letter word for "stupid," when Benny Fifth Street suddenly remembers what night it is.

"Hey, Joey!" says Benny. "Did you ever patch that hole in your roof?"

"It ain't snowing on you, is it?" shoots back Joey Chicago from behind the bar.

"That's good," says Gently Gently, looking up from his puzzle. "I wouldn't want no reindeer falling on top of me."

"Right," agrees Benny. "Then it'd be 'Off, Dancer! Off Prancer! Off all you other horned nags!' instead of 'On, Dancer! and so forth.'"

"Are you sure there was a Prancer?" asks Gently Gently.

"Absolutely," says Benny. "There's got to be, if it's going to rhyme with Dancer."

"That is all very well and good," says Gently Gently, "but I don't remember nothing rhyming with Cupid or Rocket."

"There ain't no Rocket," says Benny.

"Sure there is," says Gently Gently. "There's Dancer, Prancer, Donner, Vixen, Cupid, Cupcake, Dandy, and Rocket."

"I got a double sawbuck that says some of them are not in the sleigh-pulling business, and that I can name more of Santa's reindeer than you can," says Benny.

Gently Gently slaps twenty dollars on the bar. "Okay, wise guy," he says. "You're faded."

Benny frowns, trying to remember his childhood, when he probably knew the names of the reindeer as well as I know the morning line at Santa Anita. Finally he clears his throat and says: "Dancer, Prancer, Donner, Vixen, Buster, Blitzen, Gemini and Comet."

"I don't remember no Blitzen," says Gently Gently.

"Of course not," says Benny. "That's why you are losing the bet."

Gently Gently turns to me. "Boss, who's right?"

"Neither of you," I tell him.

"Put in your twenty bucks and take your best shot," says Benny, who is getting more than a little warm under the collar.

"I do not make bets," I say. "That is for suckers. I *book* bets, which in case it has slipped your mind is how I pay your salaries. But I will name the reindeer anyway: Groucho, Harpo, Chico, Gummo, Zeppo, Curly, Moe, and Larry."

"You're *all* wrong," says Joey Chicago. "You're forgetting Rudolph—though I cannot imagine his nose gets much redder than Gently Gently's after he has downed a couple of Old Peculiars and a chaser." He grabs the forty bucks and sticks it in his pocket. "Anyway, I guess that makes me the winner."

Benny holds out an empty glass. "If you're going to keep the money, I should at least get a free refill."

"Check the walls," says Joey. "Do you see any signs posted to the effect that this is a charitable institution?"

"Where is your Christmas spirit?" demands Benny.

"I left it in my other suit," says Joey.

Just then, before they can come to blows, or more likely curses, Dead End Dugan walks through the door. I don't mean through the doorway; I mean through the *door*. We have to make allowances for Dugan, who is a little more powerful and a lot less noticing since he became a zombie.

"I been looking all over for you, Harry," he says.

"That is probably why you haven't found me until now," I reply.

"Bet-a-Million McNabb owes you a lot of money, doesn't he?" says Dugan, and I notice that Benny and Joey have backed away, because when you've been dead and occasionally buried for the past five years you just naturally are not about to put any perfume companies out of business, or even any cologne companies for that matter. Gently Gently, who is rarely operating on more than two or three of the eight cylinders God gave him, keeps sniffing his drink, trying to figure out where the smell is coming from.

"Yes," I say. "He drops ten large betting on Horrendous Howard to knock Kid Testosterone out by the fifth round." I shake my head sadly. "Horrendous Howard might pull it off, too, if he doesn't trip and fall on his head going back to his corner after the first round. Last I hear, he still thinks he is King Arthur and he will not eat off any table that has corners on it."

"This is all no doubt very interesting," says Dugan, who as far as I can tell has not recently been interested in much besides visiting Madame Bonne Ami's House of Exotic Comforts for the Recently Departed, "but you should know that even as we speak he is playing five-card stud with Loose Lips Louie."

I do not need to hear what Dead End Dugan will tell me next, because like almost everyone else except maybe Bet-a-Million McNabb, I know that Loose Lips Louie acquires his name by beating every member of a battleship's crew out of their savings in a single night, and his specialty is five-card stud, which indeed he has used to sink more than one ship's crew.

"In fact," Dugan is saying, "he is taking such a bath that about twenty minutes ago he has to change his name to Bet-a-Thousand McNabb."

"I have to get to him and collect my ten thousand dollars before he loses it all to Loose Lips Louie," I say. "Where is this game going on?"

"At Harvey Wallbanger's Social and Sporting Club for Gentlemen of Quality," says Dugan.

"Isn't that where Morris the Mage hangs out?" says Benny.

I frown. "Come to think of it, yes, that has become his home away from home."

"Do you suppose he is helping Louie to win?" continues Benny.

"I don't know, but we might as well play it safe and take our own protection along."

"Where is he?" asks Benny.

"In the men's room, where he always is," says Joey Chicago. "He doesn't like to be disturbed."

"He will have to live with it," I say, heading off to the men's room, where I find Big-Hearted Milton seated on the floor as usual, surrounded by five black candles and reading a book.

"Why are you bothering me when I am studying the ancient grimoires?" he says, slipping the book into a suit pocket.

"Come on, Milton," I say. "I see the title before you can hide it, and it is *Meter Maids in Bondage*."

"Some grimoires are less ancient than others," he says defensively.

"Get up," I say. "We have work to do."

"Obviously someone has welched on a bet," says Milton as we emerge from the men's room and rejoin the others. "Who was it?"

"Bet-a-Million McNabb," I answer.

"Bet-a-Million McNabb always makes good his losses," Milton assures me.

"Even as we speak, he is playing five-card stud with Loose Lips Louie over at Harvey Wallbanger's establishment," I tell him.

"A taxi will not do," says Milton suddenly. "We need a nonstop jet plane."

"It is only three blocks," I point out.

"Do you know how much he can lose to Loose Lips Louie in three blocks' time?" says Milton. Then he adds: "Has Louie got a protector in his corner?"

"I do not know for sure," I answer, "but if so, there is every likelihood that it is Morris the Mage."

"That twerp?" laughs Milton. "Why, he couldn't put a spell on his own mother!"

"I would not be too sure of that," says Joey Chicago. "The last I hear of her, she is in a cage on the moon."

"Maybe McNabb put the money aside," suggests Benny hopefully. "No one will ever bet with him again if word gets out that he won't make good his marker and pay his bookie."

"How much do you think he will have left to bet after Loose Lips Louie gets done with him?" I shoot back. "Come on! We are going to Harvey Wallbanger's!"

"And a Merry Christmas to you, too," mutters Joey Chicago as the five of us walk out through the space where the door used to be.

HARVEY WALLBANGER'S Social and Sporting Club for

Gentlemen of Quality manages to put three lies in a single title, because it is not a social club unless you are of a mind to pay fifty dollars or more for a very short-term date, it is not a sporting club because all of the games are rigged and the drinks are watered, and the only gentlemen of quality are those who give the place a wide berth.

We walk in the door, and suddenly I think maybe the place is on fire because there is so much cigar smoke that I can barely see my hand in front of my face, and finally I realize that it is not *my* hand but that it belongs to something that is sort of green and kind of scaly but is mostly big, and when the smoke clears a little I realize that it is attached to Gregory the Gorgon, who is the muscle that protects Harvey Wallbanger's establishment from unwanted intruders, which is to say from those who can spot a crooked deck or a rigged roulette wheel.

"Hold it right there," says Gregory. He points to Dead End Dugan. "No zombies allowed."

"Why not?" I ask.

"What if I have to chastise him?" says Gregory. "What can one do to a malingerer who is already dead?"

I turn to Dugan and tell him to wait outside.

"Can I just stand here in the doorway?" asks Dugan. "The smoke keeps the flies away."

"This is not in the playbook," says Gregory. "I shall have to get a ruling from the Supreme Authority," which could be Harvey or God, but by the strictest interpretation of the term is probably Mrs. Wallbanger. "You may stand here until I return."

"Thank you," says Dugan.

"Just don't start doing a bunch of dead things until I get back," says Gregory as he shuffles off, and I can tell by Dugan's puzzled expression that for the life of him—or maybe it is for the death of him—he cannot think of any dead things to do, other than standing there without breathing.

"Come along," I say to Milton and Benny and Gently Gently.

"We must collect from Bet-a-Million McNabb while he still has something to collect."

We begin walking through the many rooms of the establishment, each of which features a contest that under other circumstances might be called a game of chance. There are a number of lovely young ladies selling drinks and cigarettes and occasionally themselves, and what they lack in clothing, they more than make up for in personality.

I hear a bunch of jolly laughing up ahead, and who should I run into but Nick the Saint, who is decked out in his Christmas best.

"Hi, Harry," he says. "Merry Christmas, ho ho ho."

"Hello, Nick," I reply. "Are you not supposed to be making your rounds this evening?"

"Yes," he says. "This is *my* night, ho ho ho. I just thought I'd stop off for a drink first, and see if there were any elves to recruit."

"I hate to be the bearer of bad tidings," I say, "but the young lady you are resting your hand upon is probably not an elf."

"You never know," says Nick. "But just the same, I trust news of this will not make its way up North?"

"My lips are sealed," I say.

"Mine, too," adds Big-Hearted Milton.

"I owe you one, Harry," he says, and then adds, "ho ho ho."

"If you are planning on staying here for another fifteen minutes, you can square your account with me," I say, and then I tell him how, and he agrees, and I can see he plans to spend at least fourteen of those fifteen minutes exploring every possibility that the young lady next to him is an elf in disguise.

I leave him explaining exactly the kind of Christmas present he plans to give her once his sleigh ride is over, and finally we come to a small room, and there is Bet-a-Million McNabb sitting across a table from Loose Lips Louie, and behind Louie is Impervious Irving, who calls himself Louie's financial advisor, and in truth I suppose putting people who want Louie's money into the hospital does Louie's finances more good than even twenty motivated stockbrokers.

"Gentlemen," says Impervious Irving by way of greeting, "I do not wish to be anti-social, but you are intruding in a private room and more to the point are interrupting a private game."

"We shall tarry no longer than is necessary," I say, "but I have a prior claim on ten large from Bet-a-Million McNabb."

"I am desolate to hear this," says Loose Lips Louie, who appears to be anything but desolate, "but he became Bet-a-Hundred McNabb about five minutes ago."

"I am having a terrible run of luck, Harry," says McNabb, "but it is due to change any minute."

"In *this* place?" says Benny. "It'll change about as soon as Impervious Irving changes his socks, which means seven years of bad luck will seem like a blessing by comparison."

"Boss, do I have to stand here and take this?" demands Impervious Irving.

"I believe I can solve your problem," says Big-Hearted Milton. He makes a sign in the air and mutters something that has a lot of syllables and almost no vowels, and suddenly there is a *poof* and Impervious Irving is somewhere else, though where I do not know for another minute. Then Loose Lips Louie yells for Morris the Mage, who comes in from the next room, still holding his poker hand.

"Morris," says Louie, "this goniff has vanished Impervious Irving. Bring him back!"

Morris closes his eyes and starts chanting what sounds like a song they cut out of a show that folded on its pre-Broadway tour, and then he snaps his fingers and says "Abra cadaver" and suddenly Impervious Irving is back in his accustomed position just to the right of Louie's chair.

Irving glares at Milton and says, "If you are going to vanish me to a bathroom again, next time make it one that's got a magazine to read."

"I've hexed it so he can't transport you again," says Morris. He turns to Milton. "You can still make him disappear, of course, but do you really want to be in the same room with an outraged but invisible Irving?"

Milton waves his hands wildly. "Begone!" he says.

"I was just leaving anyway," says Morris, and vanishes.

I notice that Milton is wearing a great big grin on his face, and I ask him why.

"When Morris comes in here he is holding a full house, jacks over sevens," says Milton. "But when he leaves he is holding a pair of fours and nothing else."

"Let us get back down to business," I say. "Bet-a-Hundred McNabb owes me ten thousand dollars."

"I don't deny it," says McNabb. "But even more than I don't deny it, I don't have it. It all resides within Loose Lips Louie's vest pocket, unless some of it has fallen onto the floor."

"This is the truth," confirms Louie. "I am afraid you are too late, Harry."

"I have a prior claim on the money that is in your pocket," I say.

"Then file your claim with Bet-a-Hundred McNabb," says Louie.

"I do not slake my thirst from empty glasses," I say, which I think is a brilliant rejoinder, but I can see that neither Louie nor Irving understand it, so I point out that I could get more blood from a turnip than money from McNabb.

"What the hell," says Louie. "This being Christmas Eve, I will give you a chance to win your money back from me."

"I never bet," I say. "Betting is for suckers."

"*Losing* is for suckers," says Louie. He flashes some of the money he has rescued from McNabb's clutches. "Winning is for"—he searches for the *bon mot* – "winners."

I stare at McNabb, who still doesn't know he is a sheep, let alone that he has been fleeced. "All right," I say at last. "What did you have in mind?"

"How about a nice friendly game of five-card stud?" suggests Louie.

"I have lost my trust in this establishment," I answer.

"Oh?" he says. "When?"

"When we still lived in caves," I say.

"What do you suggest then?"

"I am sure you will agree that we are the two most prodigious intellects in Harvey Wallbanger's, if not on the face of the entire planet," I begin.

"Yeah, that seems a reasonable premise," says Louie.

"What if we engage in a mental contest instead of a game of chance?" I say.

"I lost a toe in the war," he says, "so if it's a mathematical question, the answer can't be any higher than nineteen."

"No, you only have to count to eight for this one," I reply.

"I don't want you to think I distrust you, Harry," says Louie. "But I distrust you, Harry. First you tell me what the contest is all about, and then I'll tell you if we have a bet."

I stare at him and say, "I will bet you twenty large—the ten you took from McNabb, and ten more for my trouble—that I can name more of Nick the Saint's reindeer than you can."

"Don't do that, Boss!" says Gently Gently. "You tried it at Joey Chicago's and got it wrong."

"We learn from our mistakes," I tell him.

"Not always," says Gently Gently. "After all, I'm still going out with Sylvia."

"Well, it works in principle," I say.

"I just read the poem about Nick and his reindeer to my nephew," says Louie. "So if you get 'em all right and I get 'em all right, all we've done is waste a bunch of time."

I am waiting for Big-Hearted Milton to catch on, and finally he does, and just like Sandy Koufax or Roger Clemens he hurls his high hard one into Impervious Irving's brain, where it has a lot of breathing room, and Irving says, "I got an idea, Boss."

"I hope it's a small one," says Louie. "You got to take it easy with a new discipline."

"You gonna listen or not?" asks Irving.

Louie looks up at Impervious Irving, who is maybe eight feet tall and almost as wide, and he says, "I am always happy to hear your thoughts on any matter, if for no other reason than that they constitute a considerable rarity. Now, what is your idea?"

"Make him agree that you win on ties," says Irving. "If you each get three right, or six, or all eight, you win."

"It is a wonderful idea, especially for a beginner," says Louie, "but Harry is a sophisticated man of the world. He will never go for it."

"It is late and I want my money," I say. "I accept your conditions."

It is a shame that Louie is not born a hundred and fifty years ago in Tombstone, because Doc Holliday and Johnny Ringo never reach for their guns half as fast as he reaches for my hand to shake it and cement the conditions.

"You all saw that we shook on it," he says. "Now, since I am a generous and genial host and this is my private room, I will allow Harry the Book to go first."

"Okay," I say, clearing my throat. "Here goes. Dasher, Dancer, Prancer, Vixen, Donder, Blitzen, Cupid, and Flyaway."

Loose Lips Louie emits a delighted laugh. "I don't even need to invoke Irving's rule. The reindeer are Dasher, Dancer, Prancer, Vixen, Donder, Blitzen, Cupid, and Comet."

"Nosir," I say. "They are Dasher, Dancer, Prancer, Vixen, Donder, Blitzen, Cupid, and Flyaway."

"You are wrong, Harry," says Louie. "There is no reindeer called Flyaway."

"There most certainly is," I say, "and you owe me twenty large."

I wait for Milton to hurl a second idea to Impervious Irving.

"Boss," says Irving, "Nick the Saint's in the next room. Why don't we just pull him in here and ask him?"

"I'll get him," says Benny.

"I do not trust any of Harry's toadies anywhere near him," says Louie. "Irving, go get him and bring him back."

"I am not a toady," says Benny heatedly as Irving leaves the room.

"Oh?" says Louie. "And what are you, then?"

"I am one of Harry's flunkies," replies Benny with a note of pride.

Irving is back a minute later. He has Nick the Saint in tow, and Nick has his young lady in tow.

"What can I do for you gents, ho ho ho?" asks Nick.

"We need you to settle a disagreement," answers Louie.

"Okay, but it's got to be quick," says Nick. "I'm already late getting started on my rounds."

"It won't take long," says Louie. "What are the names of your reindeer?"

"Dasher, Dancer, Prancer, Vixen, Donder, Blitzen, Cupid, and Flyaway," says Nick. "I thought everyone knew that."

"*Morris!*" screams Louie, and Morris the Mage appears a few seconds later. "Morris, he says one of his reindeer is named Flyaway. Is he lying?"

Morris stares at Nick for a minute, mutters a spell, snaps his fingers, and nibbles a breath mint.

"He's telling the truth," says Morris.

"Well, if that's all," says Nick, "Elmer here and I have to be going."

"Elmer?" says Gently Gently, kind of blinking and staring at the girl.

Nick nods. "She's my newest elf," he says. "And this way if I happen to drop her name in front of you-know-who, there won't be one of her usual scenes. Well, Merry Christmas to all and to all a good night."

He and Elmer leave, Morris vanishes, and Loose Lips Louie glares at me.

"I don't know how you did it, Harry, but I'm going to find out."

"I wish you as much luck as you wish, McNabb," I say. "And now, my twenty large, please?"

He mutters such a complex curse that Morris pops into existence and Milton vanishes for a moment, and finally he shoves the money across the table to me.

"So am I off the hook, Harry?" asks McNabb.

"At least until you're Bet-a-Thousand McNabb," I say. "Come on back to Joey Chicago's with us. I'm buying."

McNabb joins us as we walk to the exit, which was the entrance on the way in, and we pick up Dead End Dugan, who still has a puzzled expression on his face, and I know he has not yet thought of any dead things to do, and a few minutes later we're all standing at the bar at Joey Chicago's, sharing a bottle of Comrade Terrorist vodka, and Big-Hearted Milton explains to everyone in the place how I do a favor for Nick the Saint and in exchange he changes Comet's name to Flyaway, and everyone seems to be having a good time, until I hear Benny Fifth Street start yelling and a minute later Gently Gently Dawkins is yelling back.

"What's the problem?" I ask, when they finally pause for breath.

"We are having an argument about the Seven Dwarfs," says Gently Gently. "Benny says they are Bashful, Sleepy, Sneezy, Dumbo, Doc, Grumpy, and Marvin, and *I* say ..."

I find myself wondering if Nick has room for one more over-sized elf on his sleigh.

A VERY SPECIAL GIRL

I am reading the *Racing Form* in my temporary office, which is the third booth at Joey Chicago's Three-Star Tavern, and coming to the conclusion that six trillion-to-one on Flyaway in the 5th at Saratoga is a bit of an underlay, as there is no way this horse gets within twenty lengths of the winner on a fast track, a slow track, or a muddy track, and I have my doubts that even a rain of toads moves him up more than two lengths. I conclude that this horse cannot beat a blind sea slug at equal weights even if he has the inside post position. Suddenly a strange odor strikes my nostrils, and without looking up I say, "Hi, Dead End," because one whiff tells me that it is Dead End Dugan, who simply cannot hide the fact that he is a zombie.

He also is an occasional employee that I use when some goniff does not wish to honor his marker, and indeed he has just returned from Longshot Lamont's, where I have sent him to collect the three large that Longshot Lamont bet on Auntie's Panties to come in first, and indeed the filly does come in first by seven lengths, but she comes in first in the 8th race after she goes to the post in the 7th race thirty minutes earlier.

"So do you pick up the three large that Harry the Book is owed?" asks Benny Fifth Street.

"Of course he picks it up," says Gently Gently Dawkins. "After all, he is half as big as a mountain, and is covered by almost as much dirt, and how much can three large weigh anyway?"

They immediately get into one of their arguments, Gently Gently saying that a three thousand dollar diamond weighs less than a cigarette, and Benny replying that it all depends who is manning the scales, and that his cousin is the clerk of scales at Belmont and has been weighing Flyboy Billy Tuesday in at 120 pounds every day for years, even though the Flyboy has not topped 108 pounds since eating some bad chili three years ago. This drives Joey Chicago, who has been standing behind the bar, wild, because he has been betting against Flyboy Billy Tuesday's horses all year, and now he learns that they've been carrying twelve pounds less than they should, but Benny points out that it's okay, because 108 pounds of Billy Tuesday is more of a handicap to a horse than 130 pounds of most jockeys, and Joey Chicago has no answer for this, so he goes back to cleaning the bar around Dead End Dugan, which requires cleaning every time Dugan moves.

"So does Longshot Lamont pay with a smile?" I ask Dugan.

He gives me that puzzled expression—he doesn't think as clearly as he used to before he became a zombie—and says, "I thought you wanted money, Harry."

"Money is even better than smiles," I say to comfort him, and because it is also true. "I trust you have it with you?"

"Well, I *had* it," says Dugan. I was going to say, "says Dugan uncomfortably," but the fact of the matter is that nothing makes him more uncomfortable than being dead, which is a permanent if not a stationary condition.

"If you do not have it any more, you had better tell me where it is and why it is not in my hand right now," I say.

"I am in love," says Dugan. "I meet the most wonderful girl this afternoon on my way back from Longshot Lamont's."

"Is this not a bit early in the relationship for an exchange of three thousand dollar gifts?" asks Gently Gently.

"Do not be so fast to misinterpret," replies Dugan. "This girl is just half a step short of perfection."

"Then she will understand that that was not your money to give, and she will be happy to hand it over to me," I say.

"Uh ... *that* is the half a step I was referring to," says Dugan, brushing away the flies that are starting to play field hockey on his face, as they always do when he stands in one place for a few minutes.

I decide to be the reasoning father figure, partially because I am a saint among men, and primarily because I have not yet figured out how to threaten a man who is already dead, and I say, "Tell us about this remarkable lady who has won your heart."

"She has left my heart right where it has always been," answers Dugan. "She is much more interested in my brain and my soul."

"I can't imagine why," says Benny. "You never use the one, and you are no longer in possession of the other."

"She is kind of a collector," explains Dugan, and it is the first time in my life I ever see a zombie swallow uneasily, or swallow at all for that matter.

"What does she collect, brains or souls?" asks Benny, who has a healthy curiosity about such things.

"I get the impression that she is not all that choosy," answers Dugan.

"Where do you meet her?" I ask.

"I am passing Creepy Conrad's Curiosity Shop, and I see her through the window, nibbling on a little snack in a feminine way, and it is love at first sight."

"What kind of snack?" asks Gently Gently, who at three

hundred fifty pounds and counting has a serious interest in such things.

"I cannot see through the window," replies Dugan, "but it is wiggling its tail just before she swallows it."

"But she swallows it in a feminine way," I say, though my sarcasm is lost on Dugan.

"Yes," he says. "She is just beautiful. And very precise. Why, she drains an entire fifth of Comrade Terrorist vodka and does not spill so much as a drop."

"I figure the tail accompanies both ears of whatever it was as a prize for her feminine appetite," says Benny.

"She should skip the Olympics and go pro," adds Gently Gently.

"Does she eat anything else we should know about?" I ask.

"Like what?" asks Dugan.

"Like small children," I say. "Or even big ones."

"You are speaking of the woman I love!" says Dugan heatedly.

"I am speaking of the woman who is holding three large that belongs to me," I say. "Maybe you should introduce me to both of them."

"Both?" asks Dugan.

"Your girl and my money," I say. "I will take it from there."

"All right," says Dugan. "I am dying to see her again anyway."

"Poor choice of words," notes Joey Chicago from behind the bar.

"But you have to approach her gently, Harry," continues Dugan, ignoring Joey's unfeeling if accurate remark. "She is a sensitive thing and takes offense easily."

"I will approach her so gently she will hardly know I am there," I assure him.

"She will know," he assures me. "She is very perceptive." He pauses. "I think it is the extra pair of eyes."

"She has four eyes?" I say.

"At the very least," says Dugan.

"Has she got four of anything else important?" asks Benny, suddenly interested.

"She comes equipped with all kinds of extras," says Dugan. "This is why I have fallen in love with her. She is unique, even among women, who are all unique, each in their own alien way."

"What kind of extras?" I ask.

"Teeth," says Dugan. "Claws. Eyes. Tails. Well, it is only one tail, but compared to everyone else it is extra."

"I cannot argue with that," agrees Benny.

"And how many women can lift an entire car?" says Dugan proudly.

"Six cylinders or eight?" asks Gently Gently.

"Why would she lift a car?" chimes in Benny.

"It is a very tight parking space, so she just walks out, picks up the car, driver and all, and sets it down in the empty space." Dugan smiles wistfully. "And she does not even break a sweat."

"I agree that she is unique among all the women of my acquaintance," I say. "Right up to the incident with the car she is running neck and neck with a redhead named Thelma, but she has sprinted into the lead."

"That is nothing," says Dugan. "You should see her fly."

"Probably I shouldn't," I say. "I have enough trouble falling asleep as it is."

"She just flaps her arms and flies away?" asks Benny.

Dugan smiles. It is maybe the first smile anyone has seen on him since he came back from the grave. "Nobody can flap their arms and fly," he says. "She flaps her wings."

"Does she imbibe anything besides vodka while you are with her?" I ask suddenly.

"Like what?" says Dugan.

"Like blood," I say.

"I will not dignify such a crude question with a response," replies Dugan.

"I doubt that there can be more than one of her," I say, "but just in case God has been asleep at the switch and there are two or more, what is she wearing so I will be able to identify her?"

"I will be right alongside you, Harry," he replies.

"True, but you are still a relative newcomer to the zombie trade, and what if you suddenly decide you don't like it? If I am to present a moldering corpse to the lady of your dreams, I at least should be sure I have the right lady. So what is she wearing?"

"I don't know," says Dugan. "I am so enraptured by her face, I never notice."

"Now I know for sure he's a zombie," says Benny.

"All right," I say, trying to hide my annoyance. "What color is her hair?"

"That's kind of difficult to say."

"How hard can it be?" I persist. "It is blonde, brunette, or possibly red."

"Well, it wriggles and hisses a lot, and it keeps changing colors under the lights," answers Dugan. "Sometimes it is red and sometimes it is green. I do not think it is ever blonde, but I could be wrong."

"Are you saying she is a medusa?" I ask.

"No, I am not saying any such a thing," answers Dugan. "For one thing, her hair is friendly."

"How can hair be friendly?" asks Gently Gently.

"It chats with me, and it sings 'Ninety-nine Bottles of Beer on the Wall' while she is drinking the vodka."

"You talk to her hair?" says Benny disbelievingly.

"No," answers Dugan.

"Then you just made that up?" says Benny.

"I made nothing up," says Dugan sharply. "Her hair chats with me, just like I say. But I do not talk to it, because I am shy and tongue-tied in her presence."

"So she has extra eyes and teeth, and comes equipped with wings and a cold-blooded hairdo," I say. "I hope you will not take it askance, Dugan, but I think I am going to bring a little protection along."

"A gun?" he asks.

I shake my head. "I have a feeling that a hail of bullets would just annoy her," I say. "No, I will take Big-Hearted Milton."

"I do not see him," says Dugan, looking around.

"That is because you are not looking in his office," I say. "I will go and fetch him."

And with that, I walk to the men's room and enter it, and there is Big-Hearted Milton, my personal mage, sitting in his usual spot on the tile floor, surrounded by five black candles which have all burned down to nubs.

"Hi, Harry," he says. "Be with you in a minute." He mutters a spell that has very little melody and even less vowels. As he says the last word of it, all five candles go out. "That'll show her," he says with a satisfied smile.

"What will show who?"

"Mitzi McSweeney," says Milton. "I take her to dinner last night, and just because I play a little itsy-bitsy-spider on her thigh under the table she throws her soup in my face and walks out." He glowers furiously. "And I do not even like chicken gumbo."

"What have you done to the poor girl?" I ask.

"When she steps on the scale this morning, vain creature that she is, she will find out that she is ten pounds heavier than last night, and nothing will take the weight off except an apologetic phone call to me."

I decide not to point out that Mitzi is bordering on anorexic anyway and an extra ten pounds will fill her out nicely. I especially decide not to mention that she can probably pack more of a wallop at 115 pounds than at 105.

"Okay, Milton," I say, "if you are done with your just and terrible vengeance, I have need of your services."

"I am the best there is at my trade," he says. "I put Morris the

Mage in the shade. Spellsinger Sol cannot hold a candle to me. But I tell you up front, Harry, that even *I* cannot bring Flyaway home a winner at Saratoga tomorrow. I could put a saddle on *you* and you could spot him eight lengths and still beat him by daylight."

"That is not the particular service I need," I say. "It seems that Dead End Dugan has fallen in love, and has given his lady friend the three large that he picked up for me from Longshot Lamont. It is my intention to retrieve it."

"And you need my help taking your money back from a girl?" laughs Milton.

"Anything is possible," I say.

"Oh, well, I have not been out of my office since I show up to wash the soup off my face last night," he says. "A little fresh air will do me good. And getting your money back should be like taking candy from a baby."

I resist the urge to ask him a baby *what*, and a moment later we emerge from the men's room into the bar, and pick up Dead End Dugan, Benny Fifth Street, and Gently Gently Dawkins, and we are about to walk out the door when Milton asks Dugan what the name of the lady we are about to visit might be.

"Anna," he says.

"And her last name is Conda, right?" says Milton, laughing at his own joke.

"How did you know?" asks Dugan.

CREEPY CONRAD'S Curiosity Shop is easy to find. You just see where all the terrified women and children are running away from, and follow the screaming to its source. On the day we go there Conrad is having a sale on shrunken heads, but these differ from every other shrunken head I have ever seen in that they are still alive and are attached to non-shrunken bodies.

They spend most of their time eating, because their mouths are so small and their bodies are so big.

Because he is on the outskirts of an Italian neighborhood, Conrad also sells a lot of full-sized wooden crosses, with or without hammers and nails. His vinyl record section—he has not yet made the jump to CDs—sells mood music, providing that your mood is either morbid or panic-stricken. He is also having a special on surplus dialysis machines, and three pale lean gentlemen, each wearing a velvet cape, are examining them.

The rest of the merchandise is *really* esoteric, especially the part that is still alive, but we have not come to enjoy a pleasant afternoon browsing through Conrad's stock. We have come for Anna Conda and my three thousand dollars, but as I look around there is no morsel of femininity to be seen, nor is there anyone who answers to Anna's description.

Finally Creepy Conrad emerges from a back room. He is missing one eye, and his left cheekbone protrudes through the skin, and those few teeth he still possesses are filed and miscolored, and the nails on his hands are about an inch long and curve like those of a leopard, but aside from that he looks every bit as normal as Dead End Dugan, which is perhaps not really an apt comparison as Dugan still possesses his hair.

"Well, curse my soul if it isn't Harry the Book and his retainers," says Conrad. "What may I do for you fine gentlemen today? Could I perhaps interest the illustrious Mr. Dugan in a coffin?"

"You couldn't interest me no matter where you were," says Dugan. "We have come to see the delectable Anna Conda."

"Well, there is an Anna Conda on the premises," answers Conrad. "But a delectable one? Possibly you want Madame Bonne Ami's House of Exotic Comforts for the Recently Departed. They might have one."

"Watch your step, sir," says Dugan, drawing himself up to his full height. "You are speaking of the woman I love."

"Now, why would the woman you love be working for Madame Bonne Ami?" muses Conrad.

"Keep a civil tongue in your head," says Dugan ominously.

"I already have one," says Conrad, sticking his tongue out at us. "It belonged to a little old lady who only used it in church on Sundays."

"Where is she?" demands Dugan.

"The little old lady?" says Conrad. "She is long gone."

"Where is Anna Conda?" says Dugan.

"I heard you mention my name," says a voice which sounds kind of like a wire-haired terrier being combed against the grain, and a moment later Anna Conda steps out from one of the back rooms.

She is everything Dugan says she is, but Dugan does not say the half of it. He never mentions the cold reptilian eyes, the pointed ears, the reticulated greenish skin, or the four-inch dew claws on each of her ankles. She offers us the kind of smile healthy cats offer to three-legged mice, and I can see that her tongue is black and forked.

"Hello, Mr. Dugan," she says, and her voice does not improve with proximity. "How nice to see you again."

"You are even more beautiful than before," replies Dugan, and Benny shoots me a look that says, *My God, what does she look like earlier in the day?*

"Who are your friends?" asks Anna.

"This is Harry the Book, my sometimes employer," says Dugan before I can whisper to him to make up a name, "and these are Benny Fifth Street, Gently Gently Dawkins, and Big-Hearted Milton."

"And what are you gentlemen here for?" she asks.

"It is Harry's fault," Dugan blurts out, so I figure I had better explain the situation.

"It would appear that Dugan, with the best will in the world, gives you a little keepsake that is not his to give," I say.

"I am just as happy to accept it from you, Harry," she says with a smile that makes me want to turn and race for the door and not stop running until I have reached Des Moines or Des Plaines or some other distant municipality beginning with "Des."

"I will handle this, Harry," says Milton, stepping forward. "Miss Conda, charming and beautiful as you are, I am afraid I must insist that you return the three large to Harry, though you can keep a couple of Ben Franklins for your trouble."

"It was given to me in all earnestness, and I am not inclined to give it back," she says, and I notice that blue vapor is starting to pour out of her nose, which means that either she is losing her temper or perhaps her spleen has spontaneously combusted, and I will give heavy odds on the former.

"Then I am afraid I shall have to resort to stringent means of recovering it," says Milton.

"You do that," says Anna.

"Very well," says Milton. "Do not say that you weren't warned."

And with that, Milton begins chanting something in a forgotten language, and making gestures in the air, and otherwise conjuring up all of the black arts at his command, and finally he ends it with a cry of "Presto!"—and suddenly there are only four of us facing Anna Conda, and Big-Hearted Milton is nowhere to be seen.

"Where did he go?" asks Gently Gently.

"Beats me," I say.

"*Get me the hell out of here!*" says Milton's voice.

I look around, but there is no sign of him.

"Get you out of where?" I ask.

"This damned dimension that she hurls me into," says Milton's voice. "And hurry! It is cold and there is something very big sniffing at me and drooling on my face."

"I do not know how to magic you back," I say. "After all, you are the mage."

"Reach out and grab my hand, of course," says Milton.

"Reach *where?*" I say.

"*Out!*" yells Milton.

I reach my hand out, and sure enough a pudgy invisible hand takes hold of it. I give it a pull, and suddenly there is a *pop* and then Milton is standing next to me, looking both relieved and annoyed.

He stares at Anna Conda with a combination of fear and awe. "Who does your protection?" he asks. "Whoever it is, he's *good!*"

"I need no protector," answers Anna.

"I can believe it," says Benny fervently.

"Enough of this chit-chat," I say. "I still want my money."

Dugan walks over and stands next to Anna. "Enough!" he says. "I will not stand idly by and let you pester the love of my life."

"Actually, she is more the love of your death," Gently Gently points out.

"Whatever she is," I say, "I am not inclined to supply her with a dowry one hour after collecting it from Longshot Lamont." I turn to her. "I hope you and Dugan will be very happy, and can find a hotel that caters to both of whatever you are, and I will even pop for a flimsy nightgown if you are going to tie the knot, but I still want my three large."

"And if I do not agree to part with it, will you put a hit out on Dead End Dugan?" she asks with a cold reptilian smile, and I have to admit that the idea of putting out a hit on a dead man can best be called counterproductive.

"Milton," I say, "have you got any other tricks up your sleeve?"

"He has nothing up his sleeve except his arm," says Anna. "And if he tries anything, he will make me lose my temper. You will not be happy if I should lose my temper. The last time I lose it they blame what happens on Hurricane Katrina, and the time before that they invent Hurricane Andrew."

"Did you do Chernobyl too?" asks Benny curiously.

"No," she says. "That was my kid sister."

"I am sure I will love her too," says Dugan.

No sooner do the words leave his mouth than Anna gets all red in the face and lets out a shriek. All the windows break, my fillings fall out of my teeth, a bus half a block away veers and plows into a fire hydrant, and every dog within a mile begins howling.

"I am sorry," says Anna a moment later. "I have a jealous and passionate nature."

"To say nothing of cataclysmic and catastrophic and a lot of other words that begin with 'cat,'" I agree.

"I see your friend is sprawled out on the floor," she says, indicating Gently Gently. "I hope I did not do him irreparable damage."

"If he can survive eighty-seven million calories," I say as Benny and I heave him to his feet, "he can survive a jealous scream."

"Where am I?" mumbles Gently Gently. "Are we at war? What day is it? Wait! I have it! Flyaway won and the world came to an end!"

"You'll be all right," I say. "Just stand there and try not to think."

"That should be very easy for him," says Benny. "Not thinking is one of the best things Gently Gently does."

Anna Conda turns to Dugan. "I am sorry I have upset your friends so much. I cherish our relationship, and to prove it I will return Harry the Book's money."

"While those are words I have been longing to hear," answers Dugan, "the part about cherishing our relationship, not the part about Harry's money, I am mildly surprised as our total time spent in each other's company has been only ten minutes, give or take."

"That is about seven minutes longer than most of my relationships last," says Anna. "I will be back with the money in a moment."

She goes into one of the back rooms, and Benny walks over to Dugan.

"I would be very careful with this girl," he says confidentially. "For example, when she suggests you go out for a bite, I will give plenty of eight-to-five that she is not talking about patronizing a restaurant."

Anna comes out and hands me a bag containing the three thousand dollars. "It is all there," she says. "You can count it if you wish."

"That is not necessary," I tell her. "Dugan would never cheat me, and if you would I prefer not to know about it, because then I will not have to do anything about it."

She gives me another of those smiles that are more frightening than a gorgon's grimace. "You are wise beyond your years, Harry the Book."

"And you are formidable beyond yours, Anna Conda," I say, bowing low, but not so low that I can't jump back if she changes her mind and reaches for the money, or maybe my neck.

As we are leaving, Benny whispers to me: "I know Love is blind, but until this minute I do not realize he is on life support."

And that is the story of Dead End Dugan's very special girl. I suppose their relationship was doomed from the start. I know that opposites attract, but there is nothing in the rulebook about anyone quite as opposite as Dugan and Anna. They decide to go away for a weekend in the mountains. Dugan never mentions exactly what happens, except that he makes a mistake by remarking that the tour bus driver is very pretty, but I am told that when the next edition of Rand McNally comes out Pike's Peak will now be Pike's Valley.

"I have learned a valuable lesson, Harry," Dugan tells me when it is all over. "From now on, I will stick to my own kind."

And so he does. The next afternoon I am sitting in the third booth at Joey Chicago's, reading the *Form*, and the smell of rotting flesh is twice as strong as ever. I look up and there is Dugan and his new girlfriend, sidling up to the bar.

"What can I get you and this beautiful young lady?" asks Joey Chicago, managing to string together three misstatements in just three words.

"What will it be, my dear?" says Dugan.

"It's been so many decades since I've drunk anything at all, I can't remember," says his companion. "Why don't we let the bartender decide?"

"I've got just the thing," says Joey Chicago, pulling out a pair of tall glasses and little paper umbrellas.

"And what is that?" asks Dugan.

"A pair of Zombies," says Joey Chicago.

How it begins is that I am sitting there in my office, which is the third booth at Joey Chicago's Three-Star Tavern, sipping an Old Washensox and taking care of business, which this particular evening concerns doping out the odds on the Horrendous Howard-Kid Testosterone rematch. Gently Gently Dawkins, all three hundred and fifty pounds of him, is sitting across from me working out a crossword puzzle, and for the past fifteen minutes has been stumped trying come up with a three-letter word for "morbidly overweight." Dead End Dugan, who is still not used to being a zombie, is standing in a corner, wondering why he isn't thirsty anymore. It is at that precise moment that Joey Chicago tells me that I've got a phone call.

"Should I come over to the bar to get it?" I ask.

"The cord is four feet long," says Joey. "What do you think?"

So I walk over to the bar and pick up the receiver, and who should be at the other end than Benny Fifth Street, but it is hard to hear him because there is a lot of barking and even more yelling going on, and I remark that I did not know they brought telephones along on fox hunts and that unlike Joey Chicago's it must have a mighty long cord.

"I am at the dog track," says Benny. "Tell me that you do not book bets on dog racing."

"I am Harry the Book," I say with a note of pride. "I book bets on everything."

"All right," says Benny. "Tell me you do not book a bet on tonight's dog races for Tabasco Sanchez."

"As a matter of fact, Tabasco Sanchez bet five large on the feature race of the night," I tell him. "Is there anything else I should not be telling you?"

"Yes," says Benny. "Tell me that Tabasco Sanchez does not lay the five thousand dollars on an animal called Devil Moon."

"I cannot tell you that," I say, "and I do not think I want to hear what you are going to tell me next."

"What odds do you give him?" asks Benny.

"Twenty-to-one," I say. "After all, the dog is a first-time starter. He has never run before."

"Well, he is now a first-time winner, though he has still not broken out of a trot," says Benny. "It is a most unusual race and this Devil Moon is a most unusual greyhound, which is why I have called you."

"What is unusual about Devil Moon?" I ask.

"I have never seen a shaggy brown greyhound before," says Benny. "Furthermore, he has a pot belly, just like Sanchez himself."

"Maybe I am hearing you wrong," I say, "because otherwise I would be inclined to ask how a shaggy, pot-bellied dog can beat all the fastest greyhounds at the track."

"It is somewhat out of the ordinary," agrees Benny. "He is in an eight-dog field."

"And?" I say.

"He kills five of them on the way to the post."

"This is clearly a new form of strategy," I say. "But that still leaves two healthy greyhounds, does it not?"

"They are two healthy, terrified greyhounds," confirms Benny. "Devil Moon just stares at them and shows his teeth. One of them climbs into the stands and will not return to the track. He is still whimpering when last I see him."

"And the other?" I ask.

"He jumps the outer fence and is still running. I figure he must be nearing the state line by now."

"The New York state line is not that close," I say.

"I am referring to the state line of Colorado, or maybe Burma," says Benny. "I have never seen a dog run that fast. Devil Moon has turned him into the Secretariat of dogs. Unfortunately, he has also turned him into the Wrong-Way Corrigan of dogs. Anyway, the race begins and Devil Moon starts trotting leisurely around the track. The mechanical rabbit makes a complete circle and is bearing down on him when Devil Moon bites its head off. He crosses the finish line and goes back to the barn, which they call a kennel here, and then he seems to vanish, because nobody can find him, although between you and me I don't know why anyone goes looking for a dog that eats his rivals and damages valuable track property."

"Do you know who owns him?" I ask.

"It says right in the program book," answers Benny. "He is owned by someone called Sylvester Sanchez."

"That is Tabasco Sanchez," I say.

"It says Sylvester," insists Benny.

"Mighty few mothers christen their children Tabasco," I note.

"You know," says Benny thoughtfully, "now that you point it out, I'll lay plenty of nine-to-five that Kid Testosterone is also an alias."

"I would stay on the phone and discuss aliases all night with you," I say, "but who should I see entering Joey Chicago's other than Tabasco Sanchez himself?"

"Perhaps he will solve the mystery of his real name," says Benny hopefully.

"I think he is more interested in collecting one hundred large from me," I say, "which I do not have any intention of paying off until all the circumstances have been explained to my satisfaction, which I put on a probability scale right up there with anacondas tap-dancing and politicians turning away from cameras."

I hang up the phone just as Tabasco Sanchez enters the bar.

"Hello, Harry," he says with a big smile on his face. "I trust you have heard the results of this evening's sporting events."

"Yes," I say. "Benny Fifth Street was out at the dog track and has so informed me."

"Have you got my money?" he asks.

"Before we talk money," I say, "we have to talk about the race, because the condition book says it is for greyhounds and I am told that Devil Moon does not exactly resemble your everyday greyhound."

"He is a most unusual greyhound, I will admit," agrees Tabasco. "But the fact remains that he wins the race."

Suddenly he coughs, and what should come out of his mouth but a bunch of dog hair.

"I thought that only cats choke on hairballs," observes Gently Gently Dawkins.

"And those are gray hairballs, are they not?" I say.

"I must have picked them up when I was back at the kennel, kissing Devil Moon for winning my hundred large," says Tabasco nervously.

"This is most interesting," I say, "because I have it on good authority that Devil Moon differs from most greyhounds in that he is brown."

"So I am nearsighted," says Tabasco. "I kiss the wrong dog."

"I am beginning to think that nearsightedness is the least of your physical problems," I say. "I am told that Devil Moon sports a pot belly just like yours."

"That is why I bet on him," says Tabasco defensively. "He reminds me of me."

"He reminds me of you, too," I say accusingly. "Especially if your name is Sylvester."

"My name is Tabasco."

"Show me your driver's license," I say.

"Nobody in Manhattan drives a car," he says. "But I am booked as Tabasco on my last three arrests."

"What are you on the first seven?" I ask.

"I don't remember," he says stubbornly.

"Gently Gently," I say, "what do you think his name was?"

"Sanchez," says Gently Gently promptly.

"You see?" says Tabasco. "Nobody knows that I was Sylvester Sanchez." He stops. "I mean, nobody remembers it." He frowns. "That doesn't sound much better, does it?" he concludes.

"So perhaps now you will deign to tell me about it," I suggest.

"Tell you about what?" he asks, suddenly scratching his left shoulder.

"About you and Devil Moon."

He leans down and scratches his thigh. "Damned fleas!" he mutters.

"So how long have you been a wolf?" I ask.

"Ever since I start noticing girls," he says, trying to smile, and I see more gray hair stuck between his teeth.

"Why don't you just admit that you are a werewolf?" I say.

"Do I look like a werewolf?" he scoffs.

"Yes," I say.

"Oh," he says unhappily. "I was hoping it wouldn't show."

"I wonder just how many rules, regulations and laws you

have broken tonight, Tabasco," I say. "You have destroyed track property. You have killed five competitors. You have chased a valuable greyhound off of the premises. You have impersonated a greyhound yourself ..."

"I do *not* impersonate a greyhound!" he says heatedly. "It is not my fault that the track steward took my entry fee. I never claimed to be a greyhound."

"All right," I say. "I will amend impersonating a greyhound to impersonating a wolf."

"I didn't impersonate a wolf," he replies adamantly. "I *am* a wolf."

"Okay, then," I say. "You have impersonated a human ..."

"I'm a human too!" he insists.

"The court is going to have a difficult time with this one," I predict. "They will not know whether to put you in jail or the dog pound."

"Have you any suggestions?" he says.

"Yes," I tell him. "I suggest you redeem your marker and pay me the five large before I decide to testify against you."

"But I *won* the race!" he says.

"Do you think the track lets the result stand once I tell them what you are?" I ask.

"Would you do that?" he says.

"Absolutely, if you don't redeem your marker," I say. "I booked a bet on a greyhound. You were at best a brownhound."

"I thought we were friends," says Tabasco.

"I am very fond of you," I assure him. "It is just that I am even fonder of the five large you owe me."

"We have a problem here, Harry," he says. "I am ashamed to admit it, because I always pay my debts, but I am tapped out. I prowl all night, which is not even a minimum-wage job, and it tires me out so much that I fall asleep at my desk during the day so often that I am given my walking papers three weeks ago. This is why I came up with the dog track idea. I am desperate for money. You would be surprised at how little a wolf can earn between midnight and six in the morning."

"If this is the case," I say, "why did you choose to become a werewolf?"

"It is not a matter of choice," says Tabasco. "I fall in love with this beautiful Gypsy woman named Yolanda Schwartz …"

"Yolanda *Schwartz?*" I say.

"Well, she is half Gypsy," he replies. "And for some unknown reason her father disapproves of me."

"Unknown," I say.

"Well, it was unknown at the time," answers Tabasco. "Only later do I find out that it is his Cadillac that I steal and sell to Straight Deal Sheldon's chop shop."

"I can see where this might cause him to view the situation with some concern," I agree.

"And a modicum of fury," adds Gently Gently.

"He winds up and hits me with his high hard one—a Gypsy curse," says Tabasco. "And from that day to this, I have had a secret identity, just like Clark Kent and Bruce Wayne, the difference being that Clark Kent is gainfully employed and Bruce Wayne is independently wealthy, and what is more, they climb into their costumes while I grow into mine."

Benny Fifth Street walks in just then.

"Hi, Tabasco," he says. "Nice race, all things considered."

Tabasco buries his head in his hands and starts crying. This causes him to choke, and he spits out still more gray hair.

"You've got to help me, Harry!" he says desperately. "This curse is ruining my life. I only enter the race to raise enough money to have the curse removed so I can get back together with Yolanda." A tear runs down his face. "She still loves me, but it is a very smart curse."

"Smart in what way?" asks Benny.

"She's allergic to dogs!" he wails, crying and coughing up hair again.

"Boy, that's some Gypsy curse," agrees Gently Gently.

"Have you talked to Big-Hearted Milton or Morris the Mage?" I suggest. "They are masterful if mendacious magicians. Possibly they can remove the curse."

"Possibly they can," echoes Tabasco. "But they will not do it for free, and I have already explained my plight to you."

"Well," I say, "it appears we must help you find a way to make a living, if only so you can pay off my five large and have enough left over to speak to Milton or Morris." I think of all the things I see dogs do in the movies. "Can you save a dying man in a blizzard?" I ask.

"I cannot even *find* a dying man in a blizzard," says Tabasco, "and besides, when I am busy being a wolf, I tip the scales at no more than ninety pounds. Can you imagine me pulling Gently Gently to safety?"

"I cannot imagine you pulling him across the room unless you know how to operate a crane," says Benny.

"Is there a market for seeing-eye dogs?" I ask.

"I am nearsighted and I have astigmatism," says Tabasco unhappily.

"I have never noticed you wearing glasses," I say.

"I do not wish to spoil my manly good looks, especially once I meet Yolanda," he says.

I am about to tell him that he is in no danger of that, that his manly good looks have gone the way of the dodo and the five-cent beer, but instead I concentrate on the problem at hand. "What else can you do besides eat greyhounds?" I ask.

Tabasco frowns. "Give me a for-instance," he says.

I shrug. "Do you herd sheep?" I say.

"That is wrong," says Gently Gently.

"How can a question be wrong?" says Benny. "It is answers that are wrong."

"Do you heard sheep is wrong," insists Gently Gently. "Have you heard sheep is right."

"Get him some calories," I say to Benny. "The crossword puzzle has sapped his mental strength, and he is now operating on two cylinders, three at the most."

Benny leads Gently Gently off to the bar for nuts and pretzels, and I go back to considering Tabasco's problem, except Tabasco isn't there anymore. I look down and there is Devil Moon, panting and drooling and looking mournfully into my eyes. Mournfully, and maybe a little hungrily too.

"Tabasco, do you still understand me?" I say.

Tabasco stares at me and yawns. He has very white teeth.

"Tabasco, howl once if you understand me and twice if you don't."

Tabasco walks over to a nearby chair and lifts his leg on it.

"I like him better as a guy," says Gently Gently, staring at Tabasco from the bar.

"Hell," adds Benny, "I even like him better as a greyhound."

"You know," says Joey Chicago, "other guys decorate their places with the stuffed heads of lions and tigers and mooses and things like that, but me, I am too gentle and too sensitive to ever show off the remains of an animal in my establishment." He raises his voice. "But if somebody lifts his leg in here again, we're going to display a mounted wolf's head over the bar." He turns to Benny and Gently Gently. "And that goes for you, too!"

All the while this is going on, I am staring at Tabasco and trying to think of how to put his transformation to economic gain. For a while I think of the movies, but even though Rin Tin Tin has gone on to his reward, I can foresee numerous problems, because out there time is money and once they get all the actors and cameras in position and yell "Action!" it would not do for the new Rin Tin Tin to appear as the old Tabasco Sanchez.

I know that guard dogs are always in demand, but I also know Tabasco Sanchez, and whether he is busy being a man or a wolf, I would not want to put him near anything that was worth guarding.

I am beginning to think that maybe he has got a handle on the situation, that there is no way for a wolf to make a decent living working the third shift, especially in Manhattan, when a newspaper delivery truck drives by, and plastered all over it are ads for the forthcoming Southminster dog show, and suddenly I see a way for Tabasco to pay off his debt to me.

"Tabasco," I say, "if you can understand me, I think I have the solution to your problem. I do not know quite how you can answer me. Clearly you do not howl on cue, and telling you to lift your leg once or twice will clearly put you in dutch with Joey Chicago. Maybe you could paw the ground once if you understand me and twice if you don't?"

Tabasco stares at me and remains motionless.

"Is that a yes or a no?" asks Benny.

"Maybe you should make it multiple choice," suggests Gently Gently.

"Tabasco," says Joey Chicago, "if you will stop being a wolf for the next ten minutes, you can have an Old Peculiar on the house."

"I call that damned sporting of you," says Tabasco, who is a man again so fast that I do not even see him change.

"How do you do that?" asks Benny.

"And how come your clothes vanish when you are a wolf and come back when you are a man?" asks Gently Gently.

"You will have to ask Big-Hearted Milton or Soothsayer Solly," replies Tabasco. "I do not seem to have any control over it—or over anything else, for that matter."

"Do you remember what I say to you while you are being Kazan of the North?" I ask as he downs his Old Peculiar.

"Yes, and I am very grateful."

"Then why do you not respond?" I say.

"When I am a wolf, I think wolfish thoughts, and I am concerned with wolfish things. I hear you say that you have solved my problem, but as a wolf I am much more interested if you can tell me where all the rabbits or the lady wolves were hiding." He pauses for a moment, then continues: "But I am interested now."

"I see that the Southminster dog show is coming up, and that first prize is six large, which means five for me and one for you. All we have to do is win it."

"Win against the best-bred best-conditioned dogs in the world?" says Tabasco doubtfully. "I haven't got a chance."

"Where would America be if Alexander Hamilton had had that attitude?" says Gently Gently reproachfully.

"Pretty much where it is today," answers Tabasco. "And so, come to think of it, is Alexander Hamilton."

"I don't know, Harry," says Benny. "I know what he did in an eight-dog field, but Southminster has thousands of dogs. How many can he kill and eat before someone gets wise?"

"Or before he gets full?" says Gently Gently.

"Tabasco," I say, "are you willing to try, or do I pass the word that you will not make good your marker?"

"I will try," he says. "I cannot have you spreading it all over town that I am a deadbeat."

"Or that he is only occasionally a human being," adds Gently Gently.

So the next morning I buy a leash and collar, making a note to add it to what Tabasco owes me, and then I go to Madison Square Garden, where they are holding this canine beauty contest that night, and ask to see the condition book, figuring I will enter Tabasco in a field for non-winners of two, and they explain to me that this does not work like Belmont or Aqueduct, and I have to enter him in the proper breed, so I request the entry form for timber wolves, and they laugh and ask me what I really want.

"I do not much care," I reply, "so long as he competes after dark."

"That is a most unusual request," says the steward.

"He burns easily," I say.

"Here is a list of the breeds that will show at night," says the steward, handing me a sheet of paper. "Is he on it?"

I look, and I do not see timber wolf or even werewolf listed, but one of the breeds is greyhound, and I figure, well, he has won a race as a greyhound so he might as well remain consistent and win Southminster as a greyhound.

I go back to Joey Chicago's, and kill some time there before we are due in the ring, and then, about an hour before post time —at Southminster they call it ring time—Benny and Gently Gently and Tabasco and I all go over to the Garden.

It is a very unusual sport, this dog show game, because they do not even have a tote board on the infield, and in fact they do not have an infield at all. There are dogs everywhere, and Benny hunts up the ring we are to appear in, and I turn to Tabasco.

"It is time to turn into a wolf again," I say, "and it would not hurt things a bit if this particular wolf happens to look just like a greyhound."

He closes his eyes and grunts.

"I am trying," he says. "But nothing is happening."

"Try harder," I tell him.

He tenses and grunts again, but when he opens his eyes he is still Tabasco Sanchez.

"This is most embarrassing," he says.

"I do not wish to be the bearer of bad tidings," says Benny, "but you are due in the ring in three minutes."

"I am sorry, Harry," says Tabasco. "It does not seem to be working tonight."

"I pay a twenty-five dollar entry fee," I tell him, "and I am going to get my money's worth." I put the collar around his neck and attach it to the leash. "Let us go."

"This is humiliating!" he says as I start dragging him toward the ring.

"Give me my five large and I will cease and desist this instant," I say.

He does not reply, and I look back at him, and he has become a wolf again.

We enter the ring with six sleek greyhounds. Tabasco looks at them and growls. It is a loud, ominous, hungry growl. Two of the greyhounds begin dragging their owners to the far side of the ring, three start shaking, and one just lays right where he has fainted.

The judge comes over and stares at Tabasco.

"I believe you are in the wrong ring, sir," he says at last.

"I am in the right ring," I answer.

"This is not a greyhound," he says.

"He is from the Mexican branch of the family," I say.

"He is not a greyhound," repeats the judge. "I am going to have to disqualify him."

"He *is* a greyhound," I insist. "He has just been out in the sun too long, and has acquired a tan."

"Get out of my ring!" says the judge, pointing to the exit.

For a minute I think Tabasco is going to bite the judge's finger off, but I jerk on the leash, and suddenly all the fight goes out of him as he realizes that we have failed and he still is penniless, and he docilely follows me out of the ring.

We are on our way to the exit when we pass a ring where they are judging these little silken-haired dogs, and suddenly Tabasco stops and digs in his heels, which is a lot of heels to dig in all at once, and I can tell he is taken with one feminine little dog.

I ask a ringsider what this kind of dog is called, and he says "Shi Tzu," and I say, "Gesundheit!" and he says, "No, that is the name of the breed."

I pull on Tabasco's leash again, and he pulls back, and before long most of the ringsiders are no longer watching the Gesundheit dogs but are laying bets on who will win our tug of war, and at the moment Tabasco is a seven-to-five favorite, and then suddenly there is a cheer, and Tabasco and I both stop pulling for a minute to see what the cheering is about, and it seems that the little dog he has been watching has won.

On the way out of the ring she makes a beeline for Tabasco, and they touch noses, and then she is led away and I start to walk to the exit again, and Tabasco bites his leash in half and runs to the big ring in the center of the building, and I have no choice but to follow him, since he is five thousand dollars on the hoof, or on the claw as the case may be, and I am not letting him out of my sight until I collect.

I am not sure what is going on, but dogs keep coming and going into the big ring, and finally there is an enormous cheer, and all that is left in the ring is the little Gesundheit dog and thirty-seven photographers. Finally the crowd starts dispersing, and as it thins out I spot Tabasco on the far side of the ring, and I race around it to reach him before he can run off, and when I get there he has forgotten to be a wolf and is just plain old Tabasco Sanchez again, still attached to a leash and collar.

"What are you trying to pull?" I demand.

"Just wait, and all will be revealed," he says.

A minute later Benny catches up with us, and I can see all three hundred and fifty pounds of Gently Gently rounding the far turn and heading for home, and then suddenly we are joined by as pretty a dark-haired girl as I have ever seen. She walks right up to Tabasco and plants a kiss on his cheek.

"Harry the Book," he says, "I want you to meet the woman I intend to marry, Yolanda Schwartz."

"You must have just arrived," I say, "because surely I would have noticed someone of your good looks before."

"You have been looking at her for the past hour," says Tabasco.

"You are mistaken," I say. "I would not forget someone like her."

"She just went Best in Show," says Tabasco. "I recognize her the second I see her, for even a change in species cannot disguise the love of my life from me."

I stare at her, and there is not a touch of Gesundheit dog to be seen, except maybe for the silken hair.

"It is true," says Yolanda. "I am so mad at my father for what he does to poor Tabasco that I run away from home, so he curses me too." She holds up a fistful of money. "It turns out to be a blessing, because now Tabasco and I can be together forever, and he can pay off the five thousand dollars he owes you."

"No," says Tabasco. "We need that money to set up house-keeping."

"Think, Tabasco," says Yolanda. "If we take our human forms, Daddy will just find us and break us up again. But if we stay a Shi Tzu and a wolf forever, he will never find us. We will sleep all day and love all night."

This sounds as good to Tabasco as it would to any red-blooded male of any species, and he turns over the money to me.

"You only owe me five large," I say. "I will invest the rest where it will do the most good."

I do as I promise, and the next day I give them their very first wedding present, which is a thousand-dollar line of credit at Morgan the Gorgon's Meat Market.

SNATCH AS SNATCH CAN

So we are sitting there in the dark, and the first one to strut across the stage is Fifi McDoll, who figures to be a thirteen on anyone's ten scale, and the audience breaks into cheers, and for a minute I figure maybe the morning line of five-to-one was a little too generous, that this Fifi McDoll makes most girls, even such high-class ecdysiasts as Bedroom Eyes Betty, look like boys.

But then out comes Bubbles La Tour, and she looks just the way a one-to-three favorite ought to look, which is to say that if there is a straight line anywhere on her it is probably between her two front teeth. I have never had the pleasure of her company, which looks from where I am sitting like this is a lot of pleasure not to have, but I can tell that she is the Secretariat or maybe the Babe Ruth of women.

I sit there, feeling No-Nose Minsky's five large in my pocket, and I am getting ready to kiss it goodbye, along with the six other bets I have booked, because there is no way Bubbles La Tour can lose the Miss Lower South Manhattan Beauty Pageant, and I am thinking that even one-to-ten would be an overlay, and that this is not going to be a good night, because each of the seven bets I have booked is on her, since a man would have to be blind and probably deceased to bet on the competition. From where I am sitting, it is clear that she can give each of the other girls a five-length lead, carry extra weights, and even if the track comes up muddy she cannot help but win by daylight.

Ten or twelve more girls walk across the stage, but there is no spring to their stride, because they have seen Bubbles La Tour and they know they are only fighting for place and show. Then the final contestant comes on, and it is Lizzie Lamont the Lizard Girl, who not only doffs her duds but also sheds her skin four times a night at Honest Ivan's Palace of Delights. She differs from the other contestants not only in the matter of her epidermis, but also her claws, her wings, and her forked tongue, and I am starting to think that the morning line of three hundred-to-one might be a little too optimistic.

The judges adjourn to a back room to deliberate, and Velvet Voice Vinnie comes out and sings half a dozen hits from yesteryear, or yestercentury as the case may be, and I look over at No-Nose Minsky and he is beaming like he has already won, and indeed you could not find a person in the audience to suggest that he hasn't.

Then the judges come back, and I notice that one of them has a black eye and one is nursing a bloody nose, and none of them looks to be in mint or even fine condition, and they hand a little blood-spattered piece of paper to Vinnie, who looks at it, laughs as if he is reading a joke, and hands it back. The biggest judge, the only one who is not bleeding, says something to him, and Vinnie looks shocked, like he has just walked in on his wife and the mailman, or like one of his records actually gets a good review.

"Ladies and gentlemen," he says, because it is easier than saying "Ladies, gentlemen, gnomes, goblins, leprechauns, elves, and assorted others," which is more accurate but long-winded. Anyway, "Ladies and gentlemen," he says, "we have a winner."

Bubbles La Tour is already smiling and bowing, and the audience is hooting and hollering, especially when she bows in the particular dress she is sort of wearing, but then Velvet Voice Vinnie holds a hand up. "And the winner," he continues, "is Lizzie Lamont."

The audience starts screaming words that should not be uttered in front of such innocent females as are standing on stage looking shell-shocked, and then Bubbles La Tour lets loose with a stream of invective that would put her no worse than third place in a county-wide cussing contest, and suddenly No-Nose Minsky is at my side, screaming that the fix was in and he wants his five thousand dollars back.

"I don't know how you and your wizard did it," he yells, "but clearly the fix was in, and I want satisfaction!"

"If you want satisfaction I suggest you visit Madame Fatima's Exotic Realm of Pleasure just above Weasel Hannity's Garage and Meat Market," I say, "or perhaps make a private arrangement with Bedroom Eyes Betty, who I am told can be quite an entrepreneur on occasion. As for me," I continue with dignity, "I am not in the satisfaction business; I am in the bookmaking business."

"You'll be sorry for this, Harry!" he promises, shaking a fist at me. "I do not take being flim-flammed lightly. You and Big-Hearted Milton are in a world of trouble."

"Just be glad Milton is over in Jersey at his favorite place of good repute or he might turn you into a horned toad," I say. "You should be careful before insulting such a powerful wizard."

Actually, Milton is hiding at his brother's place in Chicago until the current storm blows over, said storm being a redhead named Thelma who insists that certain promises were made and vows exchanged, and in truth I have no idea why Bubbles La Tour is a victim of such injustice, but at the moment I do not much care, because it means I do not have to pay off any of the bets.

"Give me back my five large and I won't take my just and terrible vengeance," says No-Nose Minsky.

"Where would I be if I refunded money to every player who bet on the wrong horse?" I say.

"Just you wait, Harry!" he hollers. "This isn't finished yet!"

I look at the stage, where Lizzie Lamont is accepting her trophy, and point out that it *is* finished, and I leave as maybe five hundred thoughtful gentlemen from the audience are lining up to offer Bubbles La Tour their condolences.

THE NEXT DAY I am sitting in my office, which is the third booth at Joey Chicago's Three-Star Tavern, doping out the line at Aqueduct. Gently Gently Dawkins, whose most recent diet lasted somewhat less than three hours and who is now pushing 375 pounds, is working on the crossword puzzle, and has spent the last ten minutes trying to come up with a three-letter word for "firearm," and is sure there has been a misprint because, as often as he tries it, "gat" doesn't work. Dead End Dugan, who still can't get used to being a zombie, keeps ordering drinks out of force of habit and then realizes that he isn't thirsty. Benny Fifth Street is arguing the finer points of tiddly winks with Joey Chicago, who is unimpressed with Benny's claim that he played left forward wink on his fourth-grade tiddly team and made it all the way to the city semi-finals before the other team's mage turned his team's tiddly winks into nickels and his teammates grabbed them and ran off to buy comics and dirty magazines, thus forfeiting all chance at the championship, which Benny regrets to this day, especially since he had a sawbuck riding on his team.

Finally Joey gets tired of hearing about Benny's great lost opportunity, and he grabs a mop.

"The place is clean," notes Benny. "Well, except for wherever

Dead End Dugan is standing." Which is true, since little pieces of dirt and even a few pieces of Dugan are constantly falling to the floor wherever he happens to be.

"As long as he is out of town, I am going to clean Milton's office," says Joey.

"His office is the men's room," Benny points out.

"Have you seen all the pentagrams and mystic signs he's drawn on the floor?" demands Joey. "It is time to scrub the place down, and it will be more entertaining than hearing about tiddly winks. In fact, not to put too fine a point on it, the black plague is more entertaining than hearing about tiddly winks."

"I could tell you about the Pick Up Sticks tournament I almost won in the second grade," offers Benny.

"Suddenly that plague is looking mighty good indeed," says Joey, disappearing into the men's room.

"I got a bad feeling about this," says Gently Gently. "Maybe some of those signs are protecting us against evil creatures from other dimensions, and we could be overrun by them if Joey washes them away."

"I think they were supposed to protect Milton from overly aggressive redheads named Thelma," I point out, "and you can see how well they worked."

Gently Gently shrugs, which almost sets the room in motion. "You're the boss," he says.

I am glad someone remembers that, for Gently Gently, Benny, and Dugan all work for me, and Benny in particular gets annoyed when anyone calls them my toadies or my stooges, and rightfully points out that what they are is my flunkies.

"I'll have another tall one," says Dead End Dugan when Joey Chicago emerges from the men's room, mop in hand.

"Why?" says Joey. "You haven't taken so much as a sip from the last six you ordered."

I can see that Dugan is pondering the question, which means we won't hear from him for another twenty minutes, because ever since he became a zombie his brain is still functioning at 33 1/3 while everyone else is running 4.7-gigabyte disks between their ears.

Gently Gently walks over to the bar to grab a fistful of pretzels, and Joey Chicago slaps his hand.

"What was that for?" demands Gently Gently.

"You're supposed to be on a diet," says Joey.

"Do you want me to starve to death?" says Gently Gently.

"How long have I got to consider my answer?" replies Joey.

"Gently Gently Dawkins is the only guy I know who *gains* weight on a diet," remarks Benny.

"Nonsense," says Gently Gently. "I feel light as a feather."

"How many four-hundred-pound feathers have you ever seen?" asks Benny.

"Really," insists Gently Gently. "I feel lighter than I've felt in years."

Joey Chicago stares at him. "Some of him is missing," he announces.

"Under my chin and around my waist, right?" says Gently Gently, standing in the middle of the tavern and turning around.

"Everywhere," says Benny, blinking his eyes rapidly.

"That is some diet!" exclaims Gently Gently. "I quit it last month, and is it still working its magic on me."

"*Something* is working its magic on you," I agree. "But I do not think it is the diet. You are becoming transparent."

Gently Gently spins like a ballerina, which is not really the case but I do not know what you call a male ballerina, and then he jumps in the air, and if there is a basket ten feet above the ground there is no question that he could stuff a basketball through it.

"I am going to have to load up on fats and carbohydrates so that I don't shrink out of my clothes by this evening!" says Gently Gently with a blissful smile on his face. "What a diet!"

He turns to Joey Chicago. "Give me an Old Peculiar, and put a cup of sugar in it."

But before Joey can even answer him, he becomes so transparent that he is gone, and there is no trace of him anywhere.

"I am no expert," says Benny, "but I do not believe a diet can do that, and especially not retroactively."

Before anyone can answer a banshee flies into the tavern with a piece of paper in its mouth, circles the room once, flies over to me, drops the paper in my hands, and flies out again.

"That is the most unusual newsboy I have ever seen," says Benny.

"They do not deliver the paper at two-thirty in the afternoon," answers Joey Chicago, "and besides, I cannot remember the last time the newspaper was only one page and printed in blue handwriting."

"It is from No-Nose Minsky," I announce.

"What does it say?" asks Benny.

So I read it aloud:

To whom it may concern:

Harry you foul swine, I still do not know how you fixed the Miss Lower South Manhattan Beauty Pageant, but I want my five large back, and to that end I have employed Morris the Mage and told him to put the snatch on your henchman, who will be returned relatively unharmed the moment you turn over my money to me.

Respectfully,

No-Nose Minsky

"So are you going to honor his request?" asks Joey Chicago.

"It was more a demand than a request," says Benny, who is still mad that Joey isn't interested in tiddly winks and is looking to start an argument.

"You are disagreeing over semantics," says Joey. "The important thing is that they've put the snatch on Gently Gently."

"Maybe Big-Hearted Milton can magic him back," suggested

Dugan, who hasn't noticed that Milton has been in hiding for the past three weeks.

"I do not pay ransoms and I do not yield to threats," I say at last. "Millions for defense, but not one cent for tribute."

"Who is Tribute?" asks Dugan.

"So you're just going to let No-Nose Minsky and Morris the Mage beat you?" says Benny reproachfully. "Milton may be out of town, but there is always Soothsayer Solly, or Maggie the Mystic, or—"

"If I give No-Nose his money back," I say, "then every plunger who backs the wrong horse will want his money back."

"I thought he was betting on women," says Dugan, who seems no more confused than usual, which is to say a great deal more than somewhat.

"This is beyond you, Dead End," says Joey. "Don't worry about it. Just busy yourself doing a bunch of dead things."

Dugan frowns, and we can see he is going to be a few hours thinking of dead things to do, and I turn back to Benny.

"I, Harry the Book, have spoken. I will be sorry to lose Gently Gently, but I am a businessman, and refunding bets to suckers is bad business."

And that is the way it stands for almost two days.

Then the banshee comes by with another message, to wit:

Where can I get five pounds of buffalo steak, potatoes au gratin made with warthog cheese, and a gallon of pickle-flavored ice cream?

Respectfully,

No-Nose Minsky

I read the note aloud, then crumple it up and toss it in the trash.

"No answer," I say to the banshee, who has been hovering above me.

It flies out the door, but it is back three hours later.

Who is likely to be selling shrimp de jongue *at four in the morning?*

Cordially

No-Nose Minsky

"No answer," I tell the banshee.

Five more hours and it is back again.

Harry, he is eating me out of house and home. How did you ever put up with it? And quick, where can I get two gallons of Wisconsin buttermilk, a pound of Rubinski's Russian peanut butter, and a loaf of Antiguan lemon bread?

Desperately,

Obidiah Minsky

This time the banshee doesn't even wait for me to say "No answer," but just flies back out the door.

"Obidiah?" says Joey Chicago with a laugh.

"He is so upset that he forgets to use his real name," chimes in Benny.

"Benny," I say, "if I were you I would move three feet to the left."

Benny looks at the ceiling as if it might collapse any second, but cannot find anything wrong with it. "Why?" he asks.

"Because," I say, "you are standing exactly where Gently Gently Dawkins stands when Morris the Mage put the snatch on him."

"So?"

"So I intuit that we will soon have a visitor," I say.

He looks at me like I am functioning on even less cylinders than Dead End Dugan, but he goes over and sits at a table, and no sooner does he do so than Gently Gently Dawkins flickers into view, becoming more solid by the instant, and by the time he is completely back, holding a half-eaten sandwich in one hand and a rhino-flavored malt in the other, he looks to have put on a quick fifteen pounds.

"Hi, Harry," he says as if he has never been away. He holds his sandwich out. "Can I offer you a bite?"

"No," I say. "A growing boy like you needs all his strength. Did they treat you well?"

"They starved me a bit," he replies, "but they never beat me or anything like that. I am glad to be back, but if you don't mind, I'm going down the street to Carla's Pie Shop to replenish my depleted strength."

And with that he is gone.

"Well, let us hope No-Nose learned his lesson and there will be no more poor sportsmanship from him," says Benny.

"I will give plenty of twenty-to-one against," I say, because even as the words leave my mouth, Dead End Dugan starts going all transparent.

"I am dying again," he announces, looking down at his body. "This is the fourth time, or maybe the fifth"—suddenly he frowns, the first emotion he has shown since he came back from the cemetery over in Brooklyn five months ago – *and it's got to stop!*"

But it doesn't, and fifteen seconds later there is no Dugan left, just a pile of dirt where he had been.

"Well, at least No-Nose won't have to feed him," says Benny.

"I hope you are not sympathizing with No-Nose Minsky," I say, "because once he figures out that I am not going to give him back his five large for Dugan any more than I did for Gently Gently, you are probably next on his list."

"If he feeds me like he fed Gently Gently, there are worse situations to be in," replies Benny.

"He knows from Gently Gently that feeding is not an answer," I say. "He will soon learn from Dugan that intelligence is not an answer. By the time he gets to you, he may be wondering if torture is an answer."

"Torture is an answer?" repeats Benny, his eyes going wide with terror. "I do not even know the question!"

Joey Chicago spends the next five minutes suggesting questions to Benny, but on a lark he does so in Polish and a couple of other languages that are popular in distant lands, and Benny is becoming more and more panic-stricken, and finally Joey takes pity on him.

"Relax," says Joey. "I personally will give plenty of eight-to-one that No-Nose Minsky and Morris the Mage do not put the snatch on you."

"You think they'll just keep Dugan, then?" asks Benny hopefully.

"No," says Joey.

"Then why do you give eight-to-one that they won't snatch me?"

"I think they will probably conclude that snatching Harry's flunkies isn't going to work. It is at least eight-to-one against." Joey pauses thoughtfully. "On the other hand, I figure it's even money that they'll kill you where you stand."

Joey spends the next half hour giving Benny the morning line on exactly how he thinks Morris will kill him, and then Gently Gently comes back with crumbs on his mouth and shirt, looking more substantial and less transparent than ever.

"You're *sure* they didn't torture you, maybe just a little bit?" says Benny by way of greeting.

"Except for starving me, you mean?" asks Gently Gently. "No, they were very cordial and friendly. Mrs. No-Nose and I spent most of the time exchanging recipes."

Just then a harpy swoops through the doorway and deposits a note in my hand.

Does he always smell this bad?

Curiously,

No-Nose

I have the harpy hover for a moment while I write an answer.

He has been dead for almost three years. What did you expect?

Yours very truly,

Harry the Book"

The harpy flies off, and five minutes later Dead End Dugan begins taking shape. We watch as all the parts fill in, except for the knife wounds and the bullet holes, and finally he is pretty much the way he was when he left.

"Welcome back, Dead End," I say.

"Did they torture you?" asks Benny anxiously.

"I don't know," says Dugan.

"How can you not know?" demands Benny.

"I do not feel pain," says Dugan, "and it is counterproductive to threaten me with death when I am already dead."

I am about to compliment him on his answer, and especially his use of big words like "counterproductive," when suddenly I feel a little flimsy, like the time I wake up with a hangover and go out to buy a paper and realize when everyone starts laughing that I have forgotten to put on my pants.

Then I feel flimsier still, and realize that my pants are fine, it is *me* that is becoming absent. Gently Gently waves at me, and Benny says "Take care, Boss," and Joey Chicago pours my drink back into the bottle, and then I am in No-Nose Minsky's living room, surrounded by No-Nose and three of his henchpeople (which is the proper term, since of one them is Sledgehammer Sally), and I see Morris the Mage decked out in his robe and conical hat, both of which are covered with the same little signs you see on the horoscope page of the newspaper.

"How do you put up with him?" asks No-Nose.

"Dugan?" I say. "He just stands in the back of the bar and doesn't bother anyone."

"I maybe could put up with the smell," says No-Nose, "and I suppose I could put up with the dirt, and I could possibly even put up with the things crawling around in his hair and under his fingernails ..."

"Then why do you send him back?" I ask.

"What I cannot put up with is Mrs. No-Nose," he says bitterly. "She takes one look at the furniture after he sits on it and says that either he goes or I go and she doesn't care which, and then she starts swinging her rolling pin." He shoots a bitter glance toward the kitchen. "It is not generally known, but I used to be Needle-Nose Minsky before our first argument."

"She sounds formidable," I say. "Maybe you should consider entering her in the Friday Night Fights."

He shakes his head. "She needs motivation, so unless I am the opponent, she figures to last no more than thirty seconds of the first round." He stares at me. "Enough small talk. I am through with toadies—"

"They are flunkies," I correct him.

"They are a dead man and a blimp with an appetite!" he yells. "From now on, I am dealing only with you. You are my prisoner, and you are staying here until I get my five large back."

"You lost it fair and square," I say. "I do not make refunds."

"I lost it unfair and crooked!" he yells. "What is the likelihood of Lizzie Lamont beating Bubbles La Tour?"

"I had it at three hundred-to-one," I say. "But on reflection, I think five hundred-to-one would have been a fairer price."

"Then you agree!" he says.

"I agree that a longshot upset the favorite," I say. "But I do not agree that I have to return your money."

"The fix *had* to be in!" says No-Nose.

"It is possible," I agree. "But I didn't put it in, and I am not refunding bets I took in good faith."

"Then you are going to stay here until you change your mind," he says.

"It cannot be any more uncomfortable and confining than the third booth at Joey Chicago's," I say placidly.

"We are not savages here," says No-Nose. "Well, except maybe for Sledgehammer Sally and Eldritch Oscar," he adds, gesturing to two of his henchpeople. "You will be treated with respect and courtesy, but you will not set foot out of here until I have my five large."

"Well, if I'm here, I'm here," I say with a shrug. "I trust you will not stop me from practicing my profession. Is there a *Racing Form* in the place?"

No-Nose nods to Eldritch Oscar, who leaves the room and comes back in a minute with a *Form.* He gives it to No-Nose, who glances at it and then hands it to me.

"I see Apricot Preserve is running in the second tomorrow," he notes. "And he is five-to-one on the morning line, which is clearly an overlay."

"You think so?" I ask.

"Absolutely."

"If you like," I say, "I will book your bet."

"I am tapped out," he admits. "That is why I need my five large back."

"You have always been an honorable man," I say, "at least until your heinous and unforgivable behavior of the past two days. I will take your marker."

"Done!" he shouts. "I will put five large on Apricot Preserve's *schnoz.*"

I write it down and have him initial it.

"Do you see anything else you like?" I ask, handing him the *Form.*

Well, he looks at it, and studies it, and also has Eldritch Oscar bring him the daily paper, and when the dust has cleared he has bet ten large on All Day Sucker in the fourth, another ten large on Ticklish Tess in the fifth, twenty large on Kid Testos- terone to kayo Hideous Horace Hochmeyer in the feature fight at the Garden, five large on the Jersey Geldings to beat the spread against the Rhode Island Ridglings, and just for the hell of it, he bets five yards that it won't rain before midnight.

It does not take me long to see why No-Nose is tapped out. Apricot Preserve comes in first, all right, but he wins the third race by a neck after going to the post in the second. All Day Sucker lives up to his name, and is still running at the end of the day. Ticklish Tess actually comes home first, but is disqualified for taking a huge bite out of Bold Nudist in the homestretch, which surprises everyone, since up until then it is generally considered that horses are vegetarians. Kid Testosterone closes his eyes and swings his money punch, a roundhouse right, which misses Hideous Horace and kayos the ref, but that is the best punch he has in him, and Hideous Horace puts him to sleep about twenty seconds after he does the same for the ref. The Jersey Geldings need to lose by less than thirty-five points to beat the spread; they are down 42-to-3 at the half, and they have used all their energy to stay that close, because they at least scored a field goal in the first half and that is three points more than they score for the rest of the game, which is played in a driving rain.

Mrs. No-Nose makes me a hearty breakfast. No-Nose waits until she has gone back into the kitchen, and then he and Morris the Mage approach me.

"Harry," he says, "I am sending you back."

"I thought I was here forever," I say.

"I cannot afford to keep you," he says. "You are here less than twenty-four hours, and I am already out fifty large plus a five-yard side bet."

"I was going to discuss that with you," I say. "How do you plan to pay me if you are tapped out?"

"I am not sure," he says. "But I am a man of honor, except for being a kidnapper and such, and I will make good on my markers, for I cannot have it spread all over town that I ever welch on a bet."

Before I can reply, Morris starts chanting in a language that was used by magicians eons ago, or maybe French diplomats, and suddenly I am back in Joey Chicago's. It takes about two minutes for all my parts to arrive, but I find I am none the worse for wear or for extra-dimensional travel.

And that is the last I hear of No-Nose Minsky for almost a month. Then one day Benny Fifth Street reads in the paper that someone has put the snatch on Lizzie Lamont. Not only that, but the big guy who was one of the judges claims that it was the work of his enemies, because he has a crush on Lizzie Lamont and beats the other judges into voting for her. He also admits that he has a major bet down on her at 250-to-one with Moneychanger McNamarra over in Queens, and the winnings are to be their nest egg. Only when he is through ranting does he realize what he has said, and I'm sure he will apologize to Bubbles La Tour and all other injured parties if Ill-Natured Sherman, who is Moneychanger McNamarra's muscle, doesn't immediately repossess his ill-gotten winnings and plant six slugs into his forehead, forming a kind of strange-looking smile a little higher up than most smiles tend to be.

The next afternoon a banshee flies into Joey Chicago's and drops a thick envelope in my lap, then flies out, so clearly no answer is expected. I open it, and there is forty-five large, and a note which reads as follows:

Dear Harry:

Like I told you, I always pay my debts. I would deliver this in person, but life is getting complicated. When I hear that Lizzie Lamont's old man is loaded I have Morris put the snatch on her, and sure enough, the old gentleman coughs up fifty large—but while she is here we fall in love. She is beautiful in her lizardly way, and kind, and gentle, and most important she has never even seen a rolling pin.

I know I am $5,500 short, but her father has put a hit out on me, and so has Esmeralda (Mrs. No-Nose to you), and I need that money to get Lizzie and me off the continent. I'll send you the rest of it when I can.

This is my dream girl, this Lizzie. She's got wings, a tail, more skins than you can shake a stick at, she even sees in the dark. She comes loaded with extras, just like a new luxury car.

Oops! Two shots just came through the window. Got to run.

Yours in haste,

No-Nose Minsky

And that is the last I hear from No-Nose and his new lady love.

Big-Hearted Milton shows up a couple of days later, and we tell him the story. I conclude by wondering where they are holed up.

"That's no problem," says Milton. "I'll find out for you."

He mumbles something that kind of rhymes, goes into his trance, rolls his eyes back in his head, stiffens like a board—which, I should add, is exactly the way he behaves after his fourth martini—and finally he opens his eyes and looks at Benny and Gently Gently and me.

"They are headed to a secluded resort on Bago Bago in the South Pacific," he announces.

"It must be pretty nice there," offers Benny.

"It used to be," agrees Milton.

"Used to be?" asks Gently Gently.

"Yes," says Milton. "Until Thelma decides I am hiding there and burns it down."

Everyone laughs at that except me. I am still busy wondering where No-Nose Minsky is going to find the five large he owes me. Eventually the solution comes to me, and a minute later I am instructing Big-Hearted Milton to put the snatch on Lizzie Lamont.

A VERY FORMAL AFFAIR

I am sitting in my office, which happens to be the third booth of Joey Chicago's Three-Star Tavern, studying the fight card and wondering if this could be the night Kid Testosterone makes it all the way to the second round before being knocked senseless. Benny Fifth Street is behind the bar, pouring himself an Old Peculiar, and Dead End Dugan, who is still having trouble adjusting to being a zombie, is standing in the corner, staring into space and trying to think a bunch of dead thoughts. Big-Hearted Milton, my personal mage, is in *his* office in the men's room, surrounded by black candles, and chanting a curse which was supposed to get Mitzi McSweeney into bed with him but so far has gotten him nothing but a slapped face, a knee in a place that I cannot mention in a G-rated story such as I am relating, and an evening explaining to the police exactly why he was playing itsy-bitsy-spider on her thigh just before she threw the wine at him. ("And it was not the house wine," he complained in outraged tones when he arrived back at Joey Chicago's. "It was Chateau Morganschlucker. Do you know what that stuff costs per glass?")

I have just about concluded that Kid Testosterone cannot last forty-five seconds with the Midtown Masher, give or take half a minute, and I am about to turn my mind to serious contemplation of the third race at Aqueduct when Gently Gently Dawkins, all 375 pounds of him, enters the tavern. He walks right up to the bar, grabs a handful of nuts and pretzels, tosses them into his mouth, repeats the procedure two more times, and then addresses the room in general. "Why is Benny Fifth Street behind the bar?" he says. "What hideous fate has befallen our beloved Joey Chicago, and before it happens does he leave the sawbuck he owes me with anyone?"

"Joey Chicago is fine," says Benny. "He is catering a formal affair across town."

"Catering?" asks Gently Gently. "You mean like with food and such?"

"These people have already eaten dinner," answers Benny. "He brings along a dozen cases of his best whiskey."

"What is the occasion?" asks Gently Gently without much interest, now that the food is off the table, so to speak.

"It is the annual Christmas Eve Dance Contest to benefit the Upper West Side Retirement Home for Warlocks and Witches of Advancing Age," says Benny. "Though with Joey Chicago catering it, I doubt that any participants will be able to pronounce it by ten o'clock tonight."

"Oh, that reminds me," say Gently Gently, walking over and pulling a wad of bills out of his pocket. "Here is ten thousand dollars, Harry."

I pick it up and start counting it.

"If I remind you of Joey Chicago, will you drop ten large on me too?" asks Benny.

"I do not wish to seem ungracious," I say, "in case this is a Christmas present, but if it is not, and I certainly do not pay you enough for it to be, then what, pray, is it for?"

"It is a bet on the dance contest from Short Odds Harrigan," answers Gently Gently.

"And who does Short Odds Harrigan pick, as if I don't know?" I say, because Short Odds plays so many odds-on favorites that he could put the chalk company out of business, and there is no way that the favored couple can lose tonight.

"This is really strange," says Gently Gently. "I ask him if he is betting on Twinkle Toes Tony and Fatima Fatale, who are the defending champions and figure to be about two-to-five to win again, and he says no, that I should tell Harry the Book—I guess that means you since you are he (or is it him?)—that he wants all ten large on Clubfoot Clarence's schnoz."

"Say that again!" I demand.

"He says the whole boodle goes on Clubfoot Clarence. I tell him he could split it five and five, half on Clarence, and half on an exacta for Clarence and Tony to come in one-two, and he says he doesn't care who comes in second, that he wants it all on Clarence."

"This is serious," I say. "I have Clarence at fifty-to-one on the morning line."

"Maybe his new partner will move him up in class," says Gently Gently.

"Who is it?" asks Benny.

"Lezli Luscious," says Gently Gently. "I am told that she is the Prima Ballerina at Salacious Sally's Palace of Exotic Delights."

"She is more like the Prima Bumpagrinda," replies Benny.

"You two are missing the point!" I say.

"Lezli Luscious does not have any points, only curves," says Gently Gently.

"The point is that Short Odds Harrigan only bets on favorites, and suddenly he has laid ten large on a fifty-to-one shot," I say. "If he wins I am out half a million dollars, and between you and me and the gatepost, I do not have half a million dollars."

"Not only that," says Gently Gently, looking around the

tavern, "but I do not even see a gatepost."

"Clearly the hex is in," I say. "We are going to have to go over there and find out what is going on."

"I can tell you what is going on," says Dead End Dugan, who has momentarily stopped thinking dead thoughts. "The hex is in, Harry."

"Thank you for that insight, Dead End," I say, because sarcasm is lost on zombies, as is logic, food, and pain. "I had better get Milton, and then we are on our way."

I walk into the men's room, and there is Big-Hearted Milton sitting on the floor, sporting a black eye and surrounded by eight big candles, and he is muttering and chanting in a language that is almost as alien as French.

"Milton," I say, "get up. We have things to do."

He puts a finger to his lips, then utters one last chant.

"Now she'll be sorry," he says, getting to his feet.

"You are referring to Mitzi McSweeney?" I say.

"That's right." He cackles and rubs his hands together. "Throw wine in *my* face, will she?"

"What terrible thing have you done to her?" I ask, not that I really care, but I do not wish to hurt Milton's delicate feelings, especially since I may need him before the night is over.

"She has left me for Bail Bond Bailey," says Milton. "I have put a curse on her undergarments. No matter how hard she or Bailey try, her bra will not come off, and neither will her girdle." He cackles again. "I guess that writes *Fini* to that romance."

I do not have the heart to tell him that as far as anyone knows, and given the texture of her blouses that is very far indeed, Mitzi McSweeney has not worn a bra since she reached puberty, and they do not even manufacture girdles any more. "That is some curse, Milton," I say, while wondering if Morris the Mage is still on vacation or is maybe available to work this evening.

"All right, Harry," says Milton, "tell me what is so

important.”

“Short Odds Harrigan just bet ten large on a fifty-to-one shot,” I say.

“Aqueduct or Santa Anita?”

“West 73rd Street,” I say.

He frowns. “What is happening on West 73rd Street?”

I tell him.

“Clearly someone has hexed Twinkle Toes Tony and Fatima Fatale,” says Milton. “We must go there before the judging is done and set things right. In fact, we haven’t a second to lose!”

“I am glad to see you so motivated,” I say.

“I have five yards riding on Tony and Fatima,” he says.

“No you don’t,” I say.

“Yes I do,” he insists. “I make the wager with Bet-a-Million McNabb.”

“You do not bet with your own employer?” I demand.

“I love you like a brother,” he says, “but McNabb gives better odds.”

I seriously consider telling him what Mitzi McSweeney does not wear under her dress, but then I decide to wait until the evening is over, because I will need him on my side when I confront whatever foul fiend has tried to rig the dance contest.

We walk out into the tavern, and my crew gathers around me.

“Harry,” says Dead End Dugan, “I have been thinking long and hard on it, and my conclusion is that we should do something. I would tell you about what, but my short-term memory has been on the blink since the last time they dug me up.”

“I second the motion,” says Gently Gently, and then adds hopefully: “Maybe there will be some free eats at the contest.”

“Do we have to dress formally?” asks Benny.

Milton walks to the coat rack and dons his red velvet cloak, the one with the signs of the zodiac emblazoned on it.

“I am ready,” he announces. “How about you, Harry?”

"I am wearing my formal straw boater and chewing on my formal toothpick," I say. "Let us away."

And away we let.

WE SHOW UP, and it seems that all the men are wearing black tuxedos, except for the few that are wearing blue, mauve, puce, or pink ones. The women are all trying their best to look like they are not wearing anything, and one or two just about succeed.

I leave Dugan at the door and tell him not to let anyone out until he hears from me, because I cannot believe that whoever has fixed the contest for Short Odds Harrigan will not be on the premises to make sure nothing goes wrong. I look around the audience and I see Joey Chicago tending bar, and it is clear that everyone has been drinking hard all night because he is serving up his cheap stuff and no one seems to notice the difference. I spot Morris the Mage is in his formal black cape (which does not match his tan Hush Puppies), and Spellsinger Solly is actually wearing a tux, though with an advertisement for Matilda's Meat Market tastefully sewn on a breast pocket. Herman the Plunger—who is not to be confused with Hyman the Plunger, the local plumber—is there, betting on every single dance, of which I gather there are an awful lot. Short Odds Harrigan is there too, smiling like the cat that is about to eat five hundred thousand canaries.

"There is magic in the air, Harry," says Big-Hearted Milton, though Gently Gently argues that it is merely the smell of pastries.

Suddenly I realize that I am getting a headache, and then I see that Velvet Voice Vinnie is standing at the microphone, singing his latest, so at least I know *why* my head hurts.

I look at the couples on the dance floor, and there, whirling and swirling like they are on ice skates, are Twinkle Toes Tony and Fatima Fatale, and it is like they are a whole different species, they are so graceful. Which is not to say that they are not a whole different species from some of the competition, because there are elves, goblins, gremlins, leprechauns, and even a ghoul or two out on the floor.

I peer into a darkened corner, and there are Clubfoot Clarence and Lezli Luscious, and I decide that Clarence has picked the ideal partner, not that Lezli can dance any better than he can, but that once you look at her you forget all about the fact that this is a dance competition. She curses as he steps on her foot, but they go right on waltzing, which is kind of strange since everyone else is doing the rhumba.

Across the way is Swivelhips McGee, whose conversion from quarterback to halfback for the Manhattan Misfits never quite worked, and who wound up playing three-eighthsback. He is dancing with Dressy Jessie Sweeney, who keeps throwing dirty looks at Lezli Luscious, but the looks keep bouncing off her superstructure and shooting off into space.

"Who is that dancing with Pretty Perky Penelope?" asks Gently Gently.

"That is Lefty Louie," says Milton.

"Are you sure?" says Benny.

"Of course I'm sure," says Milton. "Why do you ask?"

"Because I am watching him, and he seems to be right-handed," says Benny.

"He is," says Milton.

"Then why is he Lefty Louie?" asks Gently Gently.

"Because he has two left feet," answers Milton.

"He does not look that awkward to me," observes Benny.

"You do not understand," says Milton.

"Enlighten me," says Benny.

"He has two left feet," repeats Milton.

"You said that."

"And no right feet," continues Milton.

"Are you sure?" asks Benny dubiously.

"He comes to see me about it," says Milton. "But there is nothing about the condition in my grimoires, so I tell him that it could be worse, he could have two left hands growing out of his ankles." He frowns. "The ingrate does not even pay me for those words of comfort."

"Who is Bellisima Brown dancing with?" asks Benny, indicating her partner who makes even Gently Gently look thin.

"That is Biscuit Boris," I answer. "He regularly bets on the Boston jai alai games with me."

"They do not play jai alai in Boston," notes Benny.

"Probably that is why he never wins," I say. "I will not tell him if you don't."

"Why is he called Biscuit?" continues Benny. "He does not look like a biscuit, so much as a blimp."

"Because his doctor says he's about one biscuit short of five hundred pounds," I say.

The dance ends, and if Benny has any more questions they are thankfully drowned out by applause.

"Thank you, thank you, thank you," says Velvet Voice Vinnie, as if they are cheering for him, whereas half the audience is applauding the dancers and the other half is applauding the fact that Vinnie has come to the end of his song. "And now I want to introduce our all-star panel of judges," adds Vinnie. "Will you each stand up and take a bow when I call your name? First on the list is Mildred the Saint."

A sexy redhead stands up and everyone claps.

"She is a saint?" asks Gently Gently.

"By marriage," says Milton. "She is married to Nick the Saint, who is out of town on business, this being Christmas Eve."

"She's a knockout," says Benny. "No wonder he keeps her hidden up at the North Pole."

"Next is Lamont Lupo," says Vinnie, and a tall guy in serious need of a shave and haircut gets up and takes a bow.

"And our final judge is Ming Toy Epstein, who you all know as the proprietor of Ming Toy Epstein's Kosher Chop Suey House."

A lovely lady gets up, waves to the crowd, and sits down again.

"The next dance," announces Vinnie, "will be the samba, so grab your partners—no, not like that, Clarence—and let's go."

The music starts, and the dancing follows.

"This is a very unusual dance, this samba," notes Gently Gently. "Everyone moves a lot, and no one gets anywhere."

"Idiot!" screams Lezli Luscious, and I can see that Clarence has stomped on her foot yet again, and it is getting so swollen that it is almost as big as his.

The dance ends, and Vinnie announces that the jitterbug is next, followed by the two-step and then the tango, and I am looking all around the room, though I do not know what I am looking for, just something to tell me how the hex is going to work, and suddenly someone opens one of the drapes, and I hear a dismal howl coming from the judges' table, and I look, and it turns out that where there were three judges now there are only two, and between them is sitting a wolf which is still wearing Lamont Lupo's bow tie.

"Foul!" cries Twinkle Toes Tony. "It is not fair that we be judged by a wolf."

"Nonsense," says Lezli Luscious. "I am judged by wolves all the time."

A lot of the better-looking women chime in that they would rather be judged by the wolf than by the two women, but then the committee that is running the shindig holds an impromptu meeting at the bar, and decides that Lamont Lupo can continue to judge only if he can still deliberate with the other judges.

Lamont Lupo utters an ugly growl, and both Mildred the

Saint and Ming Toy Epstein immediately hide under the table.

"In English!" says the chairman.

Lamont Lupo looks like he is considering eating the rest of the committee for dinner and the chairman for dessert, but finally Morris the Mage pulls out his wand and says something only Big-Hearted Milton and Spellsinger Solly can understand, and Lamont Lupo meekly walks out of the room, pausing only long enough to lift his leg on the chairman.

"Milton," I say softly, "why do you let Morris take all the glory? You could have vanished that werewolf just as easily."

"That is true," agrees Milton, "but we know that the hex is in, and I want to see if one of the other mages rids us of the wolf, because if he does that means Lamont Lupo was never going to vote for Clubfoot Clarence."

"Come to think of it," I say, "Morris is standing very near the drapes, is he not?"

Milton nods his head. "Let me ask you one question, Harry," he says. "Do you pay off if there is a dead heat?"

"At half the odds," I confirm.

"So if one judge votes for Clarence, you are out a quarter of a million dollars, and if they both do, you are down half a million," he says. "Either way you lose, right?"

"Right," I say. "And I find this line of conversation extremely depressing."

"Well, cheer up, Harry," says Milton, "because you have told me what I wanted to know."

"You wanted to know how much I am going to lose?" I ask.

Milton shakes his head. "I wanted to make sure that no matter how the judging goes, you can't win."

"You are all heart, Milton," I say.

"You do not understand," replies Milton. "If you did not pay off on ties, then I would have to assume Morris is working for both the remaining judges, but since you do pay off, then he only has to be working for one, and I know which one."

"You do?" I say with a feeling of relief.

"Yes, I do," says Milton. "Morris the Mage is nowhere as good a magician as I am, public opinion to the contrary, but he is every bit as expensive, and Ming Toy Epstein still owes me twenty bucks from the World Series."

"You bet with *her* and not *me?*" I say, trying to control my temper. "*Again* you bet with someone else?"

"It's immoral to bet with the bookie I work for," answers Milton. "Besides, she gives me four-to-one and takes the St. Louis Browns."

"There haven't been any St. Louis Browns in more than half a century," I say.

Milton smiles. "That is another reason I bet with her. Anyway, if she cannot pay me twenty dollars, which I ask for a minimum of seventeen times a week, she cannot afford Morris, so the culprit is Mrs. Saint."

"You're sure?" I say.

"As sure as my name is Large-Hearted Milton," he replies.

"Your name is Big-Hearted Milton," I say.

"In my exuberance at unearthing this dastardly scheme I momentarily forget," he says. "Anyway, the culprit is Mildred the Saint." He smiles confidently. "Trust me on this."

"I was all set to believe you before those last four words," I say.

"We are ready for the final dance number," announces Vinnie. "This will be an old-fashioned down-home square dance, and I myself will do the call."

"Accuse her now, before she has a chance to vote," advises Milton.

"Yes, *please* accuse her now," adds Benny plaintively, "or we'll have to listen to Vinnie's version of do-si-do."

"All right, all right," I say, walking over to the bandstand. "Stop the music."

They start playing hoe-down music.

"Dugan!" I call. "Come over here!"

Dead End Dugan lumbers over and stands beside me.

"Dugan," I say, "I want you to eat the first guy who plays so much as a single note."

"I haven't eaten in more than two years," says Dugan.

Before he can tell me he doesn't like food anymore, I say, "You must be good and hungry then. Eat the first guy to play a note, and then eat the guys on each side of him."

A violinist gives me a defiant glare, tucks his instrument under his chin, and prepares to run his bow across it. The trumpet player on his left and the saxophonist on his right immediately start beating him senseless.

I have everyone's attention now, and I walk over to the judge's table, point a finger at Mildred the Saint, and say in stentorian tones: "*J'accuse!*"

"No, it's Mildred," she replies.

"Come on, Mrs. Saint," I say. "We know Morris the Mage is working for you, and that he's the one who pulled the drapes so the moon would shine on Lamont Lupo. What were you going to do to Ming Toy Epstein?"

"That's none of your business!" she snaps.

"You gave Short Odds Harrigan ten large to bet on Clubfoot Clarence," I say. "That makes it my business."

"I told him to keep his mouth shut!" cries Mildred, and suddenly realizes what she has said. "Oops," she adds. "I didn't mean that. I was just kidding."

"Dugan," I say. "Give Short Odds Harrigan ten seconds to admit his culpability, and if he doesn't, then eat him."

"All right, I admit it!" shouts Short Odds, just before Dugan can say, "What's culpability?"

"Why did you do it?" I ask Mildred.

"It's that damned husband of mine!" she says bitterly. "He keeps me cooped up at the North Pole all year. You know what it's like up there? 363 days of winter and two days of bad skiing!

If you hadn't ruined everything, I was going to take my winnings and buy a timeshare on the beach in Barbados." She glares at Short Odds. "You just *had* to make the bet with a bookie who's got his own mage. You couldn't lay it off with Morgan the Gorgon."

"Morgan was only offering thirty-five-to-one against," explains Short Odds reasonably.

"Well, it has been a fascinating evening," says Morris, heading for a door, "but I have urgent business elsewhere."

"No you don't," I say. "It is Christmas Eve."

"Then I'll *find* some," he says and leaves.

"So what's to become of our charity pageant now?" asks the chairman.

"All bets are canceled," I say. "And since all bets are canceled, I'm not going to press charges." I walk over to Mildred the Saint, pull out the ten large, peel off nine big ones for her, and hold the tenth up. "For expenses," I say, and put it in my pocket. For a moment she looks like she is going to object, but then she sighs and nods her head.

"And since we know the hex was in, you are disqualified from judging," says the chairman.

She gets up and walks out.

"That means Ming Toy Epstein is the only remaining judge," says the chairman. "Vinnie, let's have that square dance."

But the evening is not over yet, because Milton and Spellsinger Solly have been deep in conference in a corner of the room, and I see them light their pocket lighters in lieu of candles, and while I can't hear them I know they are chanting a little spell, and suddenly Vinnie has lost his voice, and the square dance is a bit of a shambles since with no one to call it the dancers don't know what to do next, but they run their way through it, and Swivelhips McGee in particular looks delighted as he dodges dancers right and left and acts like he is back on the football field again. Finally the dance is over, and the judges confer, and it is a very short conference since there is only one judge left, and then we all settle back and prepare to hear her announce that Twinkle Toes Tony and Fatima Fatale are the winners.

But then Ming Toy Epstein pulls one out of left field, and says that in the considered opinion of the judging panel all the women were equally good so there will be no female winner, but there is one male dancer who stands out from the competition, and just as Twinkle Toes Tony is getting ready to take his bows and pick up his trophy, she announces that the winner is Lefty Louie.

There is a stunned silence, and then Tony stalks out furiously, followed by all the other dancers, and then the audience starts filing out, and pretty soon there is no one left but Joey Chicago, who is packing up what's left of his goods, and Big-Hearted Milton and Gently Gently Dawkins and Benny Fifth Street and Dead End Dugan, and the judge and the winner and me.

"That was a most interesting decision," I say to Ming Toy Epstein. "I am almost sorry I canceled all the bets, because not a single person placed a wager on Lefty Louie."

"No one at all?" she asks, surprised.

"He has two left feet, you know."

"Yes, I know."

"And that does not bother you?" I ask.

She slips off her shoes, and I see that she has two right feet. "Not at all," she says, and she and Lefty walk out hand-in-hand.

"Isn't that romantic?" says Benny with a sentimental smile on his face.

"Their firstborn will inherit two feet from each of them," says Gently Gently. "In fact, he will probably qualify to run in the Kentucky Derby a few years from now." He pulls out a ten-spot and hands it to me. "Harry," he says, "will you book my bet before I forget?"

THE BLIMP AND SIXPENCE

So I am sitting in my office, which is the third booth at Joey Chicago's Three-Star Tavern, minding my own business, which at this moment is doping out the next day's races at Aqueduct, when Benny Fifth Street walks up to me.

"Hey, Harry," he says, "I got a question."

"I undoubtedly have an answer," I reply. "Now let us see if the quality of your question is up to the quality of my answer."

"How much is sixpence?" he asks.

"I will take a wild shot in the dark and say that it is probably more than fivepence and less than sevenpence," I say. "Since I do not book races at Epsom Downs or other venues across the drink, why is this a matter of importance?"

"My mother has asked me to buy her a copy of *The Moon and Sixpence* for her birthday," answers Benny, "and I was just curious."

"Ah! A classic!" exclaims Joey Chicago from where he is washing beer glasses behind the bar. "Unquestionably Stephen King's finest novel." Suddenly he frowns. "Or was it Tom Clancy's?"

Big-Hearted Milton, my personal mage, has just emerged

from his office, which is the men's room to the left of the bar, and shakes his head. "I hate to disagree with you," he says, though of course few things give him more pleasure, "but I think you will find that Stephanie Meyer writes *The Moon and Sixpence* right after she pens *Gone With the Wind*."

Suddenly there is a double sawbuck in Joey Chicago's hand. "Twenty dollars says it was King or Clancy, unless it was Dean Koontz, which is always an outside possibility."

"I will take that bet," says Milton. "It was Stephanie Meyer, no question about it—unless perhaps it was Anne Barley."

"You mean Anne Rice?" asks Joey Chicago.

Milton shrugs. "Whatever."

"Harry, will you hold our money until we settle this thing?" asks Joey Chicago.

"Anything to oblige," I say, and then add: "For fifteen percent."

"That is extortionate!" says Joey Chicago.

"That is business," I reply. "Am I not Harry the Book?"

"You are not *booking* our bet," he complains. "You are merely *holding* it."

"If you are dissatisfied with my terms, give the money to Benny Fifth Street," I say.

"The last time Benny Fifth Street gets his hands on forty dollars at one time, he runs off to New Jersey with Fifi McDoll and does not come back for three weeks," says Milton.

"Is that right, Benny?" asks Joey Chicago, but suddenly Benny has a blissful smile on his face and is impervious to sound.

"Benny is suddenly out to lunch," Joey notes.

"And possibly dinner and tomorrow's breakfast as well," agrees Milton.

"All right, then," I say. "If you are dissatisfied with my terms, give the money to Dugan to hold."

They both turn to look at Dead End Dugan, who is still

having trouble adjusting to being a zombie. He is standing in a darkened corner of the tavern, staring into space, and performing a useful social service by attracting all the flies that would otherwise be bothering the customers.

"I think he has gone comatose again," says Joey Chicago.

"Again or still," says Milton.

"Let us find out," I say. "Hey, Dugan—who writes *The Moon and Sixpence?*"

"I do not know, Harry," answers Dugan. "That is a very large marker to leave with you. The sixpence you could put in a pocket, but the moon …" His voice trails off as he goes back to thinking whatever it is zombies think about when they are not otherwise occupied, which is most of the time.

"All right," says Joey. He hands me the twenty, and Milton does likewise.

"Are you really going to charge your friends fifteen percent?" asks Milton.

"Certainly not," I say, pocketing the money. "I am charging *you* fifteen percent." Then I reconsider. "What the hell," I add. "Make it ten percent."

"What brings about this most unlikely change of heart?" asks Joey Chicago.

"I figure there are twenty million writers in the world," I reply. "You each name two. So the odds are five million-to- one that I will not have to pay off this bet to either of you."

"You are all heart, Harry," says Joey Chicago bitterly.

"It goes with Gently Gently Dawkins, who is all stomach," says Benny, who is back from dreaming about Fifi McDoll with his eyes wide open. "Which reminds me, where is he?"

Gently Gently Dawkins is one of my three flunkies. He and Benny Fifth Street get annoyed when people refer to them as my stooges or lackeys, though Dead End Dugan is impartial to whatever you call him as well as everything else in the world. Dawkins is perhaps two pieces of pie and a cheese Danish short of four hundred pounds, but he has a good heart when it is not fighting off cholesterol, which makes up for his having an IQ that can freeze water.

"He is playing Santa Claus at the Home For Retired Old Dolls on the Upper West Side," I say.

"Why him?" asks Benny.

"They have run out of padding and he is the only one who fits into the costume," I answer. I am about to add that I expect him to outgrow it by next year, but suddenly Short Odds Harrigan enters the bar, his hat and his toothpick at their usual jaunty angle, and he walks directly up to me. I notice one of his eyes is blackened, his nose is swollen, and two of his front teeth are missing.

"Good morning, Short Odds," I say. "It is good to see you up and around on Christmas Eve."

"My wife made my bail," he says bitterly. "I should have stayed in stir. I was safer there."

"I am sorry to hear this," I say.

"Steel bars do not a prison make," he quotes. "In fact, sometimes they form a safe haven."

"That is very strange," says Dugan from his corner. "I always thought they made a prison."

"Well, you live and learn," I say to him. "Except for the *live* part." I turn back to Short Odds Harrigan. "So, what can I do for you?"

He slaps five large on the table in front of me.

"That is a lot of money," I say. "What three-to-five favorite are you putting it on?"

"I am putting it on Dressy Tessie in the fifth race."

"Dressy Tessie is sixty-to-one," I say suspiciously, "and you are well-known for only betting on favorites."

"I just have a hunch," he says nervously. "I will be back tomorrow after ... I mean *if* ... she wins."

And with that he is gone.

"Something is amiss here," says Big-Hearted Milton.

"Something is five thousand misses here," I correct him. "Short Odds Harrigan has never bet a longer price than eight-to-five in all the years I have known him, and suddenly he lays five large on the longest shot of the day." I pause dramatically. "I get the distinct feeling that the hex is in."

"It is easy enough to find out," says Milton. "Come with me."

He gets up and I follow him to the men's room, where he has scrawled "Big-Hearted Milton's Office" on the door seven or eight times with everything from magic markers to Mitzi McSweeney's Kiss Me Deadly lipstick, and Joey Chicago has crossed it off just as often.

"Watch your step," Milton warns me as we enter, and indeed there are black candles all over the floor in what Milton calls occult mystical patterns and I call pentagrams.

"Now stand back," he says, stepping into the center of the biggest one. "This could be dangerous."

The only danger I can see is if he manages to catch his pants cuff on fire, but I step back as he says, and he begins chanting a spell in a tongue that could be ancient Aramaic, or maybe something even more obscure, like French. Suddenly his whole body stiffens, his eyes roll back into his head, and he looks like he should be unleashed in a film starring Boris or Bela or Basil or someone else whose name begins with a B.

"So is the hex in?" I ask.

"I do not yet know if the fifth at Aqueduct is hexed," he gasps, "but someone has definitely cast an evil spell on Panama Charlie's Chili Surprise, which I eat just before I come here. I think I am going to die."

"If you dare to die before I get my answer," I promise him, "I will follow you to the next life and make you so miserable that you turn in your white feathered wings—or your red leathery ones, depending—and beg to come back to this mortal coil. So why not save yourself the misery I am already planning for you, and just get me my answer?"

"All right," he says. "But if I die of food poisoning, it will be your fault."

"Panama Charlie's attorney will be thrilled to hear that," I say. "Now get back to work."

"I'm working, I'm working," says Milton, muttering another spell. "Gods of the Netherworld, Demons of the Ninth Circle, I implore you to tell me—" But before he can finish the question he shrieks, "*Sonuvabitch!*" and jumps out of the circle.

"What has transpired?" I ask eagerly.

"I burned my toe!" he whines.

"Play through your tears," I say. "I need to know about the race."

He mutters another spell, then looks up. "You are in big trouble, Harry. Morris the Mage has hexed the race so that Dressy Tessie wins."

"That is no problem," I say. "You have thwarted Morris before."

"But this hex requires a very complex counter-curse," he says.

"So chant it and let us be about our business," I tell him.

"You do not understand, Harry," he says. "To counter this hex, I need the whiskers of a tree-dwelling giant sloth, and I do not believe there are any in Central Park, or even Gramercy Park if push comes to shove."

"Have we got time to get to Grant Park in Chicago before they run the fifth race tomorrow?" I wonder aloud, looking at my wristwatch.

"There are no trees in Grant Park," says Milton. "At least, not any big enough to hold a giant sloth."

"Are you sure a medium sloth won't do?" I ask. "Dressy Tessie does not have to run up the track, or break a leg. I will be just as happy if she comes in second."

Milton shakes his head. "This recipe allows no substitutions."

"Well, there must be some other spell," I say.

He hems and haws and finally admits that there is one other counter-curse, but it is even more difficult to come by than the whiskers of a giant sloth.

"Tell me anyway," I say, "and we will see what we can do."

Milton clears his throat uncomfortably. "Eleven voluptuous nude virgins must approach us voluntarily and swear their eternal love."

"Eleven?" I say. "That is an odd number."

"Well, the spell calls for ten," admits Milton, "but I want a little something for my trouble."

"Voluntarily, you say?" I ask him.

"Voluntarily," he repeats.

"When was the last time you were voluntarily approached by a voluptuous nude virgin?" I ask.

He checks his wristwatch. "Damn," he says. "This thing only goes back forty years."

"Have you got a third spell hidden away somewhere?" I ask him.

He shakes his head. "Those are the only two, Harry," he answers.

"If you cannot come up with a spell to kill the horse," I say, "can you not at least come up with a spell to kill Short Odds Harrigan?"

He goes into his trance again. After a minute he comes back to the here and now. "Short Odds, too, is protected by Morris the Mage."

"Giant sloths and nude virgins again?" I say knowingly.

"Even rarer," he answers. "Six-legged rattlesnakes." He considers his answer. "Well, rarer than giant sloths, anyway."

We leave Milton's office and find ourselves back in the tavern.

"Well?" asks Benny Fifth Street.

"We have a problem," I say.

"I thought you went in there so Milton could solve your problem," says Benny.

"This is some hex that Morris the Mage has come up with," says Milton. "I would pay a pretty penny to learn where he got it."

"That is one pretty penny more than I will have if we don't find a way to make it go away," I say bitterly.

"Harry," says Benny, "I think I see a way out of your troubles."

"Highway I-95 South," suggests Joey Chicago.

"I prefer I-81," says Milton. "It's more scenic."

"Leave the academic arguments to the academs," says Benny. "Harry, I have the solution."

"I am all ears," I tell him.

"Curious," says Milton. "Mitzi McSweeney says I am all hands."

"Pay him no attention," I say to Benny, "and tell me what you have come up with."

Benny shoots me a proud smile. "Take six large and put it on Dressy Tessie to win over at Bernard the Bank's or Exuberant Eddie's."

"That is unethical!" I say in shocked tones. "Besides," I add, "they'd figure the hex was in the second I tried to put the bets down."

I go back to my office, which is the third booth, and nurse an Old Peculiar, and consider my options, none of which are looking especially bright, and I try to figure out how much I must pay off at sixty-to-one, though in truth Dressy Tessie, who has only a nodding acquaintance with the finish line, figures to be ninety-to-one by post time, and that is even after the big plungers have gone to the stores and traded in their Christmas gifts for cash.

After an hour a foul smell reaches my nostrils, and I look up and see Dead End Dugan standing before me.

"What is it?" I say.

"I have spent all evening considering it, Harry," he says, "and it is my conclusion that the hex is in."

"Thank you for those words of wisdom," I say.

"What words?" he asks, confused, and I tell him to return to his corner and go back to thinking dead thoughts.

Suddenly there is a commotion at the door, and an elderly woman in a nurse's uniform and an overcoat is pulling a blimp into the tavern, and I see that it is *our* blimp, who goes by the name of Gently Gently Dawkins, and he is wearing a Santa Claus costume and she has a death grip on his left ear.

"I believe this belongs to you!" she snaps at Joey Chicago.

"No, ma'am," he says, and points at me. "It belongs to Harry the Book."

She drags Gently Gently over to my booth. "Here!" she says. "And we never want to see him again!"

"That is a lot of him not to see," I say. "Not that I blame you in the least, but what did he do to bring about this lack of enthusiasm?"

"We picked him up and drove him to the Home For Retired Old Dolls, and fed him dinner, and gave him the Santa Claus suit, and he was supposed to pass out presents to all the old dolls who live there. It was going to be a real elegant party. We spent all day making plum puddings and wrapping presents."

"Surely he did not try to steal the presents," I say, wondering just what kind of presents you give an old doll who probably has more knitting needles and doilies than she will ever need.

"No," she says, twisting his ear until he yelps.

"What then?" I ask.

"While we were keeping him backstage, so to speak, and moving all the old dolls to the parlor for the celebration," she yells, "he ate all eighteen plum puddings!"

"You ate *eighteen* plum puddings?" I say.

"I was hungry," answers Dawkins.

"Hungry?" she screams. "Each of those plum puddings was going to feed eight old dolls!"

"Dinner was tiny," says Dawkins defensively.

"A tiny sixteen-ounce steak and three tiny baked potatoes with sour cream!" says the nurse.

"You see?" says Dawkins. "She confirms it."

The nurse stalks to the door, then turns to face us. "I never want to see any of you again!" she snaps. Suddenly she points a forefinger at Dead End Dugan, who is at the far end of the tavern. "Especially you!" she adds, and walks out into the night.

"I fear I did not make the most favorable of impressions on her," offers Dawkins, picking up a handful of nuts from the bar and nibbling on them.

"Give her three or four lifetimes and she'll forget," says Benny comfortingly. "Dugan always does, don't you Dugan?"

"Don't I what?" asks Dugan, sounding even more vague than usual.

"See?" says Benny.

"I do not wish to bring dishonor upon my friends," says Dawkins unhappily.

"That is not a problem," replies Benny. "None of us admits to knowing you anyway, and Joey Chicago tells everyone you are just here until he can afford a stuffed and mounted bear."

A cold wind whips through the tavern.

"It is getting chilly," notes Benny.

"That is because the nurse forgets to close the door when she storms out," says Dawkins.

"You are closest to the door," says Joey Chicago. "Walk over and shut it."

Dawkins walks over, and suddenly I hear the strangest jingling sound.

"What is that?" I ask.

"I don't know," says Benny. "It sounds like sleigh bells."

"No," says Joey Chicago. "It sounds exactly like a pair of chromium dice I used to own."

"You know," says Dawkins thoughtfully, "I've been hearing it on and off about an hour now, maybe even a little longer."

"But I *don't* hear it now," I continue. "I only hear it when Dawkins walks to and from the door." I turn to him. "Do it again," I say.

"Do what?" asks Dawkins.

"Walk to the door."

"But the door is closed already," he says.

"Fine," I say. "Walk to Milton's office."

"But I don't have to," he says.

"Then walk over and say Hi to Dugan."

"I can say it from here," answers Dawkins.

"But if you say it from here I will kick you as hard as I can," I say, "and if you walk over to say Hi to Dugan I probably cannot reach you."

He begins walking, and we all hear the jingling sound again.

"He is spontaneously giving birth to chromium dice," says Joey Chicago with absolute certainty.

"I think it is more likely that he has eaten a reindeer, sleigh bells and all," offers Benny.

"I do not recall eating a reindeer," says Dawkins. "All I remember is that tiny dinner."

"And the eighteen plum puddings," adds Milton.

"Oh, yes," agrees Dawkins. "I almost forgot about them." He shrugs. "They were just dessert."

"Just a minute," says Benny. "Those were Christmas puddings, weren't they?"

"I don't remember the Christmases, just the plums," answers Dawkins.

"The problem is solved," announces Benny suddenly.

"I hope this solution is more practical than your last one," I say.

"The last one was designed to keep you from waking up beneath the East River when you cannot pay off Short Odds Harrigan's bet, and I am truly sorry that it will not work and we are soon to lose you," says Benny. "This merely solves the mystery of the bells, which are not bells at all."

"I *knew* I did not eat a reindeer!" says Dawkins.

"No," agrees Benny, "it was not a reindeer."

"What was it then?" asks Joey Chicago.

"A sixpence," answers Benny. "Or more to the point, eighteen sixpences, which is why he jingles whenever he moves."

"Where would he get a sixpence?" asks Milton.

"It is a custom, one which I am sure all the old dolls honor, to bake a lucky sixpence into a plum pudding at Christmas."

"I could have chipped a tooth!" says Dawkins, who is suddenly outraged. "They should be more careful where they leave those things!"

"Puddings or sixpences?" asks Benny.

"Yes!" answers Dawkins.

"So is he doomed to jingle wherever he goes from now on?" asks Joey Chicago.

"Not to worry," says Benny. "As the great Somerset Maugham once said, 'This too shall pass.'"

"Never heard of him," says Milton.

"Me neither," adds Joey Chicago.

But as all this highbrow cerebral conversation is going on, I am busy thinking, because that is what I do best, and finally I think I have the solution to my problem, and I signal for silence. No one pays any attention, as usual, so I stand up and gently holler, *"Shut up!"*

The three of them immediately stop talking, and Dugan blinks and asks "Did I say something?" and promptly goes back to staring at a wall.

"What is it, Harry?" asks Benny at last.

"Dawkins does not merely swallow a bunch of sixpence coins," I say. "He swallows a bunch of *lucky* sixpence coins."

"So?" says Benny.

"So what if he were to bet me that Dressy Tessie comes in seventh tomorrow, and I were to book his bet?" I say. "If he cannot lose, then Dressy Tessie cannot win."

Milton walks over to Dawkins, lays his hand on his stomach, and begins mumbling spells again. After a minute he looks up at me. "Harry," he says, "it will work. The sixpences are more powerful than Morris the Mage's spell, though I am sorry about the nude virgins."

Suddenly everyone starts paying close attention, but Milton does not mention the nude virgins again. Instead he asks when post time is for the fifth race on Christmas Day.

"About five in the afternoon," I say.

He frowns. "And it is not yet midnight, and Dawkins has eaten his usual portion."

"What are you getting at?" asks Benny.

"The coins have enough power to counteract Morris the Mage's spell when they are all collected together, which they are now. But I do not know how much power they might lose once they are no longer in the same place, and I do not think Harry wants to find out."

Joey Chicago reaches under the bar and produces a cork from a bottle of wine.

"We cannot take the chance," I say. "After all, it came out of the bottle, didn't it?" I turn to Milton. "You are just going to have to cast a spell."

"For constipation?" he says. "I do not think the *Malleus Maleficarum* or the *Compendium Maleficarum* even mention it."

"Then you will have to improvise," I tell him.

"Let me see what I can find," he says, going off to his library, which he keeps in the far left-hand stall of his office. In the meantime, I loan Dawkins a dollar and tell him to bet me that Dressy Tessie will come in seventh.

"I don't know about that, Harry," he says. "I have always liked that filly. I think if the odds are right I might bet her to—"

Joey Chicago reaches over and crams a handful of bar pretzels into his mouth before he can finish the sentence.

"Gently Gently," I say, "if you do not offer to bet me that Dressy Tessie will come in seventh tomorrow, I am going to cut you into tiny pieces and feed you to Joey's piranhas."

"He doesn't have any piranhas," mumbles Dawkins as he chews on the pretzels.

"I'll buy him some," I say.

He makes the wager.

Milton emerges about five minutes later. "I think I have found what we need," he says.

"A spell for constipation?" I ask.

He shakes his head. "A spell for leprosy. No bodily parts will drop off for twenty-four hours."

"That is stretching the definition of a bodily part," I note.

"Perhaps," agrees Milton. "But it will have to do."

"It had better," I say. "I cannot afford to pay off five large at sixty or seventy-to-one."

"Not to worry, Harry," says Dawkins. "I am suddenly feeling lucky."

"Let *me* worry about the luck," I say. "*You* just concentrate on feeling full."

"Okay," he says. "Do I get to keep it when we're done?"

"The dollar?" I ask.

"The sixpences. I am growing attached to them."

"Hold that thought," I tell him.

Midnight comes and goes, and we all keep watching Dawkins like a hawk—well, like five hawks, one of them dead—and he keeps asking for nuts and pretzels and anything else there is to eat, and when Joey Chicago runs out he announces that he is going to walk down the street to Hitachi Yingleman's All-Night Kosher Japanese Bakery and pick up a dozen sushi cupcakes.

"No," I say firmly. "I cannot let you leave."

"Why not, Harry?" he asks.

"I cannot have you walking past any place with a bathroom," I explain.

"But I do not want a bathroom," he says. "I want a bakery."

"I will go to the bakery for you," I announce, getting up and walking toward the door. When I get there I stop and turn. "I do not want Gently Gently Dawkins getting up and going anywhere while I am gone. Is that clear?"

There is a general nodding of heads. I open the door, but before I can walk out I head a *thud* and then a few seconds later I hear a *CRASH*. I stop to see what has happened, and there is Dawkins lying peacefully on the floor, and Dead End Dugan is holding what is left of a wooden chair in his hand.

"Well, you said you didn't want him getting up," he explains.

"Is he alive?" I ask.

"That is probably not all that important, as long as the coins are together," says Milton.

Benny goes over and kneels next to him, and puts an ear to his chest. "I cannot hear a heartbeat," he says. He moves his head a little lower. "But his stomach is still working overtime digesting the pretzels." He pulls a breath mint out of a pocket and holds it maybe an inch from Dawkins's mouth. Dawkins's nose twitches as it smells the mint, and suddenly his mouth opens and his tongue shoots out and a second later both the tongue and the mint have vanished back into his mouth.

"He is alive!" says Benny happily.

"Leave him where he lays," I say. "And Dugan?"

"Yes, Harry?" says the zombie.

"If he wakes up, hit him again."

Then it is just a matter of waiting for post time, and everything seems to be going my way, but then disaster hits in the form of a Christmas Day thunderstorm, and suddenly the track comes up muddy and three of the nine horses scratch, and now there is no way that Dressy Tessie can come in seventh, lucky sixpences or no lucky sixpences.

Joey turns on the big-screen television in time for us to see the horses parading to the post. Then the race begins, and six horses burst out of the gate, and Dressy Tessie is dead last—and suddenly I see a horse maybe a quarter of a mile ahead of them.

"Who is that?" asks Benny, who has seen him too.

Joey Chicago stares at the screen. "That is Flyaway."

"What is he doing there?" I ask.

"He starts in the fourth race and is still running," says Joey Chicago.

Flyaway hits the far turn two hundred yards ahead of the field, and is still eighty yards in front when they come to the homestretch, but one by one they start passing him, and for a moment I think even Dressy Tessie will catch him but he digs in and is still a neck in front of her when they cross the finish line.

"She comes in seventh in a six-horse field," says Milton. "Boy, are those sixpences powerful!"

We celebrate with a drink but decide not to wake Dawkins, who is sleeping peacefully and sticking out his tongue for more mints every minute or two. Then it is back to normal at Joey Chicago's, and before long Benny and Milton are arguing about who wrote *Moby Dick*: J. K. Rowling or Mickey Spillane.

A WEIGHTY AFFAIR

So I am sitting in my place of business, which is the third booth at Joey Chicago's Three-Star Tavern, and the business I am doing is doping out the odds for the next day's races at Belmont, when I hear what sounds like an explosion, and I figure it must be a Japanese bomber left over from World War II, because the building is not shaking enough for it to be a nuclear explosion and to the best of my knowledge the Japanese do not have the H-bomb in 1944 or even in 1945.

Then Joey Chicago walks over and stands in front of me.

"Harry," he says, "it has got to stop."

"Tell General MacArthur," I say. "I am a busy man."

"Harry," says Joey Chicago, "I am not kidding. If your lackey breaks one more barstool, I am throwing you and your crew out of here."

I look to where he is indicating, and I see Gently Gently Dawkins lying on his back, surrounded by the pieces of his stool. It is clearly a disturbing and humiliating experience, though I notice that he has recovered enough to reach for the pretzels that crashed to the floor with him.

"I am not his lackey," says Dawkins with all the dignity he

can muster, which truth to tell is not all that much in his current position. "I am his flunky."

"Harry," continues Joey Chicago, "they do not make bar furniture strong enough to hold him."

"I resent that!" says Gently Gently Dawkins. "I am a svelte, fit three hundred and fifty pounds."

"You are no more than two jelly donuts short of four hundred pounds," says Joey Chicago, "and it's got to stop."

"All right," I say. "We will work something out." I look down at Dawkins. "Get up."

I hear two grunts and a groan, but I do not see any action. "I can't!" he wheezes.

I turn to Benny Fifth Street, who is sitting next to Dawkins before the stool succumbs to the laws of gravity. "Give him a hand," I say.

Benny looks down at Dawkins and applauds.

"That is not what I had in mind," I say severely.

"Come on, Harry," he says. "Even Dawkins cannot lift his own weight. How do you expect me to?"

I glance around the tavern until I find what I am looking for. "Dugan!" I say. "Get over here and help Dawkins get on his feet."

Dead End Dugan is about six feet twenty, and built like Arnold Schwarzenegger. The only difference is that he is built like a *dead* Arnold Schwarzenegger, what with all the bullet holes in his chest and head, and he has not yet adjusted to being a zombie, though he is trying, and he spends the bulk of his time standing off in a corner thinking dead thoughts.

Dugan walks over and helps Dawkins up, then freezes.

"What is the matter?" I ask.

"I can't remember what I am supposed to do next," says Dead End Dugan.

"Why don't you go back to your corner and stare at a wall until it comes to you?" I suggest.

"Thanks, Harry," he says, and walks back to where he had been.

"They make very flimsy furniture these days," says Gently Gently Dawkins, brushing himself off and grabbing another handful of pretzels.

"We are going to have to do something about you," I say. "Everybody in town knows they can find me right here at Joey Chicago's, and I do not want them to suddenly have to go searching for me and maybe find a business rival first."

"Tell Joey to get sturdier furniture," says Dawkins. "And narrower tables. I can no longer slide into a booth."

"Maybe if you cover your belly with grease or lard you could slide in," suggests Benny Fifth Street.

"Hey, that is a good idea!" says Dawkins enthusiastically. "Next time I buy some lard to nibble on, I'll remember to save a little to rub on me."

"You are missing the point," I say.

"You want me to rub it on edge of the table?" he asks.

"No," I say. "Dawkins, you are going to have to go on a diet and lose a quick fifty pounds."

You know how the lights flicker and the heroine gasps and the music builds when there is a revelation of that magnitude in the movies? Well, life is no movie, and what happens is three guys at the bar start laughing so hard they begin choking on their beer, and Dead End Dugan smiles for the first time since he came back from the cemetery up in Brooklyn, and Bet-a-Bunch Murphy, who has walked into Joey Chicago's just in time to hear me say that, pulls out his wallet and says, "I'll bet five large he can't lose fifty pounds."

Personally, I agree with him, and think even losing seven pounds qualifies as a long shot, but I am Harry the Book and booking bets is what I do.

"You're covered," I say.

"I know you are a bookie, Harry," says Murphy. "But you are

about to become a destitute bookie, because if Dawkins is a racehorse the odds are ten-to-one that he cannot even squeeze out of the gate."

"I went with a destitute once," says Dead End Dugan wistfully.

Suddenly everyone in the place except my three flunkies are lined up to lay their bets, and every bet is that Dawkins can't lose the weight.

"Boy, are we going to clean up!" enthuses Benny Fifth Street. "All we have to do is chain him in a dungeon for three or four months, and maybe sew his lips together."

"I have never gone on a diet before," adds Dawkins, "but how hard can it be? I will switch to eating small double hot fudge sundaes, and small triple-decker cheeseburgers, and drink diet pop at least once a month, and twice in every month that's got a Z in it."

Word has raced up and down the street, because suddenly it seems that every plunger in New York is lined up to bet against Dawkins, and finally I total up all the markers I have accepted and I realize that I stand to lose close to one hundred large if Dawkins can't lose fifty pounds, and I announce that the book is closed and I will accept no more bets.

"Just a minute, Harry," says Murphy. "We need a deadline. Otherwise he could weigh seven hundred pounds three years from now and you could explain that he is just warming up for his final run to the wire."

Actually, that thought occurs to me about the time I realize just how much money I stand to lose, and I am hoping that it is an anti-social thought that doesn't want anyone else thinking about it, but I have to admit that he has a point. "All right," I say. "Let us figure a pound a day, and we will make the finish line fifty days up the road."

"No," says Dawkins. "Make it twenty-five."

"Twenty-five days it is!" shouts Murphy, and everyone

cheers, and suddenly the place starts emptying out before I can explain that he means twenty-five years.

"So you really think you can lose two pounds a day?" I ask when there is no one left in the bar except me and Joey Chicago and my three flunkies.

"Of course not," answers Dawkins. "I would starve to death."

"Then why did you say that?" I demand.

"Because I do not want to starve for fifty days when I can just starve for twenty-five," he says.

"You do not have to worry about starving for fifty days or even twenty-five," says Benny Fifth Street.

"I don't?" replies Dawkins hopefully.

"No," says Benny. "If you have not lost fifty pounds by the twenty-fourth day, I think Harry will kill you and cancel all bets."

Dawkins turns to me. "You wouldn't really do that, would you, Harry?"

"Of course not," I say. "You must not believe everything Benny tells you."

"Thank you, Harry," says Dawkins.

"We would know if you're on target by the twentieth day," I continue. "Why stretch it out?"

Dawkins forces himself to laugh. It is a very insincere laugh. "What a kidder!" he says. "You are just kidding, right, Harry?"

"Have you ever known the Boss to kid about money?" says Benny.

"He *has* to be kidding!" says Dawkins desperately. "The only way I can lose fifty pounds is if you cut off my leg, and I have grown very attached to it."

Actually, I have considered both options, but I do not believe my clientele will accept an amputation as a legitimate loss of weight, and I know that two of Dawkins's cousins are cops in the Bronx and would very likely take it amiss if I killed him without first finding out if he owed them money, so I must come up with yet another alternative.

And suddenly it dawns on me that my alternative is sitting in his office, which happens to be the men's room just to the right of Joey Chicago's bar, so I get up and walk over and open the door, and there is Big-Hearted Milton, my personal mage, sitting cross-legged on the tile floor, surrounded by five black candles that are burning at the five points of a pentagram he has drawn on the floor.

"Milton," I say, "we have to talk."

He puts his finger to his lips. "*Shh!*" he hisses.

I stand still, and he chants a mystic spell in some ancient forgotten language, or maybe French, and finally he smiles and blows out the candles and gets to his feet.

"What was that all about?" I ask.

"Mitzi McSweeney," he says triumphantly. "She stands me up to go on a date with Hot Lips Hoolihan."

"Isn't he the trumpet player over at Harvey Wallbanger's club?" I ask.

"He has never played a horn in his life!" growls Milton. "It is the ladies who give him that nickname."

"So what terrible thing do you to do poor Mitzi?" I ask.

"She is a very vain woman," he says. "It is acknowledged by one and all that she has a perfect figure, or at least as close to perfect as anyone except Bubbles La Tour." Suddenly he grins. "I have made all her clothes two sizes smaller! She will be sure she is gaining weight! How is *that* for a curse?"

"Well," I say, "if you really think wearing exceptionally tight clothes will make her unattractive to everyone around her …"

His eyes widen, and suddenly he yells out another spell. "I have reverted all her clothes to their original sizes. Thank you, Harry. By not getting close enough to Mitzi, I got too close to the problem."

"It is interesting that you were thinking of making her feel she was gaining weight," I say, "because we have the opposite problem on our hands."

"You want me to make all your clothes too big?" he asks with a puzzled frown.

"No," I say. "Gently Gently Dawkins has to lose fifty pounds in twenty-five days."

"That is all the time the doctors give him?"

I explain the events of the previous twenty minutes to him.

"Cut off his head," says Milton. "It will cure his eating habit once and for all, and the added advantage is that we will never have to listen to him sing 'Sweet Caroline' again."

"Can you not just magic a quick fifty pounds away from him?" I ask.

"Yes," he says, "but if he loses fifty pounds in one swell foop everyone will know that it was magic and not willpower."

"He has willpower to spare," I say. "Unfortunately, what he lacks is won'tpower." I consider the problem for a moment, and then say: "I agree that it would look bad if you magic away fifty pounds at once, but how about two pounds a day?"

"At the rate he eats, I'll have to magic away four or five pounds a day for him just to hold even," answers Milton. "What brought this about anyway? Surely *he* didn't suggest going on a diet?"

"It was a matter of vectors and angles and stress points and gravity," I say.

"Ah," says Milton knowingly. "He broke another stool. What is that—the sixth this month?"

"The seventh," I say.

"And it's only the nineteenth," remarks Milton, who is clearly impressed. "He could hit double digits."

"I'm more concerned with my losing six digits," I say.

"I'm surprised someone hasn't put a dollar or two down on Dawkins," says Milton. "What odds are you giving on him actually losing the weight—about three gazillion-to-one?"

"You find me anyone in the whole of New York who's willing to bet on Dawkins, and I'll dope out the odds," I say bitterly.

"Well, let's go out there and hide all the bar food as a first step," says Milton.

"I thought we decided you're going to magic his weight away," I say.

"Harry," says Milton, "I can vanish a mouse, and I can vanish a bat, but I have never tried to vanish an elephant, and Dawkins is a lot closer to the one than the other."

"You just have to vanish about thirteen percent of him," I say.

"I do not know how strongly he is bonded to it," says Milton. "I may have to magic it away with an enchanted scalpel and a magical vacuum cleaner."

"Let us emerge and find out right now what you can do," I say, pushing the door open and walking back into the tavern.

"I have hidden all the pretzels," Joey Chicago informs me.

"That is all right," says Dawkins, chewing on something chocolate. "I always carry half a dozen candy bars for instant energy, and to prevent starvation."

"There he is," I say to Milton. "Do your best on him."

Milton walks slowly around Dawkins, presses a couple of fingers into his stomach, pinches the flab over his ribs, counts how many chins he has. Then he stands back a few feet, hands on hips, staring critically at Dawkins.

"I don't suppose anyone has the eye of a newt handy?" he says.

No one does.

"Or the tooth of a tree-dwelling alligator?"

Another negative.

Milton sighs. "I'll just have to work with what I've got."

He raises his hands, spreads out his fingers, clears his throat, and starts chanting: "In the names of Lucifer, Baal, Beelzebub, Albert Schweitzer, Secretariat, Willie Mays, Bubbles La Tour, and Elvis Presley ..." and then he switches to one of his ancient languages, and a minute later he's done.

"Bubbles La Tour?" I repeat. "Secretariat?"

"A job this tough, you might as well hit all the bases," he replies. He turns to Dawkins. "Do you feel any lighter?"

Dawkins frowns, lifts an arm, puts it down, does the same with a leg. "I don't know," he answers, pulling another candy bar out of his pocket.

"I forbid you to eat that!" chants Milton in his spookiest voice.

"But I'm hungry!" complains Dawkins.

Milton screams a magic word, and suddenly the candy bar turns into a salamander.

"Thanks, Milton," says Dawkins, his face lighting up. "I haven't had salamander in weeks."

Milton chants again, and suddenly the salamander is a ball-point pen. Dawkins considers eating it for a moment, then shrugs and puts it in a pocket. "You never know what flavor ink they're using," he explains confidentially.

Just then Bet-a-Bunch Murphy and five other big plungers come back into Joey Chicago's.

"You are being a bit premature," I say severely. "There are still twenty-four days and twenty-three hours to go."

Murphy holds up a scale. "We need to know what weight he starts at," he announces.

He puts the scale down on the floor. "Get on it," he tells Dawkins.

Dawkins looks at me, and I nod my approval. He walks over and stands on it. The scale groans a metallic groan and springs fly off in every direction.

Murphy looks at Dawkins in awe. "You killed the scale," he says accusingly.

I look down at it. "It only went up to three hundred pounds anyway," I say.

"I know," answers Murphy.

"Then how did you expect to weigh him?" I ask. "The house will grant that he cruises at a greater altitude than that."

"I thought he could stand on one leg, and then we'd double the total," says Murphy.

"Stand back," says Milton, and everyone backs up. He closes his eyes, spreads his arms, and chants *Tinker to Evers to Chance!* and lo and behold, a freight scale appears in the middle of the tavern. Milton opens his eyes and smiles. "It's a spell I pick up when I visit my uncle in Chicago."

Nobody challenges this, though we all know that Mitzi McSweeney knocks out three of his teeth when she learns that his uncle measures 36-23-36 and is named Fifi.

"All right, Dawkins," I say. "Climb aboard and let's get this over with."

"Just a minute!" says Murphy. "That scale was produced by your personal mage. How do we know it will give us a true reading?"

"I swear to tell the truth, the whole truth, and nothing but the truth, so help me God," says the scale in a deep voice.

"Why do I think that will not hold up in court?" says Murphy suspiciously.

"You do not have a Bible, and the scale does not have a hand to place upon it," says Milton. "This will have to do."

"Well?" I say to Murphy.

"I am thinking," he replies.

"If you distrust the scale we can cancel the bet," I suggest hopefully.

I can see his eyes go wide with horror at the thought of calling off the bet. "Climb onto the scale!" he tells Dawkins.

Dawkins walks over and puts a foot on it.

"Eighty-three pounds and fourteen ounces," says the scale. "When's the last time you washed your foot?"

"He is not done yet," I tell the scale.

Dawkins reaches up and grabs the chains that support the platform which is holding his foot.

"*Oof!*" moans the scale. "172 pounds, ten ounces."

"Hold your horses," I say. "We're not done."

"Oh my God!" says the scale. "You're loading a horse onto me?"

"Just be quiet and all will be revealed," I tell it.

"I need help!" says Dawkins.

"Dugan!" I yell. "Come on over here and give him a hand."

Dead End Dugan approaches. "Okay, Harry," he says. "But I will need the other hand to hold my beer glass."

"Don't understand me so fast," I say. "Just push him onto the scale."

Dugan pushes, and Benny Fifth Street lends a hand, and suddenly Dawkins is standing foursquare on the scale.

"The agony!" screams the scale. "No one ever told me there'd be days like this!"

"How much does he weigh?" asks Murphy.

"Who cares?" cries the scale. "I'll never dance the tango again!"

"Just tell us what he weighs and he'll get off," I say.

"Eight million three hundred and six," says the scale. "Everything's getting dark, drifting away on the winds. Tell Mom I love her."

"Milton," I say, "it's *your* scale. *Do* something!"

"*Abra caramba!*" he says, and suddenly a small screen appears at the top of the scale.

"Do you want it in drams, grains, grams, ounces, pounds, kilograms, or tons?" asks the scale.

"Pounds," says Milton.

"The horse standing atop me weighs 397 pounds," announces the scale. "Will there be anything else?"

"No, I think that covers it," says Milton.

"Good!" says the scale. "I'm going to take a long hot bath and then put a heating pad on my back."

And with that it vanishes, and Dawkins crashes to the floor and is once again lying on his back, thrashing around like a fish out of water.

"Help him up, Dugan," I say, and Dugan pulls him to his feet.

"Okay, Harry," says Murphy as he and the others walk to the door. "He has to be 377 pounds in twenty-five days." Which is the first time I appreciate the benefits of a New York public school education.

"Even twenty pounds is going to be an accomplishment of biblical proportions," remarks Benny when the door closes behind them.

"We will start right now," I say. "Milton is our back-up, but there is no reason not to win this fair and square if we can. Dawkins, I am taking you off all food and liquids, starting right now."

"What is left?" he asks plaintively.

"I don't know," I say. "When you come up with something, check with me and I will tell you if you can eat it."

"How about fingernails?" he asks.

I look at Milton and Benny to see their reaction. Milton finds it amusing, but Benny takes it seriously and shakes his head "No."

"Why not?" asks Dawkins.

"Your fingernail is too close to your finger," answers Benny. "And if you get desperate enough, you just might gobble a finger or two. Banning fingernails from your diet will keep temptation out of the way."

"I must think about this," says Dawkins, absently reaching into his pocket and withdrawing a candy bar.

"Milton?" I say.

"I'm on it," he replies. *"Presto change-o!"*

"Ow!" yells Dawkins, because just as his mouth is closing on the candy bar, it turns into a brick. "Don't *do* that! I could chip a tooth!"

"That's it, Harry!" says Benny. "Let's pull all his teeth!"

"So that all he can eat are rich puddings?" I reply. "Let him eat the brick. After all, how many calories can it have?"

Well, we argue it back and forth for maybe an hour, and then Dawkins looks around the tavern.

"What is missing?" asks Benny.

"Nothing is missing," answers Dawkins. "I just need a soft place to land."

"To land?" says Benny, frowning.

"I am about to faint from hunger," says Dawkins. "The brick was not very filling and I have had nothing to eat since then."

"How much do you suppose he's lost already?" I ask Milton.

"It's only been an hour," he replies. "Maybe an ounce."

"Cheer up, Dawkins," I say. "Only forty-nine pounds and fifteen ounces to go."

"Nineteen pounds and fifteen ounces," Benny corrects me.

"That's for Murphy," I say. "They can't *all* have gone to school in New York."

While we are talking, Dawkins wanders over to the table where Loose Lips Louie was sitting earlier in the evening and gently collapses beneath it.

"Well, that takes care of his appetite for the evening," says Milton.

"I do not think so," I say.

"But—"

"I know him better than you do," I say. "After all, he has been with me through thick and thin, except for the thin part."

I walk over, and sure enough, Dawkins is gobbling all the pretzels Loose Lips Louie has spilled on the floor.

"Oh, hi, Harry," he says when he realizes I am standing

there. "I will faint in about thirty more seconds. I can feel the weakness coming over me already."

I decide to try psychology, and I say, "I have it on good authority that Loose Lips Louie tosses those pretzels on the floor because they are carrying a Gypsy curse."

He frowns. "What kind of curse?"

"If you eat them, all your hair will fall out."

Dawkins stuffs the last five pretzels into his mouth. "Surely my hair weighs at least an ounce," he says while chewing. "We are on the road to victory."

"Dugan!" I yell. "Get over here and put him on his feet again."

Dugan walks over and lifts Dawkins to his feet.

"Now I want you to take him outside and run him six times around the block," I tell him.

"Clockwise or counter-clockwise?" asks Dugan.

"Yes," I say.

"Harry," says Dawkins, "I have not run in thirty years, give or take a decade. I have forgotten how."

"It is just like walking, only more so," says Benny helpfully.

"Harry," says Milton, "if he dies from over-exertion, he cannot lose the rest of the weight, and I do not think Murphy and the others will cancel the bet merely because he has entered a long-term state of non-life."

"All right," I say. "Dugan, *walk* him six times around the block."

Dugan escorts him out the front door, I have Joey Chicago draw me an Old Peculiar from the tap, and I go back to doping out the races, though my heart isn't in it.

They are back an hour and a half later, and Dawkins actually looks happier and healthier than when he left.

"Obviously the fresh air and exercise does you some good," I observe.

"Yes, indeed, Harry," he answers happily. "We walk around

the block six times, and I stop at Noodnik's Emporium each time to buy candy and cupcakes to replenish my depleted strength. You know," he adds confidentially, "dieting and exercising are not as terrible as I had feared they would be."

"How many candy stores do you pass on the way home?" I ask him.

"Only four," he answers. "Plus Morgan the Gorgon's All-Night Meat Market."

"Benny, call him a cab," I say.

Benny shrugs and turns to Dawkins. "You're a cab," he says.

I sigh deeply, because with absolutely no change in his condition Dead End Dugan has just become the smartest of my three flunkies.

Anyway, this is the way his diet goes for twenty-four days, and with only one day left I have Milton produce the freight scale again. The scale starts whimpering and whining the second it sees Dawkins approaching, but Milton magics it into silence and immobility, and finally Dawkins is standing atop it.

"How much has he lost?" I ask.

"A negative nine pounds," says Milton as the scale vanishes and Dawkins is standing on the floor again. "He now weighs 406 pounds."

I stare at Dawkins for a long moment. "How much do you suppose his left leg weighs?" I ask at last.

"Murphy and the others will not take kindly to that," says Milton.

"Neither will I!" shouts Dawkins.

"Milton and I are just talking business," I say. "Pay no attention to us."

"I think I am going to have to magic away a quick sixty pounds," says Milton. "Maybe sixty-five to be on the safe side, since he still has a full day left before the deadline."

"Do what you have to do," I say.

Suddenly Bet-a-Bunch Murphy enters the tavern and walks

up to Dawkins. "You do not look fifty pounds lighter to me," he says smugly.

"You know how some men beat their wives in places where it doesn't show?" replies Milton. "Well, Gently Gently Dawkins is losing his weight where it doesn't show."

"Just be prepared to be weighed tomorrow," says Murphy.

"Is that all you came here for?" I ask. "Because I am a busy man. I have no time for socializing."

"No," he says, slapping five large on the table in front of me. "I want this put on the nose of Indiscreet Prince, who is running in the feature race tomorrow."

"Done," I say. "I'll see you at Belmont tomorrow."

"I'll be there," he promises, walking to the door, "and I will have Morris the Mage with me to make sure Big-Hearted Milton has not magicked any weight off of Dawkins."

Well, the word has gone out on Indiscreet Prince, because it seems that every plunger in the neighborhood comes by to lay a bet on him, and when the dust clears at noon the next day, I am sitting on one hundred thousand dollars' worth of bets, all on Indiscreet Prince.

"Milton," I say, "it is time to perform your magic, because we are about to go out to the track, and we certainly do not want you to be seen doing it there."

He goes into his swami trance, calls upon every demon he can think of, and finally does a kind of scat dance and jive poem, and then there is a flash of light and a smell of smoke and Dawkins's pants fall to the floor.

"What has happened?" asks Dawkins.

"You are now a svelte 341 pounds," says Milton.

"I feel as light as a feather!" enthuses Dawkins, pulling his pants up, only to see them slide down again. "A lead feather, but a feather nonetheless."

"Let us go," I say. "And Dawkins," I add, "be sure to stay clear of Morris the Mage. We don't want him figuring out how you become so slender and beautiful. And on the way, we must buy you some suspenders."

So we leave Joey Chicago's, and buy the suspenders, and go out to Belmont, and I am feeling very grateful that Milton has magicked away the weight, because Indiscreet Prince is the heavy favorite in the feature race, and if there is one thing I do not want to do it is lose two hundred thousand dollars in one afternoon.

We arrive just as Indiscreet Prince is leading the parade to the post, and Bet-a-Bunch Murphy and Morris the Mage are waiting for us, and he walks up to Dawkins and says, "You look different today."

"He has been exercising all morning," I say quickly.

"Well, today we will weigh him on the jockeys' scale, and we will get a true and honest reading."

I decide not to tell him that the scale only goes up to two hundred pounds.

Morris walks over with a know-it-all grin on his face. "I see Milton has been busy," he says, gesturing toward Dawkins. "But I will expose this weight loss for what it is."

The horses enter the gate, and Milton and Benny move over to the rail to watch, and Dawkins joins them.

"You chose the wrong horse, Harry," says Morris.

"I do not choose horses," I say. "That is for suckers. I book bets."

"I mean you should have chosen me for your personal mage rather than Milton," continues Morris. "He has left his mystical fingerprints and personal aura all over this new improved Dawkins."

The bell rings, and the horses burst out of the gate. Indiscreet Prince immediately opens up a four-length lead on the field, and stretches it to six lengths as they hit the far turn.

"In fact," says Morris, "I am not even going to argue with

you, or wait to expose Milton's duplicity. I am going to set things straight right here and now."

He turns to face Dawkins, who has his back to us and is watching Indiscreet Prince extend his lead to ten lengths. Morris begins mumbling a spell, and he gets louder and louder, though of course the cheers of the crowd almost drown him out, and at the climactic moment of the chant and the race, as Indiscreet Prince is right in front of us on his way to an easy win, Morris reaches his hand out and points his finger at Dawkins, and lightning comes out of it just as Dawkins notices a discarded candy wrapper on the ground and bends over to pick it up and see if there is anything in it, and the lightning goes right over Dawkins and instead hits Flyboy Billy Tuesday, who is atop Indiscreet Prince and urging him on. And suddenly everyone can hear Indiscreet Prince grunt an enormous and heartfelt *"Oof!"* and slow down to a canter and then a trot and then a walk and then a very slow walk, and every horse in the field passes him, and finally he comes to a stop ten yards short of the finish wire.

"What has happened?" screams Bet-a-Bunch Murphy.

"Look at Billy Tuesday!" says Benny, and we all look, and Billy's belly has become so big that it has burst through his colorful silks, and his white pants have split down the middle.

"He must weigh four hundred pounds!"

I turn to Morris and say, "I think I'll stick with Milton."

He curses and promises I'll be sorry about this, and walks away in a fury. I tell Murphy that we can weigh Dawkins right now and get both bets over with, but he says no, the bet was made at 10:30 at night and he and his friends and relations will be at Joey Chicago's at 10:30, and they are bringing their own freight scale.

Since I have just won one hundred large, I take my crew out for dinner, and then I go back to Joey Chicago's and tell Dawkins to make sure he is there by 10:30. Murphy and his crowd show up at a quarter after ten, and Dawkins walks in ten minutes later, sipping an extra-thick chocolate malt.

"Hi, Harry," he says. "Thanks again for dinner. It was wonderful."

"If it was so wonderful," I say, "why are you drinking a malt?"

"I got hungry on the way back," he says, "so I had a couple of pizzas, and some Philly cheese steaks, and a French silk pie a la mode, and I needed something to wash it all down with, so …"

"Never mind," I say. "Just stand on this scale that Murphy has brought."

"Can I finish my malt first?" he asks.

I look at Murphy, and he nods. "What the hell," he says. "We've waited this long. We can wait another five minutes."

Dawkins finally finishes the malt, and steps on the scale.

"348 pounds," reads Murphy.

"Let me look at that!" I say. I look, and it really and truly says 348. I turn to Dawkins. "How can this be?" I demand. "You were 341 pounds not six hours ago!"

"Maybe I shouldn't have had that apple pie on the way to the pizza joint," he says thoughtfully.

"Give me my five large back, Harry!" says Murphy, holding out his hand, and soon they are all lined up for their money or their markers, and the end result is that I make one hundred large in the afternoon and lose it right back in the evening.

And I want to blame Dawkins, but I can't help thinking that it is my fault, that if I don't let him finish the malt he weighs in at 347 and I win the bet.

The next day I am sitting in my booth, sipping an Old Peculiar, watching Dead End Dugan standing in a corner thinking dead thoughts, listening to Joey Chicago wondering if Big-Hearted Milton is ever coming out of the men's room again so that he can mop the floor, and I notice that Dawkins is missing, so I ask Benny Fifth Street where he has gone.

"Oh, he is showing his new best friend all of his favorite ice cream parlors," answers Benny.

"His new best friend?" I say. "Who is that?"

"Flyboy Billy Tuesday," says Benny.

THE KID AT MIDNIGHT

So there I am, sitting in my office, which is the third booth at Joey Chicago's Three-Star Tavern, sipping an Old Peculiar and trying to come up with a morning line on the big game between the Mainville Miscreants and the Galesburg Geldings, when suddenly Benny Fifth Street looks up from his barstool and announces that he sees some business on the hoof approaching, and sure enough, Longshot Lamont enters the premises a moment later and walks right up to me.

"Hello, Longshot," I say. "How are you on this fine day?"

"I am well, thank you, Harry," he says, doing a deep knee bend to prove it, or maybe to pick up a quarter he sees lying on the floor, "and I am feeling very lucky today."

This is music to a bookie's ears, which happen to reside on each side of my head, because no one currently old enough to shave can remember the last time Longshot Lamont bets on anything that is less than one hundred-to-one, and most of them finish about where you would expect a hundred-to-one shot to finish. This is a guy who bets Eleanor Roosevelt to win the presidency as a write-in back in 1992, which is unlikely on the face of it and even more so when one considers that she has been dead and buried for thirty years at the time. This is a guy who bets Secretariat to go Best in Show at Crufts, which doesn't even allow American dogs, let alone American racehorses. This is a guy who bets that Willie Mays scores more touchdowns than Red Grange.

So when he pulls out a wad of bills and slaps it down on the table in front of me, I immediately try to think of the longest shot in the city on this particular day, but even I am astonished by the next words out of his mouth, which are, "Harry, I am betting two large on Kid Testosterone to beat Bonecrusher McDade in the big fight tomorrow night."

Benny Fifth Street's jaw drops down to his belly button. Gently Gently Dawkins, who had just entered, almost chokes on the candy bar he is eating. And from where he is standing at the back of the tavern, Dead End Dugan utters the first laugh I have heard from him since he returns from that cemetery up in the Bronx.

"I must be dreaming!" says Dugan.

"You are not so much dreaming as you are dead, sort of," says Dawkins.

"I thought I just heard someone bet on Kid Testosterone," continues Dugan. "But the Kid has never made it to the third round in any of my lifetimes, so I know I must be dreaming."

"I do not think zombies can dream," says Dawkins.

"Are you a zombie?" demands Dugan.

"Not the last time I check, no," says Dawkins.

"Then do not make comments about what zombies can or cannot do until you become one," says Dugan, folding his arms, staring off into space, and going back to thinking dead thoughts.

"This time the Kid will realize his full potential," says Long-shot Lamont. "I can feel it in my bones, Harry."

"His full potential has not yet seen him to the third round in forty-two tries," notes Benny Fifth Street, "and this is a ten round fight."

"O ye of little faith," says Longshot Lamont. "I will be back after the fight to collect my winnings." And with that he turns and walks back out into the street.

"Has Lamont ever won a bet with you, Harry?" asks Dawkins.

"Just once," I say.

"You must have been a long time recouping your losses," he remarks.

"Not really," I say. "It is the Godiva Handicap, for fillies and mares, and he puts five C's on Three-Legged Shirley to win."

"I remember her," says Joey Chicago, from behind the bar. "Is she not the reason that Belmont will not allow anything with less than four legs to answer the call to the post?"

"Yes," I say. "People feel so sorry for her they begin to pool their betting money and start a fund to buy her and retire her to a life of ease."

"So how does she win?" asks Dawkins.

"She doesn't," I answer. "She runs last, by 937 lengths."

"Then I do not understand," he says.

"We are standing side by side at the rail, and as they hit the far turn and she is already a furlong behind the field Lamont turns to me and says very bitterly that he can read me like a book and he bets a C-note I am feeling confident about winning his money. I feel so bad about taking his 5 C's that I accept his wager, and then admit I am feeling supremely confident. I pay him his hundred dollars as the field hits the homestretch and I write it off as an act of charity on my income tax, but it just so happens that my tax auditor knows Lamont and argues that it is an act of mercy rather than an act of charity and will not allow the deduction."

"Well, today's wager will certainly be the easiest two large you ever made," says Benny Fifth Street.

"And he will need it," adds Gently Gently Dawkins, staring out the window. "For unless my eyes deceive me, and that only happens after my fourth double hot fudge sundae of the night, I see Lamont's polar image walking down the street toward us."

"You see a snowman that looks like Lamont?" asks Joey Chicago, turning to look out the window himself.

"You mean his polar opposite," says Benny. He turns to me. "It's Short Odds Harrigan. Doubtless he is about to drop a pile on some one-to-three shot that is moving down in class."

The door swings open and sure enough, it is Short Odds Harrigan, who has probably bet a five-to-one shot once or twice in his life, but not since the glaciers departed from California.

"Hi, Short Odds," I greet him. "Are you here for business or to sample some of Joey Chicago's whiskey?"

"I had some last year," he says, making a face. "I will lay plenty of one-to-five that it was watered."

"I resent that!" says Joey Chicago.

"That is your right," says Short Odds pleasantly. "Just do not deny it or God may strike you dead."

Benny South Street and Gently Gently Dawkins immediately begin arguing which way Joey Chicago will fall if God strikes him dead, and Short Odds listens for a while and then turns back to me.

"I need the odds on the big fight tomorrow night, Harry," he says.

"About three gazillion-to-one," I reply.

"I am being serious," says Short Odds.

"So am I," I say. "I do not think the computer has been built that can compute the odds."

"I am a bettor," he says. "You are a bookie. It is against all the laws of Nature for you not to give me the odds."

"All right," I say. "I will give you one-to-five hundred that he ends it in the first round."

He considers it for a minute, then shakes his head. "I am not certain he can win in the first round. What are the odds for his winning, period?"

"One-to-four hundred," I say.

"So if I put down ten large …?" he begins.

"I will pay you twenty-five dollars when the Bonecrusher wins."

He frowns. "That is all very well and good, Harry," he says, "but I am betting on Kid Testosterone."

I put a finger into my ear, expecting to find it clogged with wax, but all it is clogged with is my finger. "Would you say that again, please, Short Odds?" I ask. "I know it's crazy, but for a second there I think you say that you are betting on Kid Testosterone."

"I am."

"But you have never bet on anything but a favorite since they invented the wheel," chimes in Benny Fifth Street. "Maybe longer," he adds thoughtfully.

"I just have a hunch," says Short Odds.

"You will have to take your hunch to Mars, or maybe Jupiter," I say. "There is not enough money in the world to cover your bet if the Kid should win."

"I will take the same odds you were giving me on Bonecrusher McDade," says Short Odds.

"Joey," I say, "pull that phone out from behind the bar and call an ambulance. Our friend Short Odds has finally gone off the deep end."

"I am the same charming and loveable character you have always known," protests Short Odds. "I do not need all the money in the world, although I admit it would be nice to have. I just need some action, so I will take a mere ten thousand-to-one odds, and I will bet a single C note."

"How can we be sure he is not ready for the funny farm?" asks Benny, staring at him.

"Is he foaming at the mouth?" suggests Dawkins, who ignores the fact that he has foam from his beer all over his mouth and dripping down onto his shirt.

"Please, Harry?" pleads Short Odds.

"I will have to think about this," I tell him.

He pulls a C note out of his pocket, pulls a pen out of his other pocket, and scribbles something on the C note.

"Bubbles La Tour's private phone number," he says, covering it with his hand. "*Now* will you take my money or not?"

"If Harry won't book your bet, *I* will," says Dawkins.

"It is against my better judgment, but in keeping with my baser instincts," I say, grabbing the C note. "I will book your bet."

He gives a triumphant shout that momentarily awakens Dugan from all the dead thoughts he is thinking, and then Short Odds is out in the street, and before I can puzzle out what is happening, in walks Bet-a-Bunch Murphy and Pedro the Plunger, and they both want to put their money on Kid Testosterone.

"That's it!" I say. "Something very strange is going on here. The book is closed!"

"You cannot do this to us, Harry," says Murphy in hurt tones. "It is your function in life to book our bets."

"There is something very fishy about this," I tell him.

"That is just the smell from Maury's Fish-and-Chips Shop next door," says Dawkins helpfully.

"It is an honest wager on an honest fight between two evenly-matched masters of the fistic arts," says Pedro.

"Who would have believed it?" says Benny.

"Believed what?" asks Pedro.

"You manage to cram five lies into an eighteen-word sentence," answers Benny.

"Maybe we should give him a door prize," suggests Dawkins.

"I do not want a door!" yells Pedro, who becomes very literal-minded when he is upset. "I want to lay my money down on Kid Testosterone!"

I look him in the eye—the blue one, not the red one—and I say, "I told you: the book is closed."

"But *why*?" pleads Murphy.

"Last month the Kid gives an exhibition of shadow-boxing in his training camp," I say. "His shadow knocks him out in forty-three seconds."

"An aberration," shrugs Pedro.

"In the fight against Brutal Boris three months ago," chimes in Benny, "he makes it through the first round. As he is coming back to his corner, his trainer sloshes water on him, and it knocks him down for the count."

"Last year the referee has him touch gloves with Yamamoto Goldberg and he breaks his hand," adds Dawkins.

"And this is the guy you think can beat Bonecrusher McDade?" I conclude.

"I just got a feeling about it," says Pedro defensively.

"Take your money and your feeling elsewhere," I say. "The book is closed."

They complain a little more, and finally they leave.

"Where is Milton?" I ask.

"Where else?" says Joey Chicago in bored tones, jerking his thumb in the direction of Milton's office, which happens to be the men's room.

Big-Hearted Milton is my personal mage, and he has chosen as his office the one place on Joey Chicago's premises where every Tom, Dick and Harry won't be able to study and perhaps even memorize his spells. It doesn't quite work out that way, but at least his spells are safe from being overheard by every Teresa, Doris and Harriet.

I enter his office, and there is Milton, standing on the tile floor, surrounded by five black candles that have burned themselves down to nubs. He is chanting something in an ancient lost language of the mystics (or maybe French), and suddenly he claps his hands, the flames on the candles go out, and he gives a triumphant laugh.

"*That'll* show her!" he cackles.

"Mitzi McSweeney again?" I ask.

He nods his head vigorously. "She slaps my face just because I give her a friendly pinch in the elevator." An outraged expression crosses his face. "I do not even draw blood." He dabs at his nose with a handkerchief. "But *she* does."

"What horrible curse have you placed upon her this time?" I ask in bored tones, because in truth Mitzi McSweeney seems to survive Milton's almost-daily curses far better than Milton survives her almost daily face-slappings.

"I have added an inch to each of her high heeled shoes," he says happily. "Next time she wears them out in public, which is every day, she will probably fall on her face."

"That is indeed a very terrible curse, Milton," I say. "So if she falls, some thoughtful gentleman will help her to her feet and brush her off here and there as gentlemen are inclined to do, and doubtless earn her undying gratitude, and if she doesn't fall but manages to locomote with them she will wiggle even more than usual."

"Why don't *I* think of that?" complains Milton.

"I would give plenty of ten-to-one that anyone in the bar except maybe Dugan could tell you, but they are all too polite," I say. "Now, if you are all through cursing Mitzi McSweeney for today, we have business to discuss."

"One minute," he says, closing his eyes and mumbling another spell. "Okay, Harry," he says when he is done. "Her shoes are all restored. Instead, I have made her belts too tight, so she will think she is gaining weight."

I decide not to tell him that if she does not wear her belt and her skirt or slacks are on the loose side, she will not only be a maiden in distress but also in undress, because past performances have taught me that we can spend all day before Milton comes up with a spell that will have a deleterious effect on anything except Milton's love life.

"All right," says Milton at last. "What is it that could possibly be more important than finding a way into Mitzi McSweeney's heart?"

"Maybe if you would stop looking for it in strange places she would stop slapping your face," I say.

"She does not slap my face every time," answers Milton with a chivalrous display of loyalty. Then he grimaces. "Sometimes she kicks my shin."

"How do you think Kid Testosterone would do against her?" I ask, subtly moving the conversation back to business.

"She would take him out in straight falls," says Milton with absolute certainty, "and she would do it with such grace and style that the referee would award her both ears and the tail."

"What if I tell you that Longshot Lamont just places two large on the Kid to beat Bonecrusher McDade?"

"I would say that in a field of slow learners, Lamont ranks somewhat behind a crippled snail," answers Milton.

"And what if I further tell you that Short Odds Harrigan also puts money down on Kid Testosterone?"

"Curious," mutters Milton with a frown. "It is sunny and pleasant out all day. It does not look like the world is coming to an end." Milton stares at me. "I hope you know a short prayer, because I am not sure you have time for a long one."

"Is there no other explanation?" I ask, and I wait for him to calm down, because Milton is an excitable sort.

"I have counted to twenty and the world is still standing," announces Milton. "If this is not the End of Days, then there is only one other possible explanation: the hex is in."

"Of course the hex is in," I say. "How else can the Kid win? In the fight against Guido van Gogh last summer, Guido throws a haymaker that misses and the wind knocks the Kid down for a seven count."

"I remember the fight, but I think it is Guido Guardino."

"That is his moniker before his girlfriend bites his ear off when she catches him cheating." I stop the sentence right there, because if I go any farther the next three words will be "with Mitzi McSweeney," and then it will take another ten minutes to get Milton to concentrate on the problem at hand, and a serious problem it is, because there is probably not enough green in all of New York to pay Longshot Lamont what I will owe him if Milton cannot counteract the hex.

"Well," says Milton after giving the matter some thought, "at least we know the culprit."

"We do?" I say.

He nods sagely as the overhead light makes patterns on his balding head. "It will take the most powerful spell in the universe and points north to bring the Kid home a winner. There are probably only two magicians alive who can cast such a spell, and I very much doubt that any dead magicians, powerful though they be, really care who wins a boxing match."

"Do we know these two geniuses?" I ask.

He pulls himself up to his full height, which is about five feet eight inches with lifts in his shoes. "You are looking at one of them," he says with dignity.

"And the other?"

"Morris the Mage, of course."

"Well, you've gone up against Morris before," I say hopefully. "So can you counteract the spell?"

"I do not know yet," says Milton. "How much time do we have?"

"The main event is scheduled for ten o'clock tomorrow night," I say. "The Kid is in the wrap-up bout, which they will hold when everyone's getting up and leaving, as the only point of interest in one of his fights is how many rows deep into the audience will he be knocked this time."

"Okay," says Milton, checking the little hourglass he wears around his neck. "It looks like I've got twenty-six hours to break the spell." He lowers his head in thought. "I will need two newts, some oil of horned toad, a cup of dragon's blood, some black mustard seeds, a bat wing with or without the bat, and a bag of jelly beans."

"Jelly beans?" I ask, surprised.

"So I like a little nosh while I work," he answers defensively. "Sue me."

I spend a few hours gathering what he needs while he goes over his ancient books of magic, and I send Benny Fifth Street into Milton's office every half hour to make sure he hasn't sneaked a copy of *Playboy* inside one of the tomes, and finally Milton emerges at about ten in the morning and plops himself down opposite me.

"So what do you find out?" I ask.

"It is a real stinker of a spell," he says wearily. "It couldn't be cast without a tooth from a tree-dwelling crocodile. Where the hell did he find one in Central Park?"

"Get to the point," I say. "Can you break it?"

"Not today," says Milton.

"Breaking it tomorrow won't do me any good," I point out.

"It's that damned tooth," says Milton. "It makes the spell absolutely unreversable until midnight."

"We are in deep trouble," says Dawkins, who is munching on a bowl of bar pretzels. "The main event won't last past eleven, and the Kid can't last past thirty seconds of the first round."

"If we cannot make a deal to buy the Denver Mint before ring time, we are doomed," says Benny Fifth Street.

"I have been doomed many times," offers Dead End Dugan from the back of the tavern. "After a while you get used to it."

"I do not have a while," I say, looking at my watch. "I have thirteen hours and forty-two minutes."

Milton checks his hourglass. "Fourteen hours and ten minutes," he corrects me.

Benny and Dawkins look at their watches.

"Harry is right," says Benny. "I have ten-eighteen."

"Me, too," says Dawkins.

Milton looks at his hourglass, then taps it with a finger and sand begins to gush to the bottom. "Damned thing needs a new battery," he says apologetically.

"How far away can we get from here in thirteen hours?" asks Benny.

"We are not going anywhere," I say, at least partially because I realize it is hard to hide in a crowd if I am to be accompanied by my flunkies, one of whom is no more than a biscuit shy of four hundred pounds and another of whom is a zombie. And suddenly a thought occurs to me, one of the few I have in the last hour that does not begin with a picture of a grave and all my friends throwing flowers and unredeemed markers into it. "Milton," I say, "if the Kid doesn't fight until midnight, can you break the spell then?"

Milton grimaces. "I have a chance, at least," he says. "But even then, I will need the claw of a Subterranean Fish Eagle."

"Benny, Gently," I say, "your job is to bring Milton that claw. We will meet at ringside at eleven o'clock tonight." I pause. "Milton, go home and get some sleep. I want you at your very best tonight."

"And what will you be doing, Harry?" asks Milton.

"I will be arranging for Kid Testosterone not to enter the ring before midnight," I say.

I wait until they all leave, and then I walk over and ask Joey Chicago for his phone. He lays it on the bar and I pull out the bill that Short Odds Harrigan gives me, and I call the number on it. A minute later Bubbles La Tour picks up the phone, and even though I am Harry the Book and am interested only in odds and money, my throat goes dry and my palms start sweating, because as everyone knows Bubbles La Tour is the Secretariat or Babe Ruth of women, an exemplar of the gender who has curves in places where most women don't even have places.

I explain who I am, and before I can get any farther she wants to know the morning line on her repeating as Miss Lower South Manhattan next month, and I tell her she is currently a one-to-ten favorite but that the serious money hasn't come in yet and I expect her to wind up at about one-to-fifty. Finally she asks what I want, and I tell her, and she says that it is an interesting proposition but she can't do it for free and what will I offer her, and I give her my very best offer which is that I will offer to cross her phone number out on the C note Short Odds gave to me and never call her again, and she says, "See you at eleven!" and that is that.

Then it is just a matter of killing time until the fight. Gently Gently Dawkins also kills four pizzas, a Belgian waffle, two bowls of chili, an eighteen-ounce steak, and a triple hot fudge sundae (but because he is on a diet, he does not eat the cherry that sits atop the sundae).

Benny challenges Joey Chicago to an afternoon of tiddly winks, but they start arguing about which came first, the tiddly or the wink, and by the time the dust clears it is eight o'clock and they have both forgotten to eat. This does not seem to be Dead End Dugan's problem, because he cannot remember whether zombies eat or not and he decides to be on the safe side and do without, though I cannot quite figure out exactly what a zombie can be on the safe side *of*.

Big-Hearted Milton wanders in nursing a black eye and a bloody nose, and Joey Chicago grins and says, "I see she is still mad at you."

"A vile canard," says Milton. "I apologize to her when we meet for dinner, and she forgives me."

"Then explain the eye and the nose," says Joey Chicago.

"I reach out to shake her hand and show her we are still

friends," answers Milton. "I am a little near-sighted, and that is not what I wind up grabbing and shaking." Suddenly he grimaces. "If you want to see a real fight, put Mitzi McSweeney in the ring against Bonecrusher McDade. I figure she takes him out no later than the fourth round."

Benny, who has seen Mitzi in action, opines that Bonecrusher cannot make it through the third round, and that reminds me that we have a fight to watch, and we walk over to the Garden, and arrive there at five minutes to eleven, just as the ring announcer is informing the crowd that Jupiter Zeus has just won a split decision over Murderous Malcolm Malone. Murderous Malcolm congratulates the winner and accidentally kicks a full water bucket onto the three judges as he is preparing to leave the ring. He holds his arms out to proclaim his innocence and that it was an accident, and in the process accidentally knocks out three of Referee Fair-Minded Freddie's teeth. Then, with a satisfied smile, he climbs out of the ring and heads off to the dressing room.

"Why have you bought seven seats?" asks Benny as we approach our seats at ringside.

"Two for Gently Gently," answers Milton, "and one each for Harry, you, Dugan and me."

"That is only six," says Benny, who is really good with math until he runs out of fingers and toes.

"Say, that's right," replies Milton. He turns to me. "Who is the seventh seat for, Harry?"

Before I can answer a hush falls over the crowd, and about ten seconds later there is a cheer that is so loud that all the mirrors in the public restrooms shatter, to say nothing of all the eyeglasses being worn anywhere in the arena. We all turn, and undulating down the aisle is Bubbles La Tour, who is wearing something very tight and very revealing that cannot possibly weigh eight ounces total. Finally she stops at the edge of our aisle and waves to the crowd, and there is another cheer, even louder than the first. She bows to acknowledge the cheers, and the seven closest men faint dead away, and everything comes to a halt while we wait for the ambulances to come and cart them off to the cardiac unit. She walks to the door with them, holding one of their hands, then walks back down to still more cheers, though I notice that almost none of the ladies in the audience are cheering, and indeed most are frowning, and a few are dabbing on lipstick and makeup.

"What time is it?" I ask.

"Eleven forty-nine," answers Benny.

"Milton," I say, "we need eleven more minutes."

"Probably only eight or nine," replies Milton. "The fighters have to make their way to the ring, and then the announcer introduces them, and then we sing the national anthem (or did we do that already?), and then—"

"Milton," I yell at him, "*do* something!"

"I could vanish her clothes," he suggests, "which are about ninety-three percent vanished already."

"There will be riots and cardiac arrests and police arrests and the fight will never come off, but just be rescheduled, and I cannot use this particular ploy to postpone it an hour the next time," I say.

"I'll think of something," says Milton.

Bubbles La Tour reaches our aisle and begins wiggling her way past Dawkins and Dugan and Benny, and then she sidles her way past Milton and utters a shriek and pivots around and slaps his face.

The crowd screams in outrage, though I get the distinct impression that most of them are outraged that *they* didn't get to give her a friendly pinch, and then Bubbles unloads a thousand-word diatribe to Milton, of which at least seventeen of the words can be printed in a family magazine, and then she pivots and wriggles her way back to the aisle and stalks out of the arena.

"Eleven fifty-nine," announces Benny.

"See?" says Milton proudly as he wipes the blood from his nose. "Nod eberythig requires magig."

A minute later, at exactly midnight, Kid Testosterone climbs up the stairs to the ring. He trips on the top step, as usual, and cracks his head against the ring post. Usually this would knock him out for the next three hours, but tonight he just smiles a self-deprecating smile, and waves to the crowd. Then Bonecrusher McDade, who looks like a walking ad for steroids, enters the ring, and the referee gives them their instructions— no biting, no kicking, no rabbit punches, no hitting below the belt, and this being Manhattan, no kissing—and then they go to their corners, and a few seconds later the bell rings, and out comes Kid Testosterone, and he doesn't look any tougher than usual, but Bonecrusher McDade lands a one-two to the Kid's belly and a left hook to his chin, and the Kid just shrugs it off.

"Okay, Milton," I say, trying to keep the desperation out of my voice. "It's past midnight. *Do* something!"

Milton mutters a spell, the Kid brushes off a haymaker that should put him to sleep for a week, and Milton tries a different spell.

"Nothing is happening," I say as the Kid misses with a left and right, and absorbs three quick punches to the ribcage, and laughs in the Bonecrusher's face.

"I cannot break through the spell," says Milton unhappily.

"It must be a real doozy," offers Dawkins sympathetically.

"It is," answers Milton. He points to Morris the Mage, who is sitting next to Short Odds Harrigan on the other side of the ring. "Look at that smug bastard," he growls.

I do look, and Morris is so caught up in the fight that he's throwing punches in the air even as he sits there. He is bobbing and weaving just like Kid Testosterone, sneering whenever the Kid sneers at McDade, and I see a way out of our dilemma and turn to tell Milton about it, but Milton has seen it at the very same time, and is already chanting a spell. It goes on for almost half a minute, during which time the Kid is pummeled mercilessly but painlessly, and finally he yells "Abra cadabra!" and suddenly the Kid shrugs off a shot to the belly but Morris moans and doubles over in his seat.

"Watch!" says Milton with a happy smile.

McDade lands a shot to the Kid's head. Nothing happens in the ring, but Morris goes flying back out of his chair.

Morris is knocked down three more times as he tries to get up, and finally we see him turn to Short Odds, and while I cannot read his lips I know what he is saying, which is that he isn't getting paid enough to take this kind of beating and he is redirecting it back to the person it is being aimed at, and he makes a mystic gesture with his hands, and the next haymaker McDade throws at the Kid knocks him out of the ring and has absolutely no effect on Morris. The referee looks out at the floor to see if the Kid can make it back by the count of ten, but it is obvious that the Kid cannot even wake up by the count of ten to the thirty-seventh power, and that is that and I do not have to pay off any bets, and I resolve to tell all the other bookies never to deal with Short Odds Harrigan again, and then I think why should I make life easier for them, so we all of us except Milton, who sees Mitzi McSweeney in the crowd and goes over to patch things up, return to Joey Chicago's to celebrate not going broke.

Milton walks in half an hour later, holding a bloody handkerchief to his nose.

"So she's still mad at you," I say.

"Well, yes and no," answers Milton, dabbing gingerly at his nose.

"What do you mean?" asks Benny Fifth Street.

"I explain to her that I have been a cad, and I apologize for all offenses I have given her, and she is clearly softening and liking what she hears, and so I throw myself at her mercy."

"That sounds like a humble approach," says Benny. "Why

should a woman get upset when you throw yourself at her mercy?"

"I miss her mercy," explains Milton, "and you cannot believe how displeased she is with what I hit."

Just then who should walk in but Mitzi McSweeney. I would say she has blood in her eye, but that would be misleading, because what she had is blood on her hand, and there is no question but that it comes from Milton's nose.

"Where is he?" she demands.

I look around, and Milton is nowhere to be seen, but I can hear a voice muttering behind the door of Milton's office, saying, "I should have let Kid Testosterone fight her when he and I still had a chance."

Mitzi hears it too, and in another twenty seconds she puts on an exhibition that would be the envy of both the Kid and the Bonecrusher.

THE EVENING LINE

"It is a truth universally acknowledged that a single man in possession of a good fortune must be in want of a wife," says Benny Fifth Street.

"I don't want to hear this," replies Plug Malone.

"I do not think that what you want enters into this," says Benny.

"What is this all about?" asks Joey Chicago, who is polishing glasses behind the bar. Well, not really polishing them, but at least flicking a semi-damp towel over them.

"I hit three long shots in a row when I am at Aqueduct this afternoon," explains Malone, "and no matter what Harry's stooge says, I plan to enjoy my winnings on my own."

"I am his flunky, not his stooge," replies Benny with dignity.

"Big difference," snorts Malone. "Either way, I am not in want of a wife."

I am sitting in my office, which happens to be the third booth at Joey Chicago's Three-Star Tavern, sipping an Old Peculiar and minding my own business, which at the moment consists of doping out the odds for the fight card at the Garden that night, when Benny turns to me. "What do you think, Harry?"

"I think Kid Testosterone lasts about thirty seconds of the first round against Tidal Wave McTavish," I say. "Forty-five if he's lucky."

"No, I mean about all the women who will soon be pursuing Plug Malone with a single-minded intensity."

"How much did you win today?" I ask Malone.

He looks furtively around to make sure no one else is listening. "Fifty-three large," he answers.

"That is nothing," says Gently Gently Dawkins, munching on a candy bar as he enters the tavern. "I myself am a fifty-eight large."

"We are talking about money, not pants sizes," says Benny. "Our friend Plug Malone has had a remarkable run of luck at Aqueduct."

"Spend it fast," says Dawkins, "before some filly spends it for you."

"No one knows except you three, and Joey Chicago here," says Malone. "No one *will* know."

"That's like saying no one will notice an earthquake because it happens on the next block," says Dawkins.

"Then no one will care," says Malone. "I will share a confidence with you. My real name is Jeremiah Malone. I know you think Plug is for the chaw of tobacco I usually have in my mouth except when I am in classy establishments like this one"—he glares at Joey Chicago—"*where they do not even have the courtesy to furnish a spittoon,* but in truth is it is short for Plug Ugly, which is a nickname they gave back at P.S. 48 and which has stuck with me ever since. I am the ugliest, least attractive husband material in Manhattan, maybe in all of New York. You have never seen me with a woman. Women take one look at me and run in the opposite direction."

"Which direction is the opposite direction?" asks Dead End

Dugan, who has been more than a little confused ever since he became a zombie, and is standing in the farthest, darkest corner of the tavern.

"Do not bother yourself with such trivialities," I tell him. "Go back to staring peacefully at a wall and thinking dead thoughts."

"You're the boss, Harry," replies Dugan, and suddenly he is as still and silent as a statue again. Benny and Gently Gently do most of my errands for me, but every now and then, when someone is reluctant to make good his marker, it is nice to have a six foot ten inch zombie on my team.

"So what are the odds of Malone's looks frightening away potential brides?" asks Benny.

"Yesterday, three thousand-to-one no one will give him a second look," I answer. "Since he won the fifty-three large, half a million-to-one that they will."

"But nobody knows!" wails Malone.

"It goes out on the wind, like news of antelope drinking at a waterhole goes out to a hungry lioness," I say. "They'll start showing up any minute now."

No sooner do the words leave my lips than Mimsy Borogrove walks in. She slithers right past my two flunkies and sidles up to Malone, who acts like he has never been sidled up to before.

"Got a light, Big Boy?" she half says and half breathes.

"A light *what*?" asks Malone.

"Come back to my place and we'll talk about it," she says, reaching out for him.

"Unhand that man!" says a voice from the doorway, and we all turn to see Almost Blonde Annie standing there.

"Unhand me?" repeats Malone, staring at his hands in horror and then trying to tuck them into his pockets. "But I *need* them!"

"Of course you do," says Almost Blonde Annie. "After all, you have to sign the marriage license."

"I beg your pardon," says Mimsy Borogrove, "but I got here first."

"And I got here last," says Snake-Hips Levine, entering the tavern and undulating right up to Malone. "Come on, Sweetie," she says. "We don't want to have anything to do with these other broads."

"Do I know you?" asks Malone.

"Wouldn't you like to?" says Snake-Hips. "Look at me," she continues, running her hands over her body just the way any healthy male of the species would like to. "Isn't this worth fifty-two thousand, two hundred and twelve dollars?"

"Fifty-three thousand," says Mimsy.

Snake-Hips shakes her head, and everything else she has just naturally shakes with it. "Fifty-two thousand, two hundred and twelve. The other seven hundred and eighty-eight dollars was the money he bet that was returned to him when he cashed in." She stares compassionately at Mimsy. "You'd better get a new source of information, honey."

Gently Gently Dawkins leans over to me. "Perhaps we should do a little something to save him from this veritable plague of potential fiancées," he whispers.

"I am a bookie, not a marriage counselor," I say. "Plug Malone's pre-marital problems are his own."

"I think Mimsy may take a poke at Snake-Hips," says Dawkins. "What will we do then?"

"I will practice my trade and offer eight-to-five that Snake-Hips takes her out in straight falls," I answer.

As we are conversing, four more women have entered the tavern, and now it is Joey Chicago who approaches me.

"Harry," he says, "we have a problem. All these women are taking up space at the bar, and none of them are buying any drinks."

"I hope you are not suggesting that I should buy drinks for

the house," I reply. "Along with everything else, I have long suspected that Almost Blonde Annie has a hollow leg."

"Can't Milton cast a spell that either makes them buy drinks or go home?" he asks. "I will tear up your tab if he does."

"All right," I say, because my tab has reached almost six dollars, and I hate spending my own money. "I will talk to him."

"Good. Where is he?"

"Where else?" I say. "In his office." I head off to the men's room, which is where Big-Hearted Milton, my personal mage, has set up shop for the past two years. I find him, as usual, sitting cross-legged inside a pentagram he has drawn on the floor just next to the row of sinks, and there is a black candle burning at each point of it.

"Milton," I say, "I need you to cast a spell."

He holds a finger up to his lips. "In a minute."

He begins chanting in a language that bears a striking resemblance to ancient Mesopotamian, or possibly French, and finally he snaps his fingers and all the candles immediately go out.

"Hah!" he says, getting to his feet. "*That* will show her!"

"Mitzi McSweeney again," I say. I do not ask, because these days it is always Mitzi McSweeney.

"We are sitting at a table in Ming Toy Epstein's Almost Kosher Chop Suey House, and she remarks that one of her garters is pinching her, so I reach under the table to adjust it, and she hits me in the face with a plate of sweet and sour pork." He frowns. "Me, who hasn't had pork since he was bar mitzvahed!"

"So what kind of terrible curse did you put on her this time?" I ask in a bored tone, because somehow Milton's curses never seem to wind up bothering anyone but Milton.

"Oh, it's a good one," he assures me with an evil smile. "Since it is her garter that causes this humiliation, I curse every garter she owns. Now none of them will work!"

"That is very brilliant, Milton," I say. "Now whenever she is out in public …"

"… her garters will unsnap …" he laughs.

"Right," I say. "And she will have to stop right there on the street and lift her skirt and try to re-snap them, and of course some handsome man will see this lovely lady with even lovelier legs in distress and will come to her aid, and try to help attach her stockings and doubtless introduce himself and tag along with her in case the garters give her further trouble, which of course they will."

"Damn!" growls Milton. "Why didn't *I* think of that?"

He relights the candles, stands in the middle of the pentagram, chants something in another unknown language, makes a mystical gesture, and then rejoins me by the door.

"All done," he announces. "Now, what can I do for you?"

"Not for me," I say. "It seems that Plug Malone made a big score and is being whelmed over by women."

"What is wrong with that?" asks Milton.

"They are taking up space at the bar and not buying anything, and Joey Chicago wants them to spend money or go home."

"Hell, have Plug Malone treat 'em all."

"There is a school of thought that opines that Plug Malone has never so much as spoken to a woman, except perhaps for his mother," I say.

Milton cracks open the door and takes a peek at the bar.

"Her?" he says. "And her too? And is that Sugar Lips Sally? And …"

He studies each of the dozen women who have gathered so far, and shakes his head in wonderment. "I have not seen such an outstanding field since the 1997 Belmont Stakes," he says at last.

"So can you do one or the other?" I say. "Send them home or get them to part with some money?"

"I will not send them home," announces Milton. "There is always a chance Mitzi McSweeney will refuse to see me again. She complains that she is getting arthritis in her hand after the last forty times she bloodies my nose."

"All right," I say. "Then cast a spell that makes them spend their money."

"Look at all those skin-tight dresses, Harry," he says. "They cannot possibly be hiding three dollars between them. I will hex Malone into buying drinks for all of them."

"Yeah," I say. "I think Joey Chicago will go for that."

So Milton mutters a spell, and suddenly Malone gets the strangest, most puzzled expression on his face, and announces that he's buying for everyone in the house.

"Everyone?" repeats Joey Chicago with a happy smile.

"Every man and woman in the place," Malone assures him.

"What about zombies?" asks Gently Gently.

"Do zombies drink?" asks Almost Blonde Annie.

"I don't know," admits Malone. "Hey, Dugan!" he shouts. "Do zombies drink?"

Dead End Dugan blinks his eyes a couple of times, and frowns. "I don't know," he answers. "It's been so long ..."

"Besides, even if he started, it would probably all pour out through those holes in his chest," says Benny Fifth Street.

"Probably," agrees Dugan unhappily. "Or maybe where I got my throat slit. That was ... let me think ... the fourth time."

"How many times have you been killed?" asks Malone.

"Five that I can remember," says Dugan.

"That's horrible!" says Snake-Hips Levine with a shudder that attracts the attention of every man in the place.

"It hardly hurt at all after the third time," Dugan assures her. He makes a face. "I really hated it when they dumped me overboard though. You think they'd have been more considerate, what with all the ice in the East River."

While all this high-brow discussion of life and death is

occurring—or to be totally accurate, death and more death—word seems to have gone out on the wind that Malone is paying, because suddenly almost a dozen men enter the tavern and ask for drinks.

Brontosaur Nelson, who is a midget wrestler, asks for a tall one, which cracks everyone up, and the laughter attracts Loose Lips Louie, who is just walking by, and Impervious Irving, who is between bodyguard jobs, and Charlie Three-Eyes (who has a scar where he claims his third eye used to be, though word on the street is that it is simply where his ever-loving wife bites him when she finds he has been watching Bubbles La Tour's Dance of Sublime Surrender at the Rialto every night, and try as he will he cannot convince her that he goes for the music, which any ever-loving spouse will agree is like buying *Playboy* for the articles.)

Everyone keeps drinking and having a good time, and finally Loose Lips Louie says, "So who's the lucky lady, Plug?" and two seconds later you can hear a pin drop. And this is not a figure of speech; Gently Gently is loosening the pin that is holding his shirt together where he has popped a button after his fourth hot fudge sundae of the day, and so silent does the tavern become that I can hear it hit the floor fifteen feet away.

"I'm not the marrying type," says Malone.

"Are you the type who buys drinks for the house?" asks Loose Lips Louie.

"Certainly not," says Malone.

"Well, there you have it," says Loose Lips Louie. "Now, who's the lucky lady?"

Malone looks like a deer caught in the headlights, except no deer ever looks so frightened, even when surrounded by a pack of elephants or whatever it is that has a taste for freshly-killed deer, and suddenly he frowns and points a finger at Milton.

"This is your doing!" he yells. "I would never stand for drinks unless I was hexed, and you're the only mage here. *You're* the reason all these gorgeous man-hungry women are after me!"

"If I am the reason all these women are here," answers Milton calmly, "than I am also the reason you win fifty-three large at Aqueduct, and I would like my fee, please."

"Never, you foul fiend!" screams Malone.

"I thought *I* was the foul fiend," says Dead End Dugan, who looks puzzled for a moment and then goes back to thinking dead thoughts.

"It is not Milton," I explain. "Not only does Milton not have a way with women, but he cannot go through a single day without Mitzi McSweeney bloodying his nose and threatening his life. It is the money that has attracted all these women."

Of course every woman in the place denies it, and Stella Houston, who claims to be Stella Dallas's better-looking sister, slinks up to Malone and offers to hold his money before Milton or I can steal it.

"So tell us, Malone," says Loose Lips Louie. "Who's the lucky woman?"

"I keep telling you," replies Malone, looking even more exasperated than terrified, "I am *not* getting married."

"Of course you are," says Brontosaur Nelson. "You don't think these lovely frail flowers are going to let you leave the place un-engaged, do you?"

"Hell, even Impervious Irving couldn't make it out the door if he was in your place," says Loose Lips Louie. "So who's your choice?"

"*I am not getting married!*" screams Malone. The nearest men jump back, startled, but the women merely look amused.

Benny Fifth Street walks over to me. "I smell a profitable enterprise here," he says.

"That thought has not escaped my notice," I say, turning to the room at large. "Let me make up a morning line, and then the book is open for business."

"It is ten o'clock at night," notes Gently Gently. "Unless you want them to stay here until daybreak, what we need is an evening line."

"The man's got a point," agrees Benny Fifth Street.

"All right," I say. "Bring me the blackboard on which Joey Chicago advertises the day's special, and a piece of chalk."

The place has fallen silent, as each of the men is studying the field and trying to decide where to put his money. It is not without incident. Almost Blonde Annie decks Charlie Three-Eyes when he tries to examine her teeth, and Mimsy Borogrove kicks Brontosaur Nelson almost to the ceiling when he tries to examine things down at his eye level.

"How's it coming, Harry?" asks Bet-a-Bunch Murphy after a few minutes.

"I'm working on it," I tell him.

"Who's the favorite?"

"That is the one thing that requires no work at all," I answer. "I make Bubbles La Tour the top-heavy favorite, you should pardon the expression."

Impervious Irving nods his head in agreement. "She is truly the Secretariat of women."

"Better," adds Short Odds Harrigan.

"Now just a minute, Buster ..." begins Stella Houston ominously.

"What are the odds on her, Harry?" asks Loose Lips Louie.

"I make it one-to-eight-thousand," I answer.

"So if I bet eight thousand dollars on Bubbles La Tour and she wins what I think we shall call the Plug Malone Sweepstakes, all I win is a dollar?" continues Loose Lips Louie.

"That's right," I say.

"An underlay," remarks Gently Gently Dawkins. "I make her one-to-ten-thousand, minimum."

"If he proposes to Bubbles La Tour, there won't be enough of him left to bury," vows Mimsy Borogrove.

"We'll kill him with such skill and dexterity that a jury will award us both ears and the tail," chimes in Snake-Hips Levine.

"You know," says Benny Fifth Street, "I never thought of it until just now, but I'll bet all the other super-heroes who come equipped with just one or two super-powers apiece do not like Superman any more than these delicate feminine blossoms like Bubbles La Tour."

"Shut up about her!" snaps Stella Houston.

"Right," says Short Odds Harrigan. "Mentioning her in front of these lovely ladies is like mentioning Babe Ruth to a bunch of minor leaguers."

Even Impervious Irving can't pull the women off Short Odds Harrigan as fast as they pile on, and I call Dead End Dugan over to help.

After about three or four minutes Harrigan is uncovered and helped to his feet. Both of his eyes are blackened, what's left of his nose is bleeding, and he spits out three teeth. Both knees and an elbow are exposed where his suit has been torn, and his face seems much larger than usual. Then Benny Fifth Street loosens his tie and suddenly he can breathe again and the size of his face goes back down to normal. He is about to say something, but then he looks into the unforgiving faces of the assembled ladies, sighs once, and trudges off to a corner.

In the meantime Gently Gently Dawkins has been whispering into his cell phone, and finally he puts it back into his pocket.

"Bubbles La Tour has scratched," he announces.

"Why?" asks Brontosaur Nelson.

"She must have thrown a shoe," muses Bet-a-Bunch Murphy.

"She says she remembers Malone, and would not marry him if he was the last man on Earth."

"This is unheard of," says Murphy. "When has a horse ever rejected his jockey?"

"Well, that makes it a more competitive field," says Loose Lips Louie. "What is the evening line now?"

"I will have to re-compute it," I say. "Losing Bubbles La Tour in the Plug Malone Sweepstakes is like doping out the odds in a golf match where Ben Hogan, Arnold Palmer, Jack Nicklaus and Tiger Woods all fail to make the cut. It is clearly a wide-open race."

But in just a handful of minutes we are given to realize that it is not as wide-open as it had seemed, because who should walk into the tavern but Morris the Mage. He walks right up to Mimsy Borogrove and holds out his hand. She puts a couple of C-notes into it, he pockets it, nods, and shakes her hand.

"What is going on here?" demands Milton, who does not like having his territory encroached upon.

"I have been retained by this lovely spinster here," announces Morris, as Mimsy kind of growls deep in her throat at the word 'spinster', "to help her nab—uh, to help her *wed* – the man of her choice." He looks at Mimsy, smiles, makes a mystical sign in the air, and says *"Presto!"* – and suddenly instead of wearing what looks like an exceptionally wide black satin belt and not much else, Mimsy is decked out in an elaborate wedding gown.

"Lacks a little something," muses Morris. "Ah! I have it! *Abra cadabra!*" And just like that, Mimsy is carrying a huge bouquet of flowers.

Almost Blonde Annie frowns. "Is that fair?"

"Don't worry," says Bet-a-Bunch Murphy. "She is still nowhere near as heavy a favorite as Bubbles La Tour was before she scratched."

The other women aren't paying much attention to Murphy *or* Mimsy. Each of them is speaking into their cell phones, and we know what is coming next, just not in what order.

Spellsinger Solly is the first to arrive. He pauses just long enough for Snake-Hips Levine to fork over some cash. Then he snaps his fingers, and Mimsy Borogrove's gorgeous wedding gown has suddenly turned into some severely-tailored widow's weeds.

"Get me outta these things!" she screams, tearing at the clothes, and Impervious Irving and Gently Gently Dawkins go over to help her, and suddenly she is standing there in nothing but her lacy underthings, and there's not much of *them*, and she is glaring at Morris. "*Do* something!" she bellows.

Morris takes a good look at her, of which an awful lot is exposed for looking at, and applauds.

"Something *else*, damn it!" she snaps.

Morris mutters a spell, and she is back in the dress she entered with.

"That's a relief," says Benny Fifth Street.

"Is it?" asks Joey Chicago curiously.

Benny nods. "Another ten seconds and I'd have proposed to her myself."

The other mages start showing up, each finds his client, and I am hoping that we are about to have a Mexican standoff, because as far as I can see, the alternative is a Mexican shootout.

The mages each have a drink, and then I assume that they begin mentally bombarding Malone with marriage proposals, because he claps his hands over his ears, scrunches up his eyes, and screams, "I *ain't* getting married!"

"What are *you* doing?" demands Morris, as I work on the blackboard.

"I am adjusting the odds," I reply.

"How?" asks Bet-a-Bunch Murphy.

"I had Mimsy Borogrove as the nine-to-five favorite," I answer, "but now I put her at six-to-one."

"Why?" demands Morris, who is clearly concerned for his client.

"She gets dressed," I explain.

"Is *that* all?" he says, muttering a spell and pointing to her—but just as he points she turns to the bar to order another drink, and the spell hits Gently Gently Dawkins full force, and suddenly he is standing there in his colorful boxer shorts and his undershirt and not much else.

"Petunias!" giggles Loose Lips Louie, pointing to the flower design on Dawkins's shorts. "Ain't that sweet?"

"He may not be much," I whisper to Milton, "but he's one of ours. Do something."

"Right," Milton whispers back. He mumbles a spell and a bumblebee crawls out of one of the petunias, flies across the room, and stings Loose Lips Louie on the nose.

Louie bellows in pain, and Stella Houston, who is standing beside him, laughs.

"Lady," says Louie, dabbing his wound with a napkin, "you might as well go home. You ain't ever gonna get a husband with an attitude like yours."

Well, there is one husband she is never going to get, and that is Loose Lips Louie, and she starts pummeling him with such intensity that it looks like no one else is ever going to get him either, unless they are heavily into necrophilia, but finally her mage, Willie the Wizard, pulls her back.

"Why are you stopping me?" she demands.

"You only give me three C-notes," he says, "which is fine for a wedding, but nowhere near enough to get you out of stir after you have been arrested for murder. Let us concentrate on marrying you to this poor unassuming bozo, who has no idea what misery is in store for him."

It is entirely possible that he is going to say more, but suddenly Stella Houston starts pummeling *him* instead. He gets loose and runs out into the street with Stella in hot pursuit.

"Another scratch," says Benny Fifth Street. "This field is getting smaller and smaller."

"Right," says Gently Gently, who actually looks more

comfortable without his suit and shirt, which are about four sizes smaller than he is. "I figure we are down to maybe only a million eligible women."

"Let us eliminate all those women who are not attracted to Malone because of the money he is carrying around with him."

"Right," says Dawkins. "Now we are down to nine hundred ninety-nine thousand, nine hundred and ninety-seven, give or take."

"Let's be reasonable," suggests Bet-a-Bunch Murphy, which I personally think would make a pleasant change. "There are so many mages on the scene that there is no way, now that Bubbles La Tour has scratched, that any woman without a mage has a chance."

"You know, he's got a point," says Brontosaur Nelson.

I find that I have to agree with him, and shortly thereafter I come up with the evening line, which reads as follows:

Snake-Hips Levine, 9-2

Bodacious Belinda, 5-1

Mimsy Borogrove, 6-1

Almost Blonde Annie, 6-1

Penelope Precious, 8-1

Lascivious Linda, 8-1

Bedroom Eyes Betty, 10-1

And the rest go up in odds from there.

"Harry, you must be out of your mind," whispers Benny Fifth Street. "You've got Lascivious Linda down there at eight-to-one. Why, she can take Snake-Hips Levine in straight falls."

"They are all utterly charming morsels of femininity," I say, "and I would never try to rank them in order of desirability, at least not without a set of body armor. But I am not ranking the ladies so much as I am ranking their mages."

"Aha!" says Benny. "Now it makes sense."

"You are forgetting something vitally important," says Malone.

"Oh?" I say. "What is that?"

"*I ain't marrying* none *of them!*" he bellows.

"Please do not interrupt us when we are having a serious discussion," says Benny. And he goes on to tell me which mages he thinks I am ranking too high.

"Milton," says Malone, with just a note of panic in his voice, "you're the resident mage here. Make them all go away."

"All the other mages?" asks Milton. "That will leave you at the mercy of the very people you wish to have nothing to do with."

"Not the mages," says Malone. "The *women.*"

"Probably their mages would object," says Milton, "and looking around the tavern I see twelve … no, fourteen of them."

"That is no problem," says Malone. He takes my chalkboard away and lays it on the far end of the bar. The mages all gather around it, studying the odds and arguing about whether their prices are too short or too long. "You see?" continues Malone. "They are only concerned with where Harry ranks them. Their interest in the women starts and stops with their fees."

Milton takes a good hard look, and sure enough, none of the mages is paying any attention to the women.

"What the hell," says Milton. "Give me ten large and I'll vanish them all."

"Forever?" asks Benny Fifth Street, who seems to have taken a liking to, or at least an interest in, Mimsy Borogrove.

Milton shakes his head. "Not for a lousy ten thousand dollars. But I'll vanish them long enough for Malone to take what remains of his stash and head out into the wild, untamed wilderness of New Jersey."

"It's a deal," says Malone, and he peels off the ten large and hands it to Milton, who stuffs it into a pocket.

"Now I'm only going to have time to cast this spell once before the other mages notice what is happening, so I need to gather all the women close together."

Having said that, Milton starts leading each of the women over to the farthest part of the bar from where the mages are. He has twelve of them standing together and is just leading Lascivious Linda over when we hear a female voice bellow from the doorway: "Since when did you become a collector?" and in walks Mitzi McSweeney with blood in her eye.

"You misunderstand, my dear," says Milton nervously, backing away a few steps as she approaches him with her hands balled up into fists. "I am just doing a service for Plug Malone here, who has no desire to be near any of these women."

"So you're carting them all off as a favor to him?" she screams.

"Certainly not," says Milton. "Women don't interest me at all. I prefer you."

"*WHAT?*" she bellows.

"I didn't mean that," says Milton, his hands stretched out defensively in front of him as he begins backing away toward his office.

"Just don't let him vanish all your clothes," says Mimsy Borogrove as Mitzi McSweeney walks by her in pursuit of Milton. "I didn't realize how cold it was in here until—"

She does not get to finish the sentence.

"You vanished her clothes?" demands Mitzi.

"Never!" protests Milton, his back to the door of the men's room. "That was Morris the Mage's spell. I cannot vanish anyone's clothes unless I say *barota nictu!*"

And as quick as the words leave his mouth, Mitzi McSweeney's clothes disappear.

Milton's eyes widen, more in terror than lust. He swallows hard and leans back against the door, which starts giving way. "You're looking ... uh ... *well* today," he says, then turns and races hell bent for leather into the interior of his office.

Mitzi is one step behind him as the door swings shut and they vanish from sight. There follows a great deal of noise, a few shrieks of pain and terror, a crash, and a lot of words I never knew existed, all screamed in a feminine voice.

"Now magic them back—or else!" yells the voice.

There is a brief pause, and then a fully-dressed Mitzi McSweeney emerges from Milton's office. She pauses and turns to him just before the door swings shut.

"I'll talk to you *later!*" she snaps and walks out of the tavern.

I head toward the men's room, with Benny and Gently Gently falling into step behind me. Just before I get there I call Dead End Dugan over, in case the carnage is so great that only a zombie can endure it on an empty stomach, and then the four of us enter.

"Any sports fans see this and they will never talk about Muhammed Ali or Mike Tyson again," says Benny.

"Who would have guessed that there was that much blood in a body?" asks Gently Gently.

"It's not *in* him," notes Benny. "It's *on* him."

"And there wasn't a mark on her," adds Gently Gently in awestruck tones.

"Thad's because I ab a gendulmad," says Milton, holding a blood-soaked handkerchief to his nose. "Helb ged me on my feed."

We help him up. He sways a bit, but then Dugan steadies him.

"Thag you," he says, blowing some more blood out of his nose. "Thad woman has a left you wouldn't believe."

"I think we're missing a bet here," says Gently Gently.

"Oh?" I say.

"Have Milton cast a spell to marry Mitzi McSweeney off to Malone. No one's bet on her, so you'll win all the money, and this way Milton will at least live till his next birthday."

"No!" says Milton. "She is the love of my life, or at least the goal of it. I will give her time to cool off and then throw myself at her mercy."

"Last time you throw yourself at her mercy you miss," I remind him, "and she is somewhat less than pleased with what you hit."

He winces in pain at the memory. "Maybe I had better just extend my hand in friendship."

"And the last time you do that," adds Benny, "she is bending over watering her flowers, and you know what happened."

"I am the greatest mage in Manhattan," groans Milton. "In all of New York City, even. How can this keep happening to me?"

"Luck," suggests Dead End Dugan.

"Luck?" repeats Milton uncomprehendingly.

Dugan nods. "With a left like she has, you should have been as dead as me months ago."

We escort Milton back to the bar, where all the other mages are still arguing over the evening line, and all the women are eyeing Malone not unlike the way a healthy cat eyes a crippled mouse.

"The women are still here!" snaps Malone, reaching into Milton's pocket and taking back his ten large.

"I see you are having your usual fine luck with the opposite sex," notes Morris the Mage.

Milton, whose nose has started bleeding again, mutters a curse. It comes out as *"Blmskph!"*

"Let us be charitable here," adds Spellsinger Solly. "You have to admit that Mitzi McSweeney is about as opposite as sexes get to be."

"You are speagig aboud the woman I love!" growls Milton. "Well, lust for, anyway," he amends.

"Let us get back to the man we all lust for," says Almost Blonde Annie. She turns to her mage, Sam Mephisto, who does most of his magicking in the Bronx. "I paid you good money for a husband. I want him."

"I am working on it," says Sam Mephisto. "These things take time."

"Work faster!" she snaps.

"Not to worry," he says. "If worst comes to absolute worst, I'll marry you myself."

That is when we learn that interacting with the female of the species is not a problem unique to Big-Hearted Milton, but may very well affect *all* mages. Dead End Dugan and Impervious Irving wait until she pauses for breath and lift him up to the bar, where Joey Chicago douses his face with water.

Sam Mephisto blinks a few times, then slowly sits up. "That was a most amazing experience," he says. "For a minute there I dream I am back in Egypt, mounted on my camel and leading my men into battle against General Sherman." Which is when we know he is not entirely recovered, unless General Sherman went further astray than most history books would have us believe.

He gets down off the bar, blinks his eyes a few more times, and finally speaks. "It has been a long, hard night," he says. "I think I am going to take a little nap." And with that he slides down to the floor and lies there, snoring up a storm.

"Some mage!" snaps Almost Blonde Annie, making the same kind of disgusted face I make whenever I see Gently Gently Dawkins pour Tabasco sauce on his oatmeal. She glares from one man to another, and finally says, "I am a woman alone, without representation. Isn't *anyone* going to do something about it?"

I decide that she has a point, so I walk over to the blackboard where I have posted the evening line and raise her odds to forty-to-one.

She takes a glass of beer off the bar, throws it in Sam Mephisto's face, and stalks out into the night, leaving him licking his lips while still snoring.

"Well, that's one less to worry about," says Malone with a sigh of relief.

"Two," says Benny. "Stella Houston's probably still chasing Willie the Wizard all over Manhattan."

"Right," adds Gently Gently, surveying the tavern. "Fourteen more and you're out of the woods."

"Well, till tomorrow, anyway," agrees Benny.

"I hadn't even thought about tomorrow," says Malone.

"Well, you had better be prepared for it, because how long do you think you can keep something like fifty-three large a secret?" says Gently Gently. "Why, even now, I'll bet women are approaching from Connecticut and New Hampshire and New Jersey, maybe even from as far away as Delaware." He furrows his brow in thought. "It must be borne on the wind, like phera … phero … those things that perfume tries to copy."

Even as he speaks three more women enter the tavern, looking neither right nor left, but with eyes trained straight ahead on Malone.

"Milton, *do* something!" says Malone, his voice shaking.

"I *ab* doing subthig!" snaps Milton, still holding his handkerchief to his face. "I ab bleeding!"

One of the three newcomers notices all the mages, and immediately pulls out her cell phone and speaks to it in low tones. The other two soon follow suit.

"Well, whatever the result," says Joey Chicago happily, "at least we are doing some business."

"Why don't they all want to marry *you* then?" asks Malone.

"Because I lose all my money betting with Harry on everything from horses to politics," answers Joey. "Why, just last night I bet on Horrible Herman to win a steel cage match at the Garden."

"And does he?" asks Malone.

Joey Chicago shakes his head. "The steel cage beats him without drawing a deep breath."

Two mages walk in the front door and a third materializes by the juke box, so I walk over to the chalkboard and adjust the evening line again.

Suddenly I am confronted by Morris the Mage.

"You really think my entry is no better than a six-to-one shot?" he says pugnaciously.

"It's a well-matched field," I say. "And unless it comes up mud, I still make Snake-Hips Levine the favorite."

"Maybe we should make her carry extra weight," suggests Gently Gently.

"Shut up!" snaps Morris. He turns back to me. "Six-to-one, that's your final odds?"

"Not necessarily," I reply. "The starting gate is far from full yet."

"But you don't expect her odds to go any lower?"

"Not unless Snake-Hips Levine or Bodacious Belinda scratch," I say.

"All right," says Morris, pulling out his wad and peeling off a dozen hundred-dollar bills. "I'm putting twelve C-notes on her to win the Plug Malone Sweepstakes."

This makes all the other mages look like they lack confidence, and soon they are all lined up, putting bets down on their entries, and when they are all done the purse is up over fifteen large, and one or two of the women are looking at me the way they look at Plug Malone, but then they remember I will have to pay most of it to the winner, and I am back to being a wallflower again.

"Well, Plug baby, where shall we go on our honeymoon?" asks Lascivious Linda.

"We don't need a maid coming along with us, Plug honey," says Bedroom Eyes Betty. "Tell her we want to be alone."

"Tell them both," chimes in Bodacious Belinda. "It's me that you love."

"I don't love anyone!" yells Malone.

"It's me he'd *better* love," says Bodacious Belinda, glaring at her mage.

"Harry, this is becoming intolerable," says Malone. "Hell, I'd almost marry the woman who tried to kill Milton if that would make the others go away."

"You can't!" says Milton, who has finally unclogged his nasal passages. "She's mine!"

"She sure didn't act like it," says Malone.

"It was just a lovers' spat."

"If the Third Reich could spat like that we'd all be speaking German," says Malone.

"Just keep away from her," says Milton. "She's *mine*." Then he pauses and adds: "Potentially."

"All right, all right," says Malone. "It was a silly thought to begin with."

"What's so silly about sharing a bed with Mitzi McSweeney?" demands Milton pugnaciously.

"I get the feeling that the bed is a hospital bed," answers Malone. "And that Mitzi McSweeney isn't sharing it, but is signing the papers about not using extraordinary means, like giving me food and water, to keep me alive."

Milton is about to object, but then he realizes that he agrees down the line with Malone, and just nods his head instead.

"It is getting near midnight, and the object of our affection still hasn't made his choice," announces Mimsy Borogrove. "I don't know about the rest of you, but I am getting tired of waiting."

"Me, too," says Lascivious Linda. "But what do you propose to do about it?"

"I say if he hasn't chosen one of us by midnight, we draw straws for him," says Mimsy.

"We could have a nude mud-rasslin' tournament, with Malone going to the winner," suggests Joey Chicago. "At least we'd get to charge admission."

The mages all nod their heads in approval, but Bodacious Belinda points out that the wrong kind of mud could ruin their complexions and did anyone really trust Joey Chicago to supply the right kind, and they spend the next five minutes arguing about what kind of contest to have, but there is no question that they plan to resolve the problem before morning comes and a whole new crowd of women shows up.

"Damn!" mutters Malone. "I wish I'd never won that money to begin with."

Which is when I begin to get a truly profound inspiration.

"Do you really mean that?" I ask him.

"Yes," he says. "Look at these women. Now I know how a seal feels when he finds himself in the middle of a flock of sharks."

"I think it is a pride of sharks," says Gently Gently.

"No, it is a school," says Benny.

"Don't be silly," says Gently Gently. "Sharks don't go to school." Suddenly he frowns. "Well, not in this hemisphere, anyway. I can't say anything about African sharks."

"Shut up!" I snap at my flunkies. I turn back to Malone. "Well?" I say.

"Yes, I really mean it."

"Bet me the fifty-three large that twelve plus twelve equals seventy-three," I say.

"But it doesn't," replies Malone.

"I know," I say.

Suddenly his face lights up. "That's brilliant, Harry!" he exclaims. He raises his voice so it can be heard throughout the tavern. "Harry the Book, I will bet you fifty-three large that twelve plus twelve equals seventy-three."

"No!" cries Snake-Hips Levine. "Do not make that wager!" Everyone turns to her. "Twelve plus twelve is sixty-seven."

"I think it is forty-one," says Mimsy Borogrove.

Even Spellsinger Solly gets into the action, opining that it is ninety-four.

"I am sticking by my guns," says Malone. "Fifty-three large says that the answer is seventy-three."

"The answer is twenty-four, and I will thank you for my money," I say.

Everyone pulls out their pocket computers, and they finally admit that I am right, and suddenly I am surrounded by women.

"Good," I announce in a loud voice. "This will just about pay off the money I owe Hot Horse Harvey for that Daily Double he hits this afternoon."

"But Hot Horse Harvey is tapped out and hasn't laid a bet since—*Ow!*" says Gently Gently as I kick him in the shin while all the women and their mages are stampeding out the door.

Finally there is just Joey Chicago, Plug Malone, my flunkies and me, and then Malone walks up and shakes my hand.

"Thank you, Harry, for saving me from a fate worse than death."

"You've really never spoken to a woman since you were a kid?" I ask.

"Well, except for Granola Gidwitz," he says. "She seemed less intimidating, what with her cock eye and her triple chin and ..." His voice trails off and he stares wistfully off into space for a minute. "You know, it's strange, but I miss her. I wonder if she still lives over on West 22nd Street?" He heads off toward the door. "I think maybe it's time I paid her a visit."

Then he is gone, and no sooner does he leave than Mitzi McSweeney re-enters the tavern.

"You came back!" says Milton excitedly.

"I have decided to forgive you this one time," says Mitzi.

"And I will never give you cause to regret it," says Milton, reaching his arms out to her and walking forward to embrace her. But he forgets that Sam Mephisto is still sprawled out on the floor, and he trips over him, and he reaches out his hands to grab hold of something, anything, to stop himself from falling, and as you can imagine Mitzi is somewhat less than thrilled with what he grabs hold of, and a moment later he has retreated to his office, she has followed him in, and the rest of us conclude that World War III will sound pretty much like the sound coming from Milton's office, only less violent.

THE FASTEST DRAGON

So I am sitting in my office, which happens to be the third booth in Joey Chicago's Three-Star Tavern, sipping an Old Peculiar and doping out the morning line at Jamaica, when Benny Fifth Street approaches me.

"How is it coming along?" he inquires.

"Slowly," I reply. "It is not as if they hold a race for dragons every day, or even every decade when push comes to shove."

"So what have you got?" he says.

I sigh deeply. "I've got Tooth and Fang at five-to-one, Green Death at six-to-one, Fire Breather at six-to-one, Cutie Pie at eight-to-one, and the filly, Dragonella, at ten-to-one."

"I didn't know they came in fillies," says Gently Gently Dawkins, entering the bar while eating an ice cream cone.

"They come in eggs," says Benny. "Only later do they divide themselves into colts and fillies."

"That's dragons and dragonettes," replies Gently Gently.

I figure I can sit there and listen to my flunkies argue until post time, or I can finish my beer and catch the subway to Jamaica five hours early, and since it is an easy choice I get to my feet and tell Joey Chicago to put the Old Peculiar and its two departed brothers on the cuff.

"In case it has eluded your eagle eye, Harry," replies Joey, "I am wearing short sleeves."

So I pull out a Washington and a Lincoln, place them on the bar, and head for the door, where I collide with Longshot Lamont.

"Just the person I am looking for," he says, leading me back to my office. "We have serious business to conduct."

"What trillion-to-one horse has elicited your interest today?" I ask.

"I have decided horses are for suckers," replies Lamont. "I will make my fortune by betting on the fastest dragon."

"I do not believe I can accommodate you," I tell him regretfully.

"You have not even heard me yet," he complains.

"In all the years I have known you," I say, "you have never put your money down on anything that is less than eighty-to-one. I regret to inform you that the longest price in the field is the filly at ten-to-one."

"Ah!" he says with a smile. "Then you have not heard the news."

"Are we at war?" I ask.

"Even better!" he exclaims with a happy smile. "Chop Suey is running!"

"Pour in some bread crumbs and it will stay on the plate," says Gently Gently who, at four hundred pounds, has a knowledge of such things second to none.

"Do not understand me so fast," Lamont growls at him and then turns back to me. "Chop Suey is a dragon, imported from China just for this race. He arrives early this morning."

"What makes you think he'll be eighty-to-one or longer?" I ask.

"He has started seventeen times at Peking Downs and has

yet to finish better than sixth," says Lamont. "I think his owner must have shipped him here looking for easier opposition."

"And how much to you wish to put on his nose?"

"First I need to know the odds."

"If it turns out that indeed he runs out of the money seventeen times in a row, I will offer one hundred-to-one against him."

"That seems fair," he says, pulling out a roll of bills that could probably choke Chop Suey. "I will put five large on him to win."

I take the money, thank him, and send him on his way, then turn to Benny. "Check with Peking Downs and find out if Lamont is telling the truth about this Chop Suey."

"I will get right on it, Boss," he answers.

"I will have one more Old Peculiar," I announce, "while you are doing my homework, and then we will head off to the track."

"That is a lot of money to walk around with," says Gently Gently. "Maybe you should leave it in a safe place."

"I plan to," I tell him, and then turn toward the darkened area at the back of the tavern. "Hey, Dugan!" I shout. "Come on over!"

Dead End Dugan, the third of my three flunkies, shambles over until he is standing directly in front of me, all six feet ten inches of him. He is not much to look at, and he will never be a nosegay, but when I encounter the occasional client who is unwilling to make good his marker, it is always nice to have an oversized zombie working on my team.

"I am here, Harry," he announces as he comes to a stop.

"I am going off to watch the dragon race," I tell him, handing him the five large, "and I want you to hold this for me until I get back."

"Right, Harry." He pauses, frowning. "Should I do anything else?"

"Just return to where you were standing and go back to thinking dead thoughts," I say.

"Right, Harry," says Dugan, shambling off between the tables.

Gently Gently Dawkins spends the next five minutes complaining that he has never found a restaurant that serves dragon, and then Benny Fifth Street gets off the phone and approaches my office.

"They have confirmed it, Harry," he says. "I ask if Chop Suey ever finishes on the board in any of his seventeen races, and they assure me that such a thing has never happened."

I scribble the one hundred-to-one on Chop Suey at the bottom of the morning line and have Joey post it on the bar for latecomers, or latebettors, whichever the case may be. I am about to head out the door and for the subway when who should enter the place than Short Odds Harrigan.

"Ah, Harry the Book!" he exclaims happily. "I was afraid I might miss you."

"And what can I do for you, Short Odds?" I ask.

"I wish to make an investment," he says.

"You mean a wager," I correct him.

He shakes his head. "This one is an investment, Harry. He can't lose, bless his scaly green heart."

"I assume you are referring to the dragon race?" I say.

He smiles. "None other."

"Then I am afraid I cannot help you, Short Odds," I say.

"This is unheard-of!" he growls. "You are a bookie. I am a bettor. We were made for each other!"

"What I mean," I explain, "is that in the twenty years I've known you, you have never bet on anything where the odds were greater than 7-to-5, and I regret to inform you that the shortest odds you can get on the Dragon Stakes is five-to-one on Tooth and Fang."

"Forget him," says Harrigan. "I'm putting three large and a

quintet of Franklins on Hideous Herman, who surely goes off at less than even money."

"Have you not heard the news, Short Odds?" I say.

He frowns. "What news?"

"Hideous Herman has been scratched," I tell him.

"How can this be?" says Harrigan. "He had the race at his mercy."

"It appears he had more than the race at his mercy," Benny chimes in.

"I do not understand," says Harrigan.

"He eats two horses and an exercise boy during yesterday morning's workout," I explain, "and the stewards have barred him from the track pending further inquiry."

"Further inquiry?" he repeats, as mad as I've ever seen him. "What are they gonna do: ask him how they tasted?"

He grabs my just-delivered beer to drown his sorrows and then wanders back out onto the sidewalk, but before I can get up and make my way to the door a seemingly endless line of plungers comes to my office, eager to do business, and of course I remain until all our business is consummated, and when it is, Dugan is holding almost twelve large plus a trio of C-Notes and half a dozen markers.

"So how do things look?" asks Benny when the bar has emptied out again.

"There seems to be a paucity of interest in Cutie Pie," I answer. "Would you believe that I have not taken a single bet on him?"

"Well, you got to admit that it isn't much of a name for a scale-covered fire-breathing dragon," says Benny.

"So what would you call him?" asks Gently Gently.

"Hortense," answers Benny.

"Hortense?" asks Gently Gently, frowning.

"For Hortense Schultz, a girl I once dated," says Benny. "I would stack her up, pound for pound, against any scale-covered fire-breathing dragon that ever lived. Hell, she could give any dragon in this field five pounds and still beat the hell out of him."

"I think we are talking different sports," I say.

"Tell that to Hideous Herman," answers Benny.

The conversation is going nowhere so fast that even Chop Suey could not run it down, so I decide that it is really time to go to the track.

"Okay," I say. "Let me just get Milton, and we're off."

"Where is he?" asks Gently Gently.

"In his office, of course," I say, and walk over to the men's room, where I find Big-Hearted Milton, my personal mage, sitting on the tile floor, surrounded by five burning black candles.

"Milton," I say, "it's time to go."

"I am almost done," he replies, and then reverts into a language that maybe twenty other mages and no one else can understand.

"Mitzi McSweeney again?" I ask in bored tones, because these days it is always Mitzi McSweeney.

He nods. "We are in the supermarket, and she is bending over to inspect some grapefruit or apple or grape—something round, anyway—and since I do not want the woman I currently love, or at least lust for, to lose her balance and fall to the floor, especially in a tiny miniskirt, I offer a steadying hand. It is as simple and straightforward as that."

"Let me guess," I say. "She is somewhat less than pleased with where you lay your steadying hand."

"An understatement," he responds. "She actually bloodies my nose."

"I believe that is the fourth time this week," I say. "At least you have the comfort of knowing that there is nothing wrong with your blood circulation."

"There is plenty wrong with it!" protests Milton. "She keeps interrupting it!" Suddenly an evil grin crosses his face. "But this time I will have my just and terrible revenge."

I stifle a yawn, because in truth Milton's just and terrible revenge is rarely just and terrible to anyone but Milton.

"You know what pride she takes in those low necklines of hers?" he says. "Well, I have hexed her right hand—the one that she uses to hold her drinks, and not coincidentally the very one she bloodies my nose with—and now every time she tries to take a sip of her drink her wrist will tilt too much and she will spill her drink right down her neckline. What do you think of *that*?"

"Oh, that is a very severe hex indeed, Milton," I say as he chuckles with glee. "Now every time she tries to drink she will spill it down her neckline—and of course any gentleman standing near her will start drying her off with his handkerchief and sympathizing when she explains *why* she is pouring her drinks there, and if he is an exceptionally thoughtful gentlemen he will invite her up to his apartment where she can slip out of her wet clothes and continue drinking without having to worry about her neckline."

"Damn!" mutters Milton. "Why do *I* never think of the consequences of my brilliance?" He utters a few words in some ancient tongue, or possibly French, which makes just as little sense, and then he turns to me. "Okay, the hex is cancelled. Where are we going?"

"To Jamaica."

"Good," he says. "I love the horses."

"So does Hideous Herman," I say.

So we gather Benny and Gently Gently, and we hop onto the subway, and in just a few noisy, crowded, sweat-and-smoke-filled minutes we get off, and suddenly we're at Jamaica. I decide that with Longshot Lamont betting on a dragon that really and truly cannot win without some serious spiritual guidance (and I have brought Big-Hearted Milton along to misdirect any spirit with the audacity to try to help Chop Suey) and Short Odds Harrigan not trying to bankrupt me by betting his bankroll on odds-on favorites, I can afford the luxury of a box in the grandstand, and a moment later my crew and I are seated and watching the last horse race of the day.

Then Near-Sighted Sam, who calls all the races at Jamaica, taps the microphone ten or twenty times to make sure it's working, which has the side effect of sending twenty thousand spectators diving under their seats on the assumption that we are being bombed by the Russians or the Canadians or some big country like that.

"Ladies and gents," he says, "it is twenty-two minutes to post time for the Dragon Stakes, the race that will determine the fastest dragon currently under saddle."

"This is a bit of a cop-out," mutters Benny. "By my count, there are only six dragons under saddle."

Milton closes his eyes, goes into his swami trance while he floats maybe four inches above the ground, and comes back to life about half a minute later.

"There are, at this very instant, eighty-three dragons under saddle worldwide, not counting those who are under riders without saddles while rounding up elephants in the Brazilian Pampas."

"There aren't any elephants in the Pampas," says Gently Gently.

Milton nods. "Yeah, those South American dragons and their gauchos do a damned good job of it."

Then Near-Sighted Sam interrupts us all again. "Ladies and gents," he says, "two days ago there was a protest filed against the Dragon Stakes by the local owners association, complaining that since Jamaica runs more than two hundred races per year for horses, and only one for dragons, that it should not be allowed to supply the purse money for this race." He waits for a chorus of hoots and boos, but none is forthcoming. Most people's attitude is: *I'm* not running, so why the hell should I care? "However," he adds, turning up the decibel level, "I am pleased to announce that the Dragon Stakes has a savior. The famed Chinese entrepreneur, Mr. Louis Throckmorton Manchu, has offered to put up a prize of $100,000 to the winner. Louis, stand up and take a bow!"

And as quick as the words leave his mouth, the guy in the box next to ours stands up. He is wearing silken robes and a strange-looking hat, and his moustache droops down past his chin, and his left hand ends in a shining steel hook, and his feet are encased in spiked slippers, which is to say that he doesn't look all that different from the plungers who are heading toward the betting windows at that moment.

I decide I could use a little something to drink, and I take my leave of the box and head to the clubhouse bar, which doesn't carry Old Peculiar but does stock Old Washensox, which is always acceptable in a pinch.

I take a sip and realize that Mr. Manchu is standing right next to me, drinking an Ogre's Blood with a cherry in it, so I turn to him and say, "So are you the insidious Lou Manchu?"

"For the moment," he agrees. "But when I finish this"—he holds up his drink—"I will return to the box to watch the race in the open air, at which point I will be the outsidious Lou Manchu."

"It was a nice gesture to put up the purse money," I tell him.

He shrugs. "It was that or spend it on"—he makes a face—"charitable institutions."

We hear the trumpet—off-key, as usual—summoning the dragons onto the track, and we walk back to our boxes together.

"Hi, Boss," says Benny Fifth Street. "Have you *seen* the entries?"

"No," I answer, "but I will now." I look up the track, then rub my eyes because I am sure they are seeing wrong. I look again. Nothing has changed.

"Who the hell is *that?*" I ask. I do not have to read off the saddlecloth number, because just about everyone in the stands is asking the same question.

"That is Cutie Pie," answers Benny.

"This is not the best-named animal I have ever seen," I say. "He has teeth longer than rowboat oars, and none of the others come up to his knee."

Lou Manchu leans over from his box to ours. "Too big, too heavy," he says. "He will have great difficulty getting a mile and a half."

"That may well be true," agrees Gently Gently. "But the Dragon Stakes is only a mile."

"Same principle," says Lou Manchu. "Sort of."

The post parade is not a thing of beauty. There is an outrider in a red jacket atop a chestnut horse, leading the parade. Fire Breather, who has drawn stall Number One, is next in line. He gets too close to the horse, who kicks at him with his hind legs. Fire Breather frowns, takes a deep breath, exhales, and suddenly both the horse and rider burst into flame. It is a race to see which of them can hurdle the inside rail and plunge into the infield pond first, but in the last stride the horse pulls ahead of the rider by a neck. Neither seems to have been done much harm, but they both adamantly refuse to climb out of the pond until the dragons move farther up the track.

While this is going on, Green Death suddenly finds Dragonella irresistible. He has about as much luck with her as Milton has with Mitzi McSweeney, and loses even more blood in the process—though as Gently Gently points out, this is perhaps not a fair assessment since he begins with more blood than Milton.

Finally they are all loaded in the starting gate, except for Cutie Pie, who could eat the starting gate for breakfast and stands to the side of it, and then the starter sends them off. Dragonella, who is used to being pursued by the male of the species, sprints into a two-length lead, followed by Fire Breather, Green Death, Tooth and Fang, and Chop Suey, while Cutie Pie is taking forever to get into gear and trails the field by maybe fifteen dragon lengths, which is even more than fifteen horse lengths.

They run down the backstretch, Cutie Pie makes up most of the ground he has lost at the start, and suddenly I realize that something is missing, but I can't quite put my finger on it.

"Omygod!" cries Benny. "Cutie Pie has eaten Chop Suey!"

"Dragons don't eat chop suey," says Gently Gently. "They are one hundred percent carnivores. Maybe one hundred and ten percent."

"I don't mean chop suey the dish!" snaps Benny. "I mean Chop Suey the dragon!"

I start counting, and sure enough I get all the way up to five and can't go any further.

"Is that legal?" asks Benny.

"I wonder how they taste?" adds Gently Gently.

Before any answer occurs to me they hit the far turn and Cutie Pie has added Tooth and Fang to his menu.

"That's got to slow him down," opines Milton.

"Unless it has increased his taste for it," I say, because as they begin turning for home Cutie Pie has moved into high gear and a few seconds later Green Death is nothing but a (possibly tasty) memory.

"If he eats one more, how does that affect show bets?" muses Benny.

And as the words leave his mouth and the three remaining dragons turn into the homestretch, Cutie Pie opens his enormous jaws again and an instant later he gulps so loud that all the railbirds can hear it, and suddenly there is only Dragonella ahead of him, and I realize that if he either passes her or eats her I will not have to pay out a single penny to my clientele, and suddenly I find myself cheering for Cutie Pie. He pulls within a length of her with one hundred yards to go, opens that huge maw one last time, and seconds later crosses the wire all by himself.

"Well, there's no doubt about who's the fastest dragon," says Benny.

"I'd say he's more the onliest dragon," replies Gently Gently.

We are getting ready to go home and celebrate our tidy little profit of twelve large and some change when Near-Sighted Sam's voice comes over the speaker system.

"Ladies and gents," it says, "there has been an official protest. Please hold onto all tickets until the stewards come to a decision."

"Now who the hell could protest that?" asks Benny. "Can anyone doubt that Cutie Pie crosses the wire first?"

"As a matter of fact, *I* filed the protest," says Lou Manchu from the next box.

"You?" says Gently Gently. "You didn't even have a dragon in the race."

"I put up the prize money on the understanding that this would be a normal race, with a winner, a place dragon, a show dragon, and the rest of the field. Clearly only one dragon finishes the race, so I want my money back, and I will divide it equitably among multi-millionaire crime lords." He looks around. "I am just waiting for my lawyer, and then we will speak with the stewards." He smiles. "Ah! Here he comes now."

An elegantly-dressed man with his hair slicked down, his moustache neatly trimmed, and not a single wrinkle on his suit, approaches Lou Manchu.

"I'm ready, Lou," he says. "Let us go win our case."

"Don't I know you?" says Milton, staring at him.

"I have no idea," says Manchu's lawyer. "Do you?"

"Aren't you Schulie Shickelmeier?"

"Not anymore," he answers with a smile. "Who'd ever hire a lawyer named Schulie Shickelmeier?"

"So what name do you go under these days?" asks Milton.

"Atticus Mason."

Milton frowns. "Atticus Mason?" he says.

Mason shrugs. "It was that or Perry Finch." He turns to Manchu. "Let's go."

They walk off to the steward's stand, and suddenly Benny Fifth Street frowns. "Do you think they got a chance?"

"Who knows?" I say.

"Well, it occurs to me that if they disqualify Cutie Pie or find any irregularity whatsoever, you might have to return all the bets."

"Damn!" I say. "You've got a point."

"Not to worry," says Milton. "I know Atticus Mason when he is just Schulie Shickelmeier, and whatever aces he thinks he's got up his sleeve, he has a hole in his elbow and they will all fall out."

"He didn't have any holes in his elbows," protests Gently Gently.

"Serves me right for wasting a poetic flourish on ingrates," says Milton. He gets to his feet. "Let us attend the stewards' meeting and right all lefts."

So we walk back through the clubhouse, down a guarded walkway, and enter the stewards' chambers just as Atticus Mason is finishing his pitch.

"So I conclude by saying that to call Cutie Pie the fastest dragon is a misstatement, when in fact at the end of the race he is the *only* dragon. I submit to you that it cannot be considered a legitimate race when only one dragon crosses the finish line."

"Does anyone else have any comment to make or add?" asks the Chief Steward.

"I do," says Milton.

"Speak up and be heard," says the Chief Steward.

"My understanding is that each dragon is legally entered in the race, that the full field of dragons goes to the post, and that none are hindered by any malfunction of the starting gate, is that correct?"

"Yes," says the Chief Steward, and the other two stewards nod their heads.

"So the race, shall we say ten seconds into it, is totally legitimate?" says Milton.

"That is correct."

"Nobody runs off the course at any point?" persists Milton.

"No."

"Then I submit that the results should be made official."

"Not so!" cries Atticus Mason. "Only one dragon crosses the line!"

"And that is the basis of your complaint?" asks Milton.

"Yes!"

Milton smiles. "Then I insist that the results be declared official. Do we have the official photo of the finish?"

"Certainly," says the Chief Steward, and has an assistant cast it up on a screen.

"You see?" says Atticus Mason. "There is only Cutie Pie."

"I beg to differ," says Milton, and mutters a spell in Enochian or Mesopotamian or some other language I never study in high school—and suddenly Cutie Pie becomes transparent and we can see the remains of the other dragons inside his stomach. "You see, all five of the other dragons cross the finish line too. Based on where their noses are, it's clear than Dragonella is second across the finish line and Fire Breather is third." He smiles triumphantly. "Q.E.D."

It takes the stewards perhaps thirty seconds to realize that he is not calling a witness named Q.E.D. and another twenty seconds of whispering to each other before they declare that the order of finish is official and that Cutie Pie is the fastest dragon in New York. They add that they hope someone will take him to New Jersey before he digests his most recent meal, since this is what New York does with almost all its unwanted garbage.

We go back to Joey Chicago's in triumph, and as I am pouring myself another Old Peculiar, who should enter but Mitzi McSweeney, who walks right up to Milton and says, "I hear you did a good thing this afternoon, so I have decided to forgive you."

"I was brilliant," he says modestly.

"That is true," Gently Gently chimes in. "Cutie Pie has no one but Milton to thank for it."

Her eyes narrow. "You help some broad named Cutie Pie?" she demands.

"Only the names are similar," he says nervously.

"In case it has escaped your attention, my name is not Cutie Pie!" she growls.

"I know, I know!" stammers Milton. "You are totally different."

"I agree," says Gently Gently. "For starters, she does not begin to have Cutie Pie's tail."

"Damned thing's a traffic hazard," Benny chimes in. "It never stops wiggling."

Milton tries to say something, cannot get the words out, and races for what he hopes is the safety of his office. Mitzi is one step behind him, and from the horrible sounds coming from the men's room we can only conclude that it is a good thing for Cutie Pie that he has never encountered anyone—human, dragon, or in between—with a temper like Mitzi McSweeney's.

THE MAYORAL STAKES

So a bunch of us are sitting around my office, which happens to be the third booth at Joey Chicago's Three-Star Tavern, listening to the big political debate, and Malcolm McNair is saying, "Elect me and there'll be a chicken in every pot," which causes Honest Fred Bellringer to chuckle and say, "My opponent is so out of touch with the 21st Century that he doesn't know that you cook chickens in microwaves."

"*After* you take them out of the cellophane," says Malcolm with a chuckle. He points to Honest Fred's bandaged hand. "How's that burn coming along, Fred?"

"Cheap shots," complains Honest Fred. "Nothing but cheap shots."

"Actually," says Benny Fifth Street, sipping his beer, "that was an expensive shot. I know the private eye that Malcolm hired."

"Besides," adds Gently Gently Dawkins, "chickens do not come in pots *or* cellophane, they come in restaurants."

"You want an expensive shot?" demands Malcolm McNair. "Tell us why you were seen going into Bedroom Eyes Betty's place three days ago!"

"She had a leak in her kitchen faucet and asked me to fix it," answers Honest Fred.

"At five in the morning?" says Malcolm with a leer.

"She works at the Club Exotique until four-thirty," says Honest Fred.

"But everyone knows that you have a key to her apartment!" yells Malcolm.

"Well, we do now," comments Benny Fifth Street.

"She is my cousin, fourteen times removed," answers Honest Fred.

"The last time I saw the two of you, she was about fourteen millimeters removed from you," says Malcolm. "And that was *before* you hugged her."

"I've heard enough," I say to Joey Chicago, who is standing behind the bar. "Turn it off."

"Aw, c'mon, Harry," he says. "I ain't laughed this much since Milton Berle went off the air." He pauses. "Well, except for the Nixon resignation and the Clinton impeachment."

"I sure do miss Uncle Miltie," agrees Benny Fifth Street.

"That may be," I explain, "but this isn't entertainment. It is homework. We've got an upcoming election for mayor, and I have to come up with a morning line or all my marks will start betting with Cold Cash Clarence."

"So how come only Malcolm and Fred are debating?" asks Gently Gently. "Last I hear, there are five or six candidates."

"The answer for the viewing public is that they represent the two major parties," I say. "But the real reason is that only these two would cross the network's hand with silver."

"Must have been a mighty heavy bag," says Gently Gently, who for some reason takes me literally. "I'm surprised that Malcolm can lift it."

I turn to Benny. "Would you please explain to your associate what a metaphor is?"

"Sure, Harry," says Benny. He turns to Gently Gently. "You

know what metaphysics is? Well, metaphor is just like that—tons and tons of numbers bigger than four."

"Then I am right," replies Gently Gently. "He has to have a lot of help carrying all that silver in." He pauses in thought, then adds, "Maybe he finds the Lone Ranger's silver mine."

Joey Chicago sighs deeply. "They're *your* flunkies, Harry." He pauses, then adds: "At least the other one keeps his mouth shut."

I turn to look at my other flunky. Dead End Dugan may not be a social gadfly, but every now and then when you have someone who won't make good his marker, it is advantageous and then some to have a six foot ten inch zombie on your team, and when he's not working, like now, he just stands in a corner, staring into space and thinking a bunch of dead thoughts.

"So how is the morning line shaping up?" asks Longshot Lamont from an adjoining booth.

"I'll let you know," I say.

"Soon," he insists. "I'm looking for action."

"The election's not for three more weeks," I say. "Wars have been won and lost in three weeks. Medical breakthroughs have taken place in less than three weeks."

"Yeah," adds Benny Fifth Street. "And Flyaway, who you bet on in the 4th race at Jamaica this afternoon, still won't have crossed the finish line in three weeks."

"So who's the longest shot in the race?" asks Longshot Lamont.

"Well," I say, "the longest shot of the six official entries is Reichmaster O'Neal, who watched one too many World War II films when he was growing up."

"What'll he go off at?" asks Lamont.

I shrug. "Maybe ninety-to-one."

He shakes his head. "Not long enough for my taste."

"Well," says Benny helpfully, "you can always bet on a write-in candidate."

"Who's running?" asks Lamont.

"No one knows until they write him in," explains Gently Gently. "That's the beauty of it. You got eight million people on this island, and only six will be on every ballot."

"So, Harry," says Lamont, looking at me, "will you give me eight million-to-one on any New Yorker I name except for the six who are on the ballot?"

"No," I say, "because probably half of them are either too young or not legal citizens, and of course I have to make a profit too, so I will give you three million-to-one against anyone you name except for the six on the ballot."

"What if I take the field?" he asks.

"The field?"

"Everyone who isn't on the ballot."

"Okay," I say, "you can do that—but I will only give twenty-to-one against the field."

He shakes his head. "No, that is no good. Okay, I will come up with a candidate."

He goes back to sipping his drink, lost in thought, and knowing Lamont that is not a prodigious amount of thought to be lost in, and suddenly in comes Short Odds Harrigan, who walks right up to my office and pulls a chair over.

"Hi, Harry," he says. "How's it going?"

"Hi, Short Odds," I reply. "What one-to-ten shot have you come to place your money on?"

"I need the morning line for the Mayoral Stakes," he says.

"I think it is called the Mayoral Election," interjects Benny Fifth Street.

Short Odds shrugs. "Whatever."

"I regret to inform you that there is no overwhelming favorite," I say. "Especially for a player like you, who considers an even-money horse a longshot."

"This is not fair, Harry," he complains. "How can there be a race without a favorite?"

"I have yet to come up with the odds," I tell him, "but I cannot imagine that any of these losers goes off at less than three-to-one, which is probably an underlay for anyone else, but too long a price for you."

He frowns. "Politics is a strange racket, I freely admit it," he says, "but these guys have been serving the public for decades. How can there not be a shorter price?"

"Probably because these guys have been serving the public for decades," suggests Gently Gently.

"Maybe instead of having elections, we ought to have a draft, like the NFL does," says Short Odds.

"You'd have to speak to the commissioner about that," I reply.

"Maybe I will," says Short Odds thoughtfully. Then: "*Is there a commissioner?*"

"Well, yes," I say, "but we call him the governor."

"I will write to my congressman about this," promises Short Odds.

"You will write to your congressman about the governor or about a draft?" I ask as he gets to his feet.

"Yes," says Short Odds, walking over to the bar and ordering an Old Washensox.

"So who *is* gonna win the Mayoral Stakes?" asks Gently Gently, drinking the chocolate bourbon malt that Joey Chicago makes especially for him, and sitting on the reinforced bar stool, which is the only one that can withstand his four hundred pounds.

"I really don't know," I answer. "If this was a field of claiming horses, the most expensive one would have a price tag of about $37.50." Then I add: "Including the clothes."

"They should just stick to yelling at each other in City Hall and not interfere with real people," offers Joey Chicago, who is polishing glasses behind the bar.

"Yeah," adds Benny. "And they shouldn't waste so much

money. If they paid the cops a living wage, Harry wouldn't have to slip a twenty to Officer Brannigan every Wednesday in order to stay in business."

"The cops are part of it," argues Gently Gently Dawkins.

"Oh, come on," says Benny. "When did a cop ever harass or arrest you?"

"Never," admits Gently Gently. "But they do worse things."

"Oh?" says Benny.

"Three nights ago they try to shut down Madam Fifi's Emporium, right in the middle of Bubbles La Tour's world-famous Dance of Sublime Surrender!"

"*No!*" gasps Joey Chicago.

"Yes!" responds Gently Gently. "And this is not the first time!"

"This is unconscionable!" says Joey Chicago, slamming a fist down on the bar and forgetting that it is wrapped around a delicate champagne glass, which shatters into a hundred pieces.

"Unconscionable, hell—I was perfectly conscious the whole time," answers Gently Gently. "I would have comforted poor Bubbles, but there were already two hundred thoughtful guys in line ahead of me to do the same thing."

"Yeah, her fans are the best," agrees Joey Chicago.

"And the most," adds Benny Fifth Street. "I walk by Madame Fifi's tonight on the way back from collecting three dollars and fifty cents from Short Cash Alex"—he holds up the bloody, bandaged fingers of his right hand to prove he's been working —"and the line to see Bubbles do her dance is two blocks long, and so wide I have to cross over and walk on the other side of the street."

"It is nice to know that true talent will always be rewarded," says Joey Chicago.

"Maybe that's why Harry is having so much trouble with the morning line," suggests Benny. "There ain't no true talent in the field."

"He should be used to it by now," says Joey. "There wasn't any talent the last five times."

"Maybe they ought to move the Mayoral Stakes off the dirt and onto the grass," muses Gently Gently.

"Or make them carry different weights, like in a handicap," says Benny.

"They're handicapped enough as it is," I say. "Or weren't you watching the debate?"

"The problem," says Bet-a-Bunch Brady, who is sitting at a table near the window, "is that they go about it backward."

"I do not follow you," says Benny.

"In horses, you win a few stakes races and a bunch of money to prove you're worth the bother," explains Brady, "and *then* you retire to stud. But these politicians, they're all busy littering the ground with yearlings and two-year-olds before they've won anything worthwhile —or even anything at all."

"Man's got a point," agrees Short Odds Harrigan.

"Maybe I'll run for Mayor myself," says Gently Gently Dawkins.

Benny Fifth Street shakes his head. "You couldn't afford the rent on Gracie Mansion."

"Wasn't she married to George Burns?" asks Longshot Lamont.

"I don't know about that," answers Benny. "All I know is that Gracie Mansion is where the Mayor lives."

"They turned her into a *house*?" demands Lamont. "The foul fiends!"

"You're getting all upset," says Gently Gently soothingly. "Go back to doing something restful, like figuring out what longshot you want to write in on your ballot."

"You got a point," agrees Lamont. He closes his eyes, which is how we know he is thinking or perhaps asleep, and finally he shakes his head. "I cannot nominate Babe Ruth, because he starts with the Red Sox and winds up in that other league."

"Also, he's dead," says Benny.

"Some of our greatest leaders are dead," says Lamont. "Washington, Lincoln, King George ..."

"Uh ... King George wasn't one of *our* leaders," notes Joey Chicago.

Lamont frowns. "King Lyndon? King Barak? I know it was King Somebody."

Benny shakes his head. "This is America, Lamont," he says.

"America's out *there* somewhere!" growls Lamont, waving his hand toward the door. "This is Manhattan."

I am getting annoyed with Lamont, but what the hell, when you're right, you're right.

I have another Old Peculiar, and while I am busy digesting it, who should enter but Spats McConnell, who is so addicted to his lucky spats that he wears them even when he goes barefoot to the beach in the summer.

"Where is he?" demands Spats, looking around.

"Where is who?" I ask.

"Big-Hearted Milton, of course," he replies.

Milton is my personal mage, and he has set up his office in the men's room for the past few years, because he says Joey Chicago's customers bother him much less than when he spent a week working out of the ladies' room. Well, a week there, and then two months in the hospital.

"Okay," I say, "I will take you to him, but if he is casting a spell, we must not talk or bother him until he is through."

"Not a problem," says Spats. "Hell, I got straight A's in spelling, so I can help him if he runs into trouble with his spell."

"Straight A's?" I repeat, dubious a bit more than somewhat.

"Yeah, in P.S. 43. It was my teacher who couldn't spell. She gave me straight F's. Can you imagine that?"

"Not without using up three calories thinking about it," I say. "Maybe two."

So we go into Milton's office, and as usual he is sitting in the middle of a pentagram he has scrawled on the floor, and there is a candle at each point, and he is muttering in a truly incomprehensible language, maybe Enochian or possibly French.

"Milton ..." I say.

He gestures me to silence. "I'll be done in less than a minute."

He chants a little louder, winds up with a scream that makes my fillings want to run out of my mouth, claps his hands, and the candles flare up like fireworks and then go out.

"Mitzi McSweeney?" I say. Despite the question mark I have included here, it is not really a question, because these days it is always Mitzi McSweeney.

"Yes, Mitzi McSweeney," he growls.

"What terrible thing did she do to you this time?" I ask in bored tones.

"We are having an intimate dinner at the Burnt Kettle, which is a truly outstanding one-star restaurant, and while we are waiting for them to clean off the main course and bring the dessert, I am playing a friendly game of itsy bitsy spider on her thigh."

"A friendly game, you say?" I interject.

"I would certainly not be inclined to play an *unfriendly* game on that particular playing field," he assures me. "Anyway, just before I get to the goal line she throws what's left of her pickled pig's feet in my face." His face contorts with rage. "*Me*, who has kept kosher since ..." He pauses and frowns. "Since last week, anyway," he concludes.

"I dunno," says Spats. "You wanted a response, you got a response."

"I could have pulled a better one, to say nothing of a less painful and less humiliating one, out of a hat," replies Milton.

"So what terrible curse did you put on her this time?" I ask, stifling a yawn.

"Oh, this time it is a really good one, Harry," says Milton

with an evil grin. "I have taken an inch and a half off the right shoe of every pair of high heels she owns. This way, if she tries to speed up to catch a bus or make a green light, she will stumble all over and maybe even fall." He smiles triumphantly. "What do you think of *that*?"

"Oh, that is certainly an evil and effective curse," I say. "Of course, it will give even more wiggle to her walk, and should she actually fall down no doubt some helpful strangers will lift her back to her feet, brush her off here and there as gentlemen will—"

"Especially there," interjects Spats.

"And may very well help her back to her apartment to make sure she doesn't fall again," I conclude.

"Why do I never think of the consequences of my own brilliance?" growls Milton. "I am too smart and creative and subtle for my own good." He roars a chant that almost rhymes, the candles go out, and he turns to me. "It is undone." He seems to notice Spats for the first time. "I cannot undo the terrible curse that has turned your feet white," he says. "You will just have to live with the deformity."

"Those are not my feet," replies Spats. "Those are spats."

Milton shrugs. "Well, it had to be one or the other." He pulls a lit cigar out of thin air and takes a puff of it. "So how may I help you?"

"My brother-in-law, Izzy, has announced that he has decided to become a write-in candidate in the Mayoral Stakes, in which a victory would have much the same effect as a dozen H-bombs followed by a rain of toads."

"There's only three weeks to go, and nobody has heard of your brother-in-law," says Milton. "He is not going to win."

"Curse him anyway," says Spats.

Milton frowns. "Why?"

"Because I have bet five large that he can't get twenty write-in votes," answers Spats.

"Not a problem," replies Milton. "Pay me four large and I will guarantee he does not get twenty votes."

"Isn't that a big price for what is, when all is said and done, a very small curse?" asks Spats.

"Okay, don't buy the curse," says Milton with a shrug. "I take it that math was not your long and strong suit in school?"

"Why does everyone always say that?" complains Spats. "I got straight 63's on every math test I ever took."

"Beats me," says Milton, and Spats turns and leaves the office.

"So what can I do for you, Harry?" asks Milton.

"I'm doping out the morning line for the Mayoral Stakes," I tell him, "and I need to know if there is any write-in I should take into consideration."

"Not at the moment," says Milton. He tests the wind inside his office with a forefinger and examines it. "No, none that I can see." He pauses for a moment, then adds: "If the ones already on the ballot were horses, they'd be getting weight from every write-in in the field. Even blinkers couldn't make Honest Fred run straight and true. Especially true." He shakes his head sadly. "Whatever happened to the good old days, when we had candidates like King Arthur and Wild Bill Hickock?"

"I do believe King Arthur lived across the pond," I say.

"So?" says Milton.

"He was a Brit," I explain.

"So he couldn't move?" demands Milton. "Was Bobby Kennedy a native New Yorker? Was Hillary Clinton?"

"They ran for the Senate," I note.

He shrugs. "Yeah, maybe the track conditions are different for the Senate Handicap."

"I wonder what makes it a handicap, when the mayor's race is just a normal stakes race?" I say.

"Have you seen the baggage those Senate candidates have to lug around?" answers Milton. "Mistresses, bribes, gambling debts, payoffs." He shakes his head. "Talk about having to carry extra weight!"

"But you don't see any write-in who could make Malcom McNair or Honest Fred Bellringer work up a sweat?"

"Fiorello La Guardia's dead, isn't he?" asks Milton.

"For close to seventy years," I tell him.

"Then I can't see any guy out there with a chance to upset," he concludes.

We leave Milton's office and go back into the bar, where a number of my regulars have gathered, and they all want to know the morning line. I borrow Milton's quill pen—well, it is actually a ballpoint with a feather glued to it, but it makes him feel more magical—and I scribble down the line:

Honest Fred Bellringer, 3-1.

Malcom McNair, 7-2.

Saint Christopher, 6-1. (Actually, his name is Christopher Saint Patrick, but this is the name on all his posters.)

Good Neighbor Charlie Chisel (whom his opponents keep referring to as Charlie Chisel 'Em), *10-1.*

Mordecai Montromorcy, 12-1.

Whacko Marx, 50-1.

"You know," says Saratoga Slim, "they should *all* be eighty-to-one." He shudders. "I don't mind betting on them, but I'd hate to live under them. I may just stay upstate until the next election."

"Oh, I've seen worse," replies Loose Lips Louie. He pauses and scratches his bald head. "Of course, none of 'em were ever elected."

"What we need," opines Clubfoot Clarence, who is not really a clubfoot but never remembers which shoe goes on which foot, "is the Mickey Mantle of politics."

"No," says Hitachi Yingleman, who is taking a break from running Yingleman's All-Night Kosher Japanese Bakery. "What you need is Takeda Katsuyori, the great 16th Century samurai."

"Don't be ridiculous," says Short Odds Harrigan. "You need the Muhammed Ali of politicians." He pauses thoughtfully. "Though maybe the Jack Dempsey would do."

Pretty soon they are all arguing passionately about who they want to see on the ballot, the Red Grange of politics, or the Michael Jordan of politics, or the Josef Stalin of politics (but that comes from a New Jerseyite), and finally Joey Chicago reaches behind the bar and pulls out his trumpet and blasts out a few notes, and suddenly everyone is quiet.

"Enough screaming and yelling!" he yells. "I expect you to behave with some decorum. After all, this is a bar, not City Hall."

Everybody agrees that he has a point, and voices are lowered, but the discussion does not end, and very soon they have also wished for the Gordie Howe, Eddie Arcaro, John Wayne, Enrico Caruso, and Seattle Slew of politicians.

"You know," says Gently Gently during a brief lull in the conversation, "you are never going to agree on the best man for the job. If it was the best woman, it'd be a piece of cake, because everybody knows that Bubbles La Tour is a woman without equal, but ..."

"So who says we can't write in a woman?" demands Clubfoot Charlie.

"Yeah!" chimes in Bet-a-Bunch Brady. "Where does it say that in the rulebook?"

I turn to Milton for an official opinion.

He shrugs. "You know," he says, "they got a point."

"Okay, Harry," cries Saratoga Slim, "what are the odds on Bubbles La Tour?"

I do some quick mental calculations, and announce that she has just become the three-to-five favorite.

"She's not even on the ballot!" says Longshot Lamont.

"How many healthy able-bodied men live in New York?" I ask.

He shrugs. "I dunno. Maybe two, three million."

"Two-to-five," I amend.

Well, within five minutes everyone at the bar has placed their bets on Bubbles La Tour, and I am holding almost eight thousand dollars' worth of money and markers.

Then Short Odds Harrigan goes to the door. "Come on, men!" he yells. "My brother-in-law owns a print shop over in Brooklyn. We'll get him to print up thirty or forty thousand posters and glue or nail 'em onto every wall and door in the city!"

And quicker than you can say Jack Robinson—well, I assume it's quicker; actually I hardly ever say Jack Robinson any more—they are gone, and the bar is empty except for me and my crew.

"Ain't you a little worried, Harry?" asks Joey Chicago.

"About what?" I ask.

"Every man who's healthy enough to make it to a polling place is going to write Bubbles in on his ballot. You could go broke."

"Nonsense," I say. "There are a couple of hundred bookies in town. They'll spread it around. And if I lose a few hundred, I lose a few hundred. It's an occupational hazard, like going up against Clint Eastwood in a gunfight. Lee Van Cleef always came back in the sequel. So will I."

It sounds reasonable when I say it, and it remains reasonable all the way to midafternoon the next day, when I climb out of bed, get into those clothes that I'd remembered to take off before going to sleep, and walk to my office, which is jammed with maybe eighty guys I have either never seen before or at least not recently.

"What's going on?" I ask Joey Chicago. "Are drinks on the house?"

"They absolutely are not, you should perish the thought," he replies. "These guys are all here to see you."

"I'm flattered," I say, sliding into my office, "but why are you guys not betting with your own bookies?"

"It is hideously unfair," says one plunger I recognize from Belmont Park. "Half of them close the book on the Mayoral Stakes once word gets out that Bubbles La Tour is in the field."

"She is not in the field until someone writes her name on the ballot," I say.

"She is already on five thousand absentee ballots," he says.

"Just since last night?" I ask.

He nods his head. "A lot of guys are so anxious they do not wait for the mailman, but hand-deliver their absentee ballots."

"Okay," I say, "half the bookies are not taking bets on the election. But what about the rest?"

"That is why we are here, Harry," says another.

"I don't follow you," I say.

"You are an incredibly generous man," he says, "for an evil, self-centered, probably immoral bookie. No other bookie has her listed at more than one-to-ten. My own has got her at one-to-fifty."

"One-to-fifty?" I repeat, frowning, because that comes to a payoff of two cents on the dollar.

"Well, she *is* the most perfect woman who ever lived," he continues. "She makes Sophia Loren and Marilyn Monroe look like boys. *Ugly* boys."

"Don't forget Clara Bow," says an old geezer by the door.

"Sophia and Marilyn *and* Clara Bow," he corrects himself.

"Well," I say after about five seconds of mental calculations, during which I figure one-to-ten-thousand on Bubbles La Tour is probably an overlay, "I'm afraid you boys are going to have to go somewhere else. I can't handle this volume of wagers."

"But our bookies have closed up shop, or cut the odds!" cries another.

"Try Off-Track Betting," I suggest.

"The State of New York won't let them take bets on politics."

"Well, as of this minute, neither do I," I proclaim.

Spats McConnell steps forward. "Not a problem," he announces. "*I'll* book your bets." Then he adds: "But just on the Mayoral Stakes."

"Who are you?" demands one of the men.

"Spats McConnell," he says. "A lot of you know me, or at least have seen me at Belmont and Aqueduct and Jamaica."

"The guy with the white feet, right," says another man.

"How do we know you won't run off with our money?" asks a third guy.

"I will sit here in Joey Chicago's, right across from Harry the Book's office, until the polls close," answers Spats. Suddenly he frowns. "Except for two hours in the afternoon toward the end of next week, when I have to see my lawyer and stop by the courthouse, but you can accompany me or follow me, whichever you choose."

"Just a minute," I say. "I have reconsidered my position. I *will* accept bets on the Mayoral Stakes."

Spats gives me a dirty look and shoulders his way out of the bar.

"Harry, are you sure?" asks Benny Fifth Street in a low whisper.

"He's worth about sixty dollars, total—including the clothes," I whisper back. "He knows something, or he wouldn't have offered to let them watch him every second until the polls close."

"So what does he know?" asks Benny.

I shrug. "We've got three weeks to find out."

"Twenty days," he answers with a worried frown.

Pretty soon it is fifteen days, and then ten, and then five, and suddenly it is two days and I am sitting on maybe twenty-two thousand bets of various denominations, all but one of them on Bubbles La Tour, and that one is probably not legit because it is on Fatty Arbuckle and the lady who makes the bet giggles nonstop.

Gently Gently Dawkins walks up to my office. He is clearly distressed, because he tries to slide in opposite me, and he has not been able to do that for the last seventy-five pounds.

"I have been doing some reconnoitering, Harry," he says.

"You've been spying on Bubbles La Tour?" I ask.

"Damn!" he says, pulling up a chair. "I never thought of that."

"So what *have* you been doing?" I say.

"I follow Spats McConnell," he says. "And just like he announces a couple of weeks ago, he goes to Go For the Jugular Julius's office ..."

"Who is Go For the Jugular Julius?" I interrupt.

"His shyster," answers Gently Gently. "And ten minutes later the two of them go over to the court building. I do not follow them in, because I have a well-known allergy to courts, but I hang around on the sidewalk, and half an hour later they come out, grinning as if they just hear Laughing Linus telling one of his jokes, and they shake hands, and Julius heads back to his office, and Spats pulls an official-looking sheet of paper out of his pocket, holds it up and stares at it for a minute, then giggles, kisses the paper, and puts it back in his pocket."

"Then what?" I ask.

"Then I realize that it is almost three o'clock and I have not eaten since noon, so I grab a couple of cheeseburgers and a sixteen-ounce soda to replenish my depleted strength, and then I come right here to report to you."

"You forget to mention the hot fudge sundae," I say, pointing to the fudge on the corner of his mouth.

He pulls out a handkerchief and wipes it off. "That was my mid-morning picker-upper," he explains.

I nod. "That makes all the difference."

The next day I book another four thousand bets.

"Where do we stand now?" asks Benny Fifth Street.

"We have booked 26,709 bets," I tell him.

"And how many are for Bubbles La Tour?"

"26,706," I answer.

"Boy!" he says, impressed. "That is a lot of people not to bet on the exquisite Bubbles. I know about Fatty Arbuckle. Who are the other two on?"

"Luke Skywalker and Pogo Possum," I tell him.

We hang around Joey Chicago's, I book a final fifty bets, and then it is Election Day. I go home and try to go to sleep, but I lay awake most of the night wondering how I am going to pay off all these bets, because Bubbles La Tour is far and away the surest thing I have seen in all my years as a bookie, and when I drag myself out of bed in the morning I still do not have an answer.

I make it to my office and slide into the third booth at about five in the afternoon, and at seven Joey Chicago turns on the television so we can watch the results.

"It's starting to look like a rout, folks," Headline Herb is saying. "As of this moment, Honest Fred Bellringer has 78,023 votes, Malcolm McNair has 66,289—but running away with it is"—he stops and blinks, as if he's having trouble reading the paper that has just been handed to him—"Bubbles La Tour, with"— he blinks again—"1,493,471 votes."

"Oh boy, are we in trouble!" moans Gently Gently Dawkins.

"When you get right down to it," says Benny Fifth Street, "the really surprising thing is that Malcolm and Fred got damned near 150,000 votes. Against"—he utters a heartfelt sigh —"Bubbles La Tour."

I am about to answer when who should enter the bar than Spats McConnell, with a huge smile on his face and even a clean pair of spats on his shoes.

"What a night!" he says enthusiastically. "What a race!"

"Making two cents on the dollar ain't that much to brag about," says Benny.

"Actually, she closes at one-to-three hundred," says Spats. He turns to me. "Someday you'll thank me for this, Harry."

"We'll talk about it when I get out of debtor's prison," I answer him.

"Sooner than that!" he says with a laugh. "Drinks for the house, Joey!"

Joey Chicago looks around. "Four drinks coming up."

"Five," says Spats.

"Four," Joey corrects him.

"Me, Harry, and his three flunkies," says Spats.

"Hey, Dead End!" Joey yells across the tavern. "Do zombies drink?"

Dead End Dugan frowns. "It's been so long I don't remember."

"I know they don't eat," says Joey. "He's been standing in that corner for two weeks now."

Spats raises his glass in a toast. "To Short Odds Harrigan!"

None of us can figure this out, since we should probably be toasting our new mayor, who is three thousand times easier on the eyes, but we grunt and mumble something and down our drinks, and then he's gone again, and it is just the regular crew. I figure I should make one last-ditch attempt to avoid the poorhouse, so I go to the men's room to see if Milton can reverse the election, but he is so busy trying to come up with an effective curse against Mitzi McSweeney that I can tell he won't be able to concentrate on my problem until he solves his own, and given his lack of success creating a curse that affects Mitzi even half as much as it affects him, I figure he's going to be occupied for the next couple of days.

So I go back out to my office, and the television is still on, and Headline Herb is still announcing results, and I nurse an Old Peculiar and consider running far, far away, like maybe to New Jersey or even Connecticut, and then Herb announces that the election is over and the result has been declared official, and that the winner is that exquisite morsel of femininity, Bubbles La Tour.

The crowd of politicians and millionaires on the floor of City Hall all break out in a very insincere cheer, since none of the parties have nominated her and therefore she won't be beholden to any of them, and suddenly Benny jabs me in the ribs.

"Is that Spats McConnell there?" he says, pointing to the screen.

"You know, I do believe it is!" says Gently Gently.

"What the hell is he doing there?" asks Joey Chicago.

"He is standing on a platform and signaling for a microphone," I point out. "So we should have our answer any second now."

"Thank you, thank you, thank you!" says Spats. "And I will have my bed and my easy chair and all my clothes moved into Gracie Mansion by tomorrow morning."

"Who the hell are you?" yells some politician.

"I'm your new mayor," answers Spats.

"I know you!" cries another. "You're Spats McConnell. Our new mayor is Bubbles La Tour!"

"No, sir!" says Spats. "Bubbles La Tour is unquestionably the finest woman ever to prance the face of the Earth, but she is *not* your mayor!"

"Throw this bum off the stage!" yells Three-Ton Tony Tobasco, one of the more prominent Councilmen, especially around the waistline.

"You lay a finger on me and you're off my City Council!" says Spats, and the threat is dire enough, especially since Three-Ton Tony hasn't held a real job in twenty years, that he stops dead in his tracks.

"So why do you insist that you are the mayor instead of the exquisite Bubbles La Tour?" demands Wall Street Wally, who himself does not sit on the City Council but who admits to owning four Councilmen and has made down payments on half a dozen more.

"I'm glad you ask," says Spats, unrolling one of Short Odds Harrigan's forty thousand posters and holding it up.

"Okay, it's a poster," says Wall Street Wally. "It's the reason she won. Big deal."

"It was created by my friend Short Odds Harrigan," says Spats. "Look at it carefully."

"It's a photo of the magnificent Bubbles," says Three-Ton Tony. "So what?"

"Do not look at the photo of the unsurpassed Bubbles," says Spats. "Look at the writing."

"'Write in Bubbles La Tour for Mayor,'" reads Wall Street Wally.

"No!" cries Spats.

"What do you mean, no?" demands Wally. "It's right there in black and white."

"Short Odds knows no more about French than most of you know about governing," says Spats. "It does not say Bubbles La Tour. It says Bubbles *Le* Tour."

"Big difference," snorts Three-Ton Tony.

"Bigger than you think," answers Spats. "Two days ago I legally change my name to Bubbles Le Tour." Suddenly he flashes his teeth, new and false alike, in a huge grin. "I have checked, and Bubbles Le Tour gets 300,000 more write-in votes that the voluptuous Bubbles La Tour."

There is a stunned silence in the chamber.

Finally Wall Street Wally speaks up. "Come on over to my place for dinner, Bubbles. We've got things to talk about."

Pretty soon everyone is showering Spats—I mean Bubbles—with promises of gifts and dinners and front-row Broadway seats, and I tell Joey Chicago he can turn the television off, and once more it is just Joey and me and my three flunkies alone in the tavern.

"*We* should have thought of that," says Gently Gently Dawkins.

"Yeah," chimes in Benny Fifth Street. "Think of what kind of mayor Dead End Dugan would have made. I mean, hell, when you're already dead you're pretty much immune to threats and bribes."

"It's a lost opportunity, that's for sure," says Gently Gently.

"You know," I say at last, "there's a governor's race coming up next year."

And thirty seconds later we are all gathered around Joey Chicago's blackboard, where he posts the day's special drinks, and trying to decide whether Bubbles Li Tour or Bubbles Lo Tour looks more natural.

THE GREAT MANHATTAN EAT-OFF

I am sitting in my office, which is the third booth at Joey Chicago's Three-Star Tavern, doping out the morning line at Saratoga. I am feeling exceptionally flush since last night, because Kid Testosterone made it all the way to the second round before Malicious Monty knocked him out, and of the 713 bets I booked on the fight, only Longshot Lamont bet that the Kid would make it past the first round. In fact, he bet that the Kid would still be conscious by the fifth round, which had me worried for about four minutes, since the odds were three thousand-to-one against it.

Then Joey Chicago walks up to me and lays a sheet of paper on my table, right between my bottle of Old Peculiar and my bicarbonate.

"Good afternoon, Joey," I say, because no one in my circle of acquaintances has ever seen a morning from the tail end. "And what, pray, is this paper about, because as you can plainly see I already have a napkin."

"I have always been a good friend and landlord to you, have I not?" asks Joey Chicago.

"Absolutely," I say, wondering where this is leading. "And of course it is mutual, because surely I have doubled your business since word went out that I had set up shop here."

"So we are agreed on that," he confirms. "Yet we have a serious problem"—he frowns—"*and it has got to stop!*"

"What is our mutual problem?" I inquire politely.

"It's Dawkins," he half-says and half-yells, "and you've got to do something about it!"

Gently Gently Dawkins, who is maybe a donut short of four hundred pounds, is one of my flunkies.

"We have had this problem before," I say, "after he broke your sixth barstool."

"My ninth!"

"Sixth, ninth, what is the difference?" I reply. "I paid for new stools, did I not?"

"That was *then*," he says. "This is *now!*"

I look over at the bar. "I do not see any more broken stools," I tell him.

"Look a little higher," says Joey Chicago.

"He cannot reach the ceiling," I answer.

"The bar," says Joey.

"Okay, I see the bar," I say. "Almost clean and nearly polished, as usual."

"Can you not see what is missing?" demands Joey Chicago.

"Customers?" I ask.

"Nuts!" he yells.

"I am sorry you are so distressed," I say, "but I must compliment you on your choice of language. Usually you would just curse and be done with it."

"No," he says. "*Nuts!*"

"If you've seen any hanging around, call Bellevue and report it to them."

"Stop understanding me so fast!" snaps Joey Chicago. He points to the paper he has laid on my table. "That is a bill for $1,538.60."

"And what is it for?" I inquire.

"That's the wholesale cost of the nuts your lackey has eaten off the bar just this month!"

Just as he says this, who should wander in but Gently Gently Dawkins, nibbling what's left of a candy bar.

"Hi, Harry," he says, then turns to Joey Chicago. "You forgot to put nuts and peanuts and niblets out on the bar."

"Ask your boss," growls Joey Chicago.

Dawkins wanders over. "I wish you'd get a bigger office," he says. "I cannot slide into this one."

"That is just as well," says Benny Fifth Street, another of my flunkies. "If I were you, I would keep out of the boss's reach for the next few years."

"Why?" asks Dawkins, pulling another candy bar out of his pocket. "The Kid made it to the second round. We should be rolling in money."

"Yes, we should be," I agree. "Instead, one of us is rolling in bar food."

"That is immoral!" says Dawkins. "It might even be sinful. Bar food is for eating, not rolling in."

I glare at him for a minute, then pull out my wallet and peel off fifteen hundreds and a forty some guy tried to pass to me. "Dawkins, take these and give them to Joey Chicago."

"Right, Harry," he says, grabbing the bills from me.

"And Dawkins?" I say.

"Yes, Harry?"

"If you eat any of them, I will cut your head off and use it as a bowling ball."

"I didn't know you bowled, Harry," says Dawkins.

"I'll learn."

Nothing much happens for the next hour except that Dawkins leaves the building for five minutes and returns with a bag of cheeseburgers in one hand and a chocolate malt in the other.

"To keep my energy level up until mealtime," he explains.

"Has *anyone* ever had an appetite like that?" muses Benny Fifth Street.

"Oh, someone must have," says Joey Chicago.

"Of course they have," says Short Odds Harrigan, looking up from his beer for the first time in maybe an hour.

"You sound very sure of yourself," says Benny Fifth Street. "Perhaps you would like to put some money on that idle speculation."

"It is not an idle speculation," answers Short Odds. "In fact, it is a speculation that could give Seattle Slew a three-length head start and a beating."

"And which of Ripley's many tasteful museums did you see his corpse in?" asks Benny.

"That is three misstatements in thirteen words," notes Short Odds, "which is a lot, even for you. He is not in Ripley's, he is not dead, and he is a she."

"You are saying that a dame can out-eat Gently Gently Dawkins, who could be mistaken for a small elephant if his nose was a couple of feet longer?" demands Benny.

"Check the record books," says Short Odds. "She is the champion of all she surveys. Well, before she eats it, anyway."

"Granting that this woman has a major appetite," I interject, "I still want to know why you mention her in such superlatives."

"Surely you have heard of the Great Manhattan Eat-Off," says Short Odds.

"Not until three seconds ago," I say.

"They hold this contest in Manhattan every five years, and Miss Priscilla Nibbles is the reigning champion."

"Oh, come on," says Benny. "No one is called Nibbles."

"She used to be Miss Priscilla Smith," answers Short Odds, "but she changed it legally after she won for the fifth—no, make that the sixth—time."

"She is undefeated for thirty years?" I ask.

"Longer. The contest is now entering its thirty-fifth year."

Benny Fifth Street turns to me. "You know what I am thinking, Boss?"

"Probably," I say. "But go ahead and tell me, just in case I am wrong."

"I think we could enter our very own dark horse—well, dark hippo or elephant or whatever—and no one who hasn't seen him, no one who bets based on past performances, will bet on him. Think of the odds!"

"I'm all in favor of it!" adds Joey Chicago. "He'll finally have enough to eat. Think of my bar snacks!"

"I will consider it," I say.

"Don't I have a say in the matter?" asks Dawkins.

"Shut up," says Benny. "You're just the horse or whatever."

"Okay," I say. "Benny, find out everything you can about the eat-off: when is it, where is it, are there entry fees, how much winning is worth, whatever."

"I'm on my way," says Benny, heading out the door.

"Damn, I'm getting peckish again," says Dawkins. "I think I'll pop out for a pizza. I'll be back in a few minutes."

"Stay where you are!" I growl.

He looks startled, but he stands still.

I look to the farthest, darkest corner of the tavern, and yell "Dugan! Get over here!"

A few seconds later there is some movement, and then the cause of the movement appears and it is Dead End Dugan, the third of my flunkies—and let me tell you, when you've got a plunger who won't make good his marker, it is a handy thing to have a six-foot ten-inch zombie on your team, even if his brain is only working on a couple of cylinders.

"Yes, Harry?" he says, blinking his eyes furiously as if trying to focus, and I can tell he's spent a little too much time today thinking dead thoughts.

"Dawkins is not allowed to leave the building," I say. "He is your responsibility. Do you understand?"

"Sort of," answers Dugan.

"But why can't I go out for a pizza?" asks Dawkins plaintively.

"You're in training for the Great Manhattan Eat-Off," I tell him. "I figure we'll hold you to two hundred calories a day to work up a *real* appetite." I pause thoughtfully. "Maybe one hundred and fifty."

His screams of agony are still ringing in my ears as I cross the street and treat myself to lunch at Horatio the Grub's Pizza Emporium.

"So what did you learn about the contest?" I ask when Benny Fifth Street shows up back at Joey Chicago's and walks over to my office.

He frowns. "The main thing I learned is that it's not a contest at all."

"There is no Great Manhattan Eat-Off after all?" I ask, at which point Dawkins stops sobbing and looks alert and alive again.

"Oh, yes, there is a Great Manhattan Eat-Off," says Benny. "But it is not a contest, except for second money."

"Explain," I say.

"Miss Priscilla Nibbles is the Man o' War, Babe Ruth, and Michael Jordan of the eating fraternity. Every eat-off follows the same pattern. A bunch of half-ton guys show up, and this dainty little lady eats 'em all under the table"—he pauses for effect —"and *then* asks for more food because she is still hungry."

"A soulmate!" says Dawkins. "I wonder if she's dating anyone?"

"According to the program book for the last eat-off, she

should be turning eighty-seven this month," says Benny. "Any day now she should be a perfect mate for Dead End Dugan."

"Do not malign the woman I probably love!" snaps Dawkins.

"Anyway," says Benny, "the eat-off is slated for this Friday. Entries close Thursday at noon."

"And what does it cost to send our steed to the post?" I ask.

"Five hundred dollars," he answers.

"They're going to lose money on a lot of the entries," I say. Then: "What's first place worth?"

"Five thousand," answers Benny.

"Okay," I say, pulling another five C's out of my pocket, still thanks to Kid Testosterone, and lay them in Benny's hand. "Enter him, and see if we need to bring anything besides Dawkins."

He frowns. "Like what, Harry?"

I shrug. "A saddle cloth number, a feed bag, whatever."

"Okay, you got it," he says, saluting (without poking himself in the eye for a change) and walking out the door.

"You believe all this about a Miss Priscilla Nibbles?" asks Joey Chicago.

"I believe she exists and that she'll soon be eighty-seven," I answer. "But beyond that ..." I shake my head. "It'd be more likely for Upset to beat Man o' War."

"Uh ... Harry," says Short Odds Harrigan, who I would have sworn was dozing off at the bar, "Upset *did* beat Man O' War in the 1919 Sanford Stakes."

I feel I need a cutting reply, so I say "I said *more* likely, not *as* likely," and, my dignity salvaged, I start doing some serious thinking about the eat-off.

The one thing I can't do is book bets at Joey Chicago's. Anyone who's ever come by since I set up shop here a few years ago has seen what Dawkins can do to a dozen Big Macs and a gallon of root beer just to see him through until his next official meal. I'd have to make him a one-to-a-thousand favorite, and even then I can't imagine anyone betting on anyone else once they've seen him in action.

So I figure the thing to do is get a box at Madison Square Garden or wherever they're holding it, assume Miss Priscilla Nibbles has established not only a reputation but also a fan following over the decades, and hope that most of the money will be placed on her nose (or mouth, or stomach, or whatever), and that very few people will know Dawkins by sight, and he'll just look like any other massive meal on feet who is looking for more than five hundred dollars' worth of food before he collapses or falls asleep.

So when Joey returns, I sent him right back out to reserve a box for us. I decide not to bring Dugan along, because anyone who gets a good look at Dead End Dugan before he's used to it might pass out or run screaming in the opposite direction before he can lay his bet down on Miss Priscilla Nibbles.

Suddenly I feel a pudgy finger tapping at my shoulder. I look up and it is Dawkins.

"I do not wish you to think I am unappreciative of your confidence in me, or your willingness to come up with the entry fee, but if I don't get something to eat in about thirty seconds I will collapse due to malnourishment."

I think about it and nod my consent.

"Joey," I say, "give him a peanut."

"Just one?" demands Dawkins, with the kind of look on his face that most people get when they're watching horror movies starring Boris and Bela and Basil and other people whose names begin with a B.

I stare at Dawkins for a moment, and decide that the eat-off is in the bag, and I relent.

"Okay," I tell Joey Chicago. "One peanut an hour."

I FIGURE AS LONG as there's serious money likely to be riding on the eat-off I could probably use some serious insurance, so I go to Big-Hearted Milton's office. Milton is my personal mage, and his office is in the men's room at Joey Chicago's.

I enter, and Milton is standing in the middle of a pentagram he's drawn on the tile floor, with a burning candle at each of the five points, mumbling a spell.

"Milton," I say, "we've got to talk."

He shakes his head, places a forefinger to his lips, and goes back to mumbling, louder and louder in some alien tongue, and after maybe a minute he screams, *"So shall it be!"*

Then he turned to me. "Sorry, Harry," he says. "But I couldn't stop in the middle of a spell."

"Let me guess," I say. "Mitzi McSweeney again?"

He nods and flashes me an evil grin. "Oh, this time it's a dandy one, Harry. We are at Pudgy Otto's for dinner last night, and she gets a drop of wine on her white blouse, and since I have a better view of it than she does, I reach over and start patting it dry."

"And she throws her food in your face," I say in bored tones, because this is a recurring story between Milton and Mitzi, and only the details change from week to week.

He nods his head. "And it was pork chops!" he growls. "No pork has passed my lips since I was bar mitzvahed! Well, hardly any." He rubs his hands together. "But I have hexed her good!" he chortles. "Wait'll the next time she gets a drop of anything on her blouse or skirt!"

"What terrible thing will happen then?" I ask, stifling a yawn.

"The garment will vanish, and she'll be sitting around her kitchen half dressed! What do you think of that?"

"I think it is truly a terrible curse," I say. "On the other hand, doesn't she eat at Greasy Gus's on nights she doesn't dine with you?" I lower my tone and add confidentially, "I don't know about you, but I've *never* gotten out of there with a clean shirt."

His face contorts into a frown. "Why am I always the victim of my own brilliance?" he says, then mutters another spell. "Okay, the curse is lifted. She can drip all the wants." He pauses. "So what can I do for you?"

I explain the situation to him.

"So do you want her to fill up sooner, or do you want him to eat even more?" he asks.

"Yes," I say.

"You know," he adds, "I used to have a teacher named Miss Nibbles. Must have been, oh, fifty years ago." He shook his head. "Can't be the same one. She was no spring chicken then."

"Okay," I say. "Just as well you said it here."

He looks puzzled. "Said what?"

"Spring chicken," I reply. "Gently Gently is in the bar, and if he hears it there's no telling what he might do."

"Okay," says Milton. "What time Friday is the eat-off?"

"Dinnertime," I tell him. "Six o'clock. But we want to get to the Garden by one-thirty, so I can open up shop."

"Will there be anyone there?" he asks.

"It sold out two weeks ago. Benny had to bribe some friends to get our tickets."

"Sold out?" he repeats, surprised.

I nod my head. "The old lady has a hell of a fan following." I smile. "All the better for us when Dawkins eats her under the table."

"I wonder how that expression ever came into being?" muses Milton.

"Easy," I say. "Someone must have seen Dawkins on his hands and knees, looking for crumbs."

WE ARRIVE at the Garden at one-thirty, and by three o'clock I have booked maybe seven thousand dollars' worth of bets, sixty-six hundred on Miss Priscilla Nibbles, three hundred on Three-Ton Tony from Brooklyn, and the other hundred spread around among longshots.

"And not a penny on Dawkins so far!" whispers Benny Fifth Street. "Are they crazy?"

I shake my head. "Just uninformed. But when he steps out into the arena that'll all change."

By five o'clock I have enough bets in that I can post a morning line, though it is actually a late afternoon line, or possibly an early evening line:

Miss Priscilla Nibbles 1-5

Slim Sandy 15-1

Three-Ton Tony 20-1

Hogpen Harvey 40-1

Pizza Pete 50-1

Really Big Fred 100-1

Maury the Mooch 400-1

Gently Gently Dawkins 500-1

Mealtime McGuire 750-1

More money comes in, and I have to knock the favorite down to 1-10, which means to win a dollar on her you have to bet ten.

"And Dawkins is five hundred-to-one," says Benny Fifth Street. "Isn't *anybody* betting on him?"

"So far just you and Milton and, of course, not with me," I answer. "Let's hope it stays that way. I don't feel like paying off five large for every sawbuck that's bet on him."

"At least Milton and I knew enough to bet on Dawkins with Quick Cash Quenton. But wait till the horses line up at the gate," says Benny, who is fresh out of metaphors. "People will take one look at him, and suddenly you'll be whelmed over with bets."

"Let us hope not," I say. "Miss Priscilla has the largest fan base, I freely admit that—but Dawkins has the largest appetite. I expect him to finish lengths ahead of the field."

"As long as he doesn't throw a shoe and come up lame," says Benny. "And hell, even if he does, he'll be sitting down." He leans over and whispers confidentially: "He's so hungry he might start gnawing on a table leg before the starter sends them off."

"Won't make much difference," says Milton. "Hardly any calories in a table leg. It's good for his teeth, and he won't find it at all nourishing."

Comes a quarter to six, I expect the bugler to sound the call to the post, but there isn't any bugler. Instead there is a middle-aged lady sitting at a pipe organ, and as the sound fills the Garden the contestants come out from wherever they've been kept since we dropped Dawkins off about five hours earlier.

"We're saved!" whispers Benny Fifth Street excitedly.

"What do you mean?" I ask.

"Look!" he says as the contestants take their post positions. Well, their chairs. "Three of them are even bigger around the middle than Dawkins. If you don't know him, if you haven't seen him in action, you'll never pick him over Maury the Mooch or Really Big Fred."

I look, and he's got a point, but it's a point of logic, not experience. I had never seen those other two eat (knock wood!) but when Dawkins springs into action I expect him to leave the field far behind.

"And look at the favorite!" he continues. "It must be a ringer. Nobody who looks like that could have gone win, place, or show at this contest even once!"

I look, and sure enough Miss Priscilla Nibbles looks like a customer who walked in through the wrong door. In fact, she is dressed for an evening at the opera, or perhaps the ballet, not for an all-American sport like an eat-off. She is maybe an inch or two under five feet, her gray hair is piled atop her head, she wears thick glasses in a delicate golden frame, she's got a pearl necklace and a gold wristwatch which she can certainly afford after winning the eat-off six times but which don't seem streamlined enough for a contest that requires speed as well as capacity. And finally, she can't weigh as much as Dawkins can eat when he gets up a head of steam.

The crowd gives her a standing ovation, and she smiles, waves to them, and finally sits down at the table.

"Ladies and gents," says the announcer, who is wearing a turtleneck sweater beneath his tuxedo, "are you ready for action?" The crowd screams its assent, and I realize that the guy with the mike is Horatio Bridge, who calls all the wrestling matches and was obviously hired to lend a little class to the eat-off.

The crowd assures him it is ready.

"Okay, then, let's introduce the combatants one by one," says Horatio. "Please stand up when I call your name."

He calls off their names, but only Miss Priscilla Nibbles is able to get up out of her chair with ease, or at least without capsizing the table. The roars for the favorite are deafening, and Horatio lets them scream for a whole five minutes before he shouts for silence into his microphone.

I notice that Milton is paying no attention to the contestants, but instead is scanning the ringsiders, so I ask him what he is looking for.

"Anyone who looks out of place," says Milton. "Remember— you stand to lose a bundle if the favorite wins."

It is a telling argument and I resolve not to bother him again, but mere seconds later he utters a mighty "Aha!" and, of course, I have to ask him what brought forth such an exclamation.

"Sitting right across the arena from us, third row center," he says, and I look, and sure enough Morris the Mage is sitting there.

"So, is he working for Miss Priscilla, or one of the other entrants?" I ask.

"I'm not sure yet," answers Milton, and then gives vent to a second "Aha!"

"What now?" I ask.

"Tenth row, maybe thirty seats to the left of Morris," answers Milton.

I look, and it is Spellsinger Solly.

"You wouldn't think there's enough money to draw so many mages," says Benny.

"You're just considering the prize money," I say, "which is as nothing if you're putting it all on yourself at forty or fifty-to-one." I turn to Milton. "Just keep it fair. You don't have to help Dawkins, who never needs help to consume entire barnyard animals; just don't let any of the others cheat."

"I'm onto it already," Milton assures me, in between mumbling chants in indecipherable ancient mystic languages, or maybe French.

"For the first course," announces Horatio Bridge, "salted chimeras!"

The waiters, most of whom I recognize from Friday Night Rasslin', bring out the plates, sweating under their burden, and all the contestants dig in. When the last of them finishes, they are given a thirty-second break to renew their appetites, and then the waiters bring out a large pile of *something*.

"What the hell is *that*?" I ask.

"Chopped dragon," answers Milton. "It's like chopped liver, only different."

"We're in luck!" exclaims Benny. "Dawkins *loves* chopped dragon."

Indeed, Dawkins digs in like there's no tomorrow, and so do most of the others, except for Miss Priscilla Nibbles, who is daintily eating her chopped dragon like it is the rarest delicacy in the world (which, for all I know, it may well be), but I also notice that when all the others except Dawkins have stopped gobbling down their dragon liver, Miss Priscilla is still consuming forkful after forkful with small, ladylike bites. By the time they reach the bottom of the bowl, which probably held thirty pounds to begin with, only she and Dawkins are still eating.

"Does anyone concede yet?" asks Horatio Bridge, but no one does.

The next course is a huge bowlful of Abaddon's Locusts covered with jalapeno jelly. Just as I am wondering how many locusts are in the bowl, Horatio announces that there are a thousand, which he explains—for those who learned their math in the New York public school system—comes to one hundred locusts for each contestant.

Except it does not come to one hundred apiece, because Mealtime McGuire has collapsed and fallen to the floor, and Slim Sandy says, "I cannot eat these!"

"You refuse to eat Abaddon's Locusts?" demands Horatio.

"I have no problem with the locusts," Slim Sandy answers, "but I am allergic to jalapeno."

Horatio walks over to where the track stewards, four men in tuxes and three women dressed almost as well as Miss Priscilla, hold a quick conference, and then he speaks into the mike again and announces that Slim Sandy and Mealtime McGuire are both disqualified, though for different reasons. The wrestlers drag McGuire's body off to the dressing room, and come back to do the same to Slim Sandy, but he eludes them and actually outruns them to the nearest exit.

The next course is leviathan, basted in gargoyle blood, and Hogpen Harvey, Maury the Mooch, Pizza Pete, and Really Big Fred all concede defeat before the course is finished, Really Big Fred by announcing he isn't hungry anymore and the other three by sliding or falling to the floor with a minimum of grace.

"Hot damn!" exalts Benny Fifth Street. "Only Three-Ton Tony to go and we've won!"

"What about the defending champion?" I ask.

"She's already eaten more than half her body weight, and they're just getting to the main course," he says, "How much longer can she last, a petite little old lady like that?"

"They probably asked that the last six times," I mutter.

"The next course," announces Horatio, "is broiled behemoth basted with creamed innards of tree-dwelling wooly mammoth."

The waiters lug out the next course. Three-Ton Tony takes one good look at it, sniffs at it twice, and then gets to his feet.

"I concede," he announces. He looks at his wristwatch. "Thanks for the meal. If I hurry, I can just make Bubbles La Tour's Dance of Sublime Surrender at the Rialto."

He heads for an exit, and about half the men in the audience, after checking their own timepieces, follow him out.

So now it is just down to Miss Priscilla and Dawkins. They each dig in, and I look for a sign that either of them is slowing down, but the food is vanishing before our very eyes, and after another ten minutes the last of it is gone.

"Let's give the remaining players—well, contestants—a hand!" says Horatio. "There will now be a five-minute break before the first of the dessert courses."

I wander down to ringside to see how Dawkins is doing.

"Hi, Harry," he says, but without his usual sparkle.

"Hi, Dawkins," I say. "How are you holding up?"

"I don't know if I can make it through one more course," he admits very softly, so that only I can hear him.

"But you jammed that behemoth into your mouth like you were starving!" I say.

"That was to fool my stomach into thinking it hadn't already eaten forty or fifty pounds of beautifully-prepared delicacies." He looks like he is on the verge of tears. "I hate to let you down, Harry."

"All you can do is your best," I say, and add mentally *Until I get Milton to cast a spell to help you.*

I return to my seat and whisper the situation to Milton, who listens and nods sagely.

"Can you do anything to help him?" I conclude.

"Let me give it a shot," he says, and starts mumbling in incomprehensible languages again. In half a minute he stops and turns to me. "Okay, he's got five minutes of voracious appetite left."

"Only five?" I ask.

"Harry, the man's eaten the equivalent of a small automobile."

"Okay, how about Miss Priscilla. Can you magic her appetite away?"

"I can but try," he says with false modesty. A few seconds later he is muttering in English, and they are not words I can repeat in a story which might be read by any youngsters under the age of forty-five.

"What is it?" I ask.

"She's protected."

"So?" I say. "You've broken through Morris the Mage's spells before."

He shakes his head. "This isn't Morris's. This is a lot more powerful, and has been building for thirty-six years."

I am about to say something else, but Horatio starts speaking into the microphone again.

"Ladies and gents!" he hollers. "The dishwashers are working overtime, but they're still having trouble cleaning the creamed wooly mammoth innards off the plates, so our first few desserts are going to be finger foods until the state inspector assures us that the contestants can't catch more than two or three hideous diseases from the plates and silverware." He pauses, waiting for the applause that trickles in.

"If you're going to do something," I tell Milton, "you'd better do it quick!"

"Normal spells aren't working," he says. "I think I'd better come at this from the other side."

"The other side of what?" I demand.

"There's no sense trying to magic away her appetite," he says. "Like I told you, it's protected."

"So give Dawkins an even bigger appetite," I say.

"He'll burst right in front of everyone," answers Milton. "No, I think the only way to approach this is from the left side."

I am about to ask: the left side of *what,* but Horatio interrupts me.

"For our first dessert course," he continues after a moment, "we present miniature éclairs. Our judges have examined them, and not one of these baby éclairs is more than an inch and one-half in length."

The waiters bring out a huge bowl filled with maybe five hundred little éclairs.

"We're washing *all* the plates, just to be on the safe side, so we urge you to sit next to each other since we have only the one bowl." Dawkins tries to get up and finds that he can't budge. Miss Priscilla thoughtfully gets up, carries her chair with her, and sets it down right next to Dawkins. "And now, since we're capturing this on video for re-runs all over the country, I ask the two finalists to shake hands and come out eating!"

They shake, and then each is grabbing handfuls of baby éclairs and stuffing them into their mouths. But an expert eye—and I have one on each side of my face—could tell that Dawkins is slowing down, that he isn't grabbing éclairs as fast as his opponent is. I am totaling up all the bets I'd have to pay off on her, and subtracting the five large that we weren't going to win, and deciding that I wish I'd never heard of the damned contest when suddenly we were deafened by an agonized scream—and when I looked around the arena, I realize that the scream has come from Dawkins, who has wrapped his left hand in a bloody napkin.

"Time out!" cries Horatio, and then "Medic!"

A doctor comes out from behind the grandstand. "I was watching the ballgame," he says. "What seems to be the problem?"

Dawkins waves his hand and bloody napkin at the doctor.

"She bit off half my index finger!" he whines.

Miss Priscilla Nibbles frowns. "I *knew* one of those éclairs didn't taste quite right."

"I suppose we could pump your stomach and get it back if it's not digested yet," says the doctor.

"No!" yells Dawkins. "I don't want anything that's been *there*"—he points to her stomach, realizes he has nothing to point with, and uses his other hand—"attached to me!"

I can see Morris the Mage and Spellsinger Solly and the others glaring at Milton, who smiles triumphantly. "It'll be our secret, okay?"

I agree, of course, and turn my attention back to the proceedings.

Well, the judges put their heads together for maybe a minute, and the upshot is that Miss Priscilla Nibbles has been disqualified and placed second, and that Gently Gently Dawkins, who goes to the post as a 453-to-one outsider, is awarded first prize in the seventh running of the Great Manhattan Eat-Off.

WE WAIT for the medics to stop the bleeding and bandage what's left of his finger, and then we all return to Joey Chicago's to celebrate.

"So you're the defending champion now!" says Longshot Lamont. "They're gonna be training for the next five years to dethrone you."

"Not me," says Dawkins. "I retire undefeated."

"What kind of talk is that?" says Lamont.

Dawkins holds up his bandaged hand. "I only got one forefinger left. I might want to point it at something sometime."

"So who else can we enter?" asks Benny.

I look around the tavern, and in its farthest, darkest corner I see a lone figure staring off into space.

"Maybe we'll run Dead End Dugan," I say. "After all, look at all the bullet holes in his chest. I'm thinking that he won't care if they eat three or four of his fingers."

"You know," says Benny, "that just might work."

"Hey, Dugan!" I holler.

"Yes, Harry?"

"What's your favorite food?"

"You mean, back when I used to eat?" he asks.

"We'll work on that," I mutter.

I go back to the conversation at the bar, which mostly concerns whether he should remain Gently Gently Dawkins or change his name to Nine-Finger Dawkins to celebrate the first thing he has ever won.